THIS IS NOT YOUR COUNTRY

Previous winners of the
G. S. Sharat Chandra Prize for Short Fiction

A Bed of Nails by Ron Tanner,
selected by Janet Burroway

I'll Never Leave You by H. E. Francis,
selected by Diane Glancy

The Logic of a Rose: Chicago Stories by Billy Lombardo,
selected by Gladys Swan

Necessary Lies by Kerry Neville Bakken,
selected by Hilary Masters

Love Letters from a Fat Man by Naomi Benaron,
selected by Stuart Dybek

Tea and Other Ayama Na Tales by Eleanor Bluestein,
selected by Marly Swick

Dangerous Places by Perry Glasser, selected by Gary Gildner

Georgic by Mariko Nagai, selected by Jonis Agee

Living Arrangements by Laura Maylene Walter,
selected by Robert Olen Butler

Garbage Night at the Opera by Valerie Fioravanti,
selected by Jacquelyn Mitchard

Boulevard Women by Lauren Cobb,
selected by Kelly Cherry

Thorn by Evan Morgan Williams, selected by Al Young

King of the Gypsies by Lenore Myka,
selected by Lorraine M. López

Heirlooms by Rachel Hall,
selected by Marge Piercy

The Owl That Carries Us Away by Doug Ramspeck,
selected by Billy Lombardo

When We Were Someone Else by Rachel Groves,
selected by Hilma Wolitzer

Stone Skimmers by Jennifer Wisner Kelly,
selected by Stewart O'Nan

One of Us by Scott Nadelson,
selected by Amina Gautier

THIS IS NOT YOUR COUNTRY

Stories

AMIN AHMAD

Winner of the G. S. Sharat Chandra Prize for Short Fiction
Selected by Stephanie Powell Watts

BkMk Press
University of Missouri-Kansas City

BkMk Press
www.bkmkpress.org

Executive Editor: Christie Hodgen
Managing Editor: Ben Furnish
Assistant Managing Editor: Cynthia Beard

Financial assistance for this project was provided by the Missouri Arts Council, a state agency.

For a complete list of donors, see page 260

The G. S. Sharat Chandra Prize for Short Fiction wishes to thank Ann Marti Friedman, Rachel Hall, Jennifer Wisner Kelly, and Linda Rodriguez,

Library of Congress Cataloging-in-Publication Data

Names: Ahmad, A. X., author.
Title: This is not your country : stories / by Amin Ahmad.
Description: Kansas City. MO : BkMk Press, [2021] | Summary: "These stories, set in Boston, New York, Washington D.C., Chicago, Spain and Barbados, all have ties to India. This Is Not Your Country captures the plight of the "new immigrant": savvy, cosmopolitan, connected by cell phone and video chat, but lonelier than ever, and yearning for connection. Such characters as an emergency-room doctor, a genius computer programmer, a lonely livery car driver, and a teenage runaway desperately seek solace in the bodies and lives of others. The book won the G. S. Sharat Chandra Prize for Short Fiction, selected by Stephanie Powell Watts"-- Provided by publisher.
Identifiers: LCCN 2021010856 | ISBN 9781943491285 (paperback)
Subjects: LCGFT: Short stories.
Classification: LCC PS3601.H573 T47 2021 | DDC 813/.6--dc23
LC record available at https://lccn.loc.gov/2021010856

ISBN: 978-1-943491-28-5

CONTENTS

Lychees—7

The God of Datamatics—29

The Architecture of Desire—43

Mummy—61

The Acrobats—83

Barcelona—101

The Second Lady—117

The Palmview Hotel—137

Emergency Room—159

El Caballo Amarillo—185

Rosetta Stone—203

How to Bury Your Grandmother—225

Chinese Food—233

Interview with Amin Ahmad—253

Discussion Questions—259

When my country, into which I had just set foot, was set on fire about my ears, it was time to stir. It was time for every man to stir.

—Thomas Paine

LYCHEES

The Air-India 747 had flown a great distance, New Delhi-Chicago, fifteen hours direct, and when land appeared, a cheer went up, and the atmosphere became electric. Diana Gonzalez joined the Indian passengers as they crowded around the porthole windows: The tourists from India—clad in clumsy, hand-knitted sweaters—were the most excited, while the American-born Indians, in their performance parkas and sturdy boots, hung back and looked bored. Mediating the two extremes were the techie Indians, born in India, but with H-1B visas and jobs in America; they wore bright windbreakers over cheap department-store clothes and simply looked uncomfortable, as though they didn't belong anywhere.

Eighteen months ago, when she left for India on a PhD research grant, Diana couldn't tell the groups apart, but now she could parse their differences with one expert look. In fact, her Indian seatmates had assumed that she, Diana—with her olive skin and black hair and faded green *salwar kameez*—was Indian too and were disappointed when she told them, no, she was half Cuban, half Polish. She was from here, she said, pointing toward the earth: Here. Chicago. USA.

But really, was she? The plane landed, and the other passengers grabbed their suitcases and crowded into the aisles, but Diana remained in her seat, staring at the banks of dirty snow lining the runway. Men in bright-orange insulated jumpsuits stood on the tarmac, their breath fogging the air. This was March in Chicago? How had she forgotten?

She heard Rahul's voice in her head: *What is there in America for you? It's a frozen garbage heap where people die alone.*

The plane's doors hissed open, and the passengers surged anxiously ahead, clutching their passports, but Diana remained in her seat. An exhausted flight attendant plodded down the aisle and spoke to Diana in Hindi. "Madam, do you need help deplaning?"

I think I made a mistake, Diana wanted to say. *Please let me go back to Delhi with you.* Of course, she did not say that. She stood up, smiled apologetically, and grabbed her dusty backpack. She walked down the length of the empty plane, and it was like getting married, but in reverse—there was no one waiting for her at the end of the aisle.

Diana paused at the door and inhaled the familiar scent of India for the last time: spicy food, body odor, and from the open lavatory door, the sweet stink of urine. She ducked her head and walked out into the freezing, odorless cold. She stood in the line for US citizens and made it easily through immigration, but she was stopped at customs by a young white guy in a crisp blue uniform.

"Ma'am," he said, frowning at her. "Hold up. Do you have any agricultural products? Meats, cheeses, fruits?"

Diana abruptly remembered the bag of lychees at the bottom of her backpack. Rahul had given them to her for the plane ride, but she hadn't eaten a single one. She could not bear the thought of throwing them away.

"Hey, I heard the Cubs won." Diana smiled brightly and pulled her hair back into a ponytail, a pretty gesture that men liked.

"That was last year." The young man's hand rested on her backpack. He squinted at her. "You from Chicago?"

"South Side. I was in India, doing fieldwork for my PhD. Watching the World Series over there really sucked. One billion people, and me, the only Cubs fan."

The young man laughed. "Welcome home," he said and waved her through.

The automatic doors that led into the arrivals area were right in front of her, and the icy cold of Chicago seeped through them. She remembered the warmth of Rahul's body as they embraced at Delhi airport: he was unshaven, his white linen shirt hung out of his pants, and he smelled of cologne and desperation. He had said: *This is your decision, Diana. Always remember—I don't want you to go.*

An Indian family pushed past Diana, activating the automatic doors. They swung open, and there was good old Marnie waiting by a pillar, her round face beaming. Before Diana knew it, she was weeping and hugging her sister's soft, familiar body. Marnie hugged her back and said, "There, there. It's okay. You're home now. You're home."

Marnie had brought Diana's old North Face parka, the one with the furry hood. Diana put it on, and it felt heavy and unfamiliar, and also smelled faintly of a deodorant that she had stopped using a long time ago.

⁓

"What are these?" Marnie crinkled up her snub nose and pointed into the back of the refrigerator. "I thought you're not supposed to bring fruits and vegetables into the country."

It was early the next morning. Marnie was already dressed in her white nurse's uniform, but Diana was half asleep. She sat in the bay window of Marnie's tiny apartment, drank tea, and stared out at the gray Chicago sky.

"Yeah, you're not supposed to, but these were a present. They're lychees."

"Lychees. Ah, from the street kids. You must miss them."

"Yes, I do." The lychees were from Rahul's orchard in the hills, but Diana didn't correct her sister. She sipped her tea, sweetened with four spoons of sugar, a habit she had developed in India. "I miss the kids a lot."

Marnie nodded and shut the refrigerator door. With her big-boned Midwestern build and pale blonde hair, she belonged in Chicago. People never believed that Diana and Marnie were sisters.

Marnie slowly pulled on her knee-length black parka, pushing one arm through and then the other. "What will happen to the street kids? Now that you're gone?"

"They don't really depend on people. They're survivors." Diana went into anthropologist mode. "They live in a state of impermanence. People come, people go. All that survives are their kinship networks. That's what makes them fascinating to study."

"Didn't you say one kid grew attached to some people? And then he killed himself?"

Diana stared out of the window. Through a scrim of bare tree branches she could see the rooftops of Logan Square. Rahul had said: *Dee, why are you always so alone? Why can't you see that other people need you?*

Diana turned to her sister. "That's the problem with these European do-gooders. They get attached to the street kids and make promises. This boy, Chotu, he was ten, he was fine—or as fine as you can be, I guess—but then these two German backpackers promised they'd take him home with them. Of course, they couldn't."

"Okay. Sure." Marnie wrinkled up her nose. "But how can you study something when your presence will change the behavior of those you are studying?"

"Exactly. That's what anthropologists are always grappling with. All we can do is be explicit about our biases and—"

"Okay, okay." Marnie smiled, and her round cheeks tightened. "I gotta get going. Dee, are you sure you're okay?"

"Me? I'm fucking freezing. It's like every molecule in my body has been swapped out. But it's good to be home. So much stuff I want to do. Walk by the lake, eat some dim sum, see the new Gauguin exhibit at the Art Institute. And it'll be good to get my old apartment back."

"Take it slow, Dee. It'll take a while for your body to adjust." Marnie put a warm hand on Diana's shoulder. "I'll be back early. We'll get Chinese, and I want to hear everything. I really missed you." She paused at the door. "Oh, the storage company called—they'll drop the container off at your apartment day after tomorrow. Meanwhile, just wear my stuff, okay? I know it's a bit big, but—"

"I'll be fine. Don't worry."

Marnie left. Diana stood in the bay window and waved down at her, and Marnie waved back and then waddled down the street, breath shrouding her face. She worked in the cancer ward at Cook County Hospital, and when their mother was sick, tubes coming out of her nose, Marnie was the one who had handled it all. Diana was in her first year of the PhD, and yes, it was hard, it was strange, all that theory, but she'd used it as an excuse not to visit Mom. She couldn't bear to see her so frail and unfocused, the same woman who, with a will of iron, had raised two daughters on a postal-worker's income, the same woman who had drilled into them her view of the world: "There is no place for weakness. Never let your guard down. Never depend on anyone. Do you hear me? Never."

Mom had gotten religion at the end, and Marnie had spent hours praying with her. Diana had visited just once, and Mom had been asleep, her skin sickly yellow, her face fallen into itself, already looking like a corpse. Diana took the elevator back down, ran out into the street, and walked blindly for hours, till the cold numbed her. She hadn't been there when Mom died. It was Marnie who'd made the arrangements, even found the strength to comfort Diana. Marnie didn't know it, but she was the extraordinary one.

When Diana was in Delhi, she'd barely thought of those terrible days, but now it was all coming back; the heartache was woven into the very fabric of Chicago. Diana remained at Marnie's bay window, but not one single person went by. Mornings in Delhi were an explosion of crows cawing and traffic rumbling by; from the window of her rooftop *barsati* apartment she could hear the chatter of the maids as they hung out wet laundry, and the neighborhood housewives filled the air with the tang of frying onions. Here, it was like being wrapped in thick, soundless cotton wool.

Rahul had said to her: *Why do you lie to your sister? Why won't you tell her about me? I thought you two were close.* He had said: *I'll talk to my family. They'll have to accept you. I'm their only son.*

～

Diana took a hot shower and was sweating when she walked outside. The warmth didn't last. Within a block, she was chilled again, but it was worse now, because of her clammy T-shirt. She headed for the tall monument at the heart of Logan Square and strolled across a wide avenue to reach it;

when she saw a speeding car, she stuck out her palm, Indian style.

Brakes screeched and a blue SUV halted a few feet from her. A bald man rolled down his window and yelled, "What the fuck. Want to get killed?"

Diana hurried to the curb. Obviously, people drove much faster here. She had forgotten that. Nothing to get upset about.

She reached the monument and stared at the stone eagle at the top. It was carved by the same man who did the Lincoln Memorial in Washington. How did she know this? Was it something she'd learned in middle school? She couldn't remember.

She was cold now and decided to walk on, down Milwaukee Avenue.

The massive old furniture warehouse on the corner, boarded up for years, was under scaffolding, and a billboard said that it was being converted into a gleaming, glass-fronted hotel. Why would anyone want to stay here, in Logan Square? It seemed incredible. She hurried on, looking into the shop windows. The dusty old jewelry store was still there, but the Mexican department store was gone, the one that Mom loved, where you could buy a doll, sheets, or a piñata. In its place was a brand-new food co-op, staffed by young people in kerchiefs and denim overalls. Well, not all change was bad. Fresh fruits and vegetables were probably a good thing.

She passed two new coffee shops with gleaming blond wood counters, packed with hipsters hunched over laptops. Funny how this style, which had originated in Brooklyn or San Francisco, had spread all over the globe; there were coffee shops like these in Delhi. Rahul had said: *Look at those fools. Cappuccinos, chai lattes, matcha smoothies. They're copies of copies of copies and they don't even know it. Come on, let's go to the chai stall on the corner, get the real stuff.*

She was faithful to Rahul, even now. She hurried past the coffee shops, but she would have to go inside soon, just to warm up. Maybe she'd stop at the Gap and buy a new pair of gloves, but then, incredibly, she saw a sign: *Chiya Chai Café*. It was probably some phony new-age place, but when she stepped inside the large, sunny room, she smelled the thick, tannic odor of *chai*. One high wall had been left unfinished: bare brickwork showed between tattered patches of emerald-green plaster, and someone had inserted, at random, glazed ceramic tiles painted with Hindu gods: Krishna, Vishnu, Shiva. That wall, distressed by time, modified by a hidden intelligence, evoked India perfectly.

She took a seat at the counter, next to a young black man who was reading a book. She saw that it was Christina Sharpe's new book on race, *In the Wake*, and felt a surge of kinship. He was clearly a grad student.

She ordered *chai* and *samosas* and ate rapidly with her fingers, wiping away the red tamarind chutney that dribbled down her chin. The man stared at her.

"Are the *samosas*," he said, smiling painfully, "any good? It's my first time here."

"Excellent." She talked through a mouthful of potato filling. "It's the real thing. I'm impressed."

The young server behind the counter overheard them. She had a nose ring and a lip ring. "Our owner is from Nepal. It's his mom's recipe."

"This," said Diana, "is what I need today. This is like a sign from the heavens. How long have you guys been here?"

"A year," said the server. "If you like us, write a review on Yelp. It helps."

The server walked away, but the young man continued to stare at Diana. He already had a receding hairline, but at least he didn't shave his head. He wore a collared shirt under his blue V-neck sweater, and his round, gold-rimmed glasses gave him a harmless, nerdy air, and so she thought, *Fine, I'll talk to him. Why not?*

"You know, it's my first time here, too. I just got back from India."

"Christian."

He saw her confusion. "That's my name."

"Oh." She found it wildly funny. "I was going to say, *Agnostic*. I'm Diana."

"Where in India were you? I always wanted to go."

"New Delhi. You're a grad student, right?"

His eyes widened.

"The book. No one would read that for fun. Are you in American studies?"

Christian said that he was in African-American studies at Northwestern. Like Diana, he had finished his coursework and then moved down to Logan Square to be away from the academic craziness. Like her, he was working on his PhD thesis. He felt isolated at home, he said, so he'd decided to walk out to a different coffee shop every day and read. It was, he said, an economical solution to his self-enforced isolation.

Diana was astounded at the intimacy of his tone; she had forgotten that in America conversation consisted of mutual revelation. In India, people held forth for ten or fifteen minutes without interruption: Conversations there were a series of definitive statements and counterstatements.

"So," Christian said, "what was India like? Life changing?"

He waited patiently for her to speak. His eyes were hazel and intensely alive. She liked that he waited, while Rahul would have said, *Well, what is it? Come on, Dee, don't be so wishy washy.*

There was no way Diana could explain what India meant to her. Instead she said, "I was in Delhi for a year and a half. I missed Chicago a lot. Now it's strange to be back. I mean, my body is here, but my mind hasn't caught up. My stuff is coming out of storage in a couple of days, and maybe that'll make things more real."

Christian nodded slowly. He closed his book, meticulously marking the page with a strip of torn paper. He sat up straight.

"Want to go out sometime?"

"But we're out now."

"I mean, a date. To use a word that is out of fashion. But I can't think of anything else. I hate the phrase *hang out.*"

"Me too," she said, smiling.

They exchanged numbers, and Diana walked back through the cold, deserted streets, her stomach full of hot *chai.* She thought about Christian's question and realized that she couldn't explain her time in India.

She couldn't describe her small, cramped apartment in Old Delhi, with its single shelf of books. She would be hard pressed to describe the street kids she studied through Apna Bacche—a non-profit which tried to help them, without reforming them—and especially Chotu, with his ragged clothes and bright eyes, Chotu who had swallowed a bottle of rat poison. She could not describe how the other street kids had cried and tried to convince themselves that Chotu was with *bhagvan* now, in heaven, eating his fill of food.

She could definitely not talk about Rahul, the scion of a fabulously wealthy Punjabi family. She had met him out in the field. He'd arrived in a chauffeured Land Rover, auditing the charities his family supported, and the connection was immediate. Within a week, they ended up in her *barsati*, and headed straight for her small, hard bed.

Afterward, Rahul had—still naked—made her *chai*, carefully measuring out the milk and water and tealeaves, crunching the *elaichi* pods between his teeth. It was the most delicious *chai* she had ever tasted. She could not explain how all this had happened—and continued to happen for over a year—even though Rahul was engaged to pale, haughty Indira, a wealthy heiress from a family of industrialists.

She definitely couldn't explain why Rahul had fallen in love with her. *Love.* What did that word mean, anyway?

That evening, Marnie returned home, smelling of the hospital, and Diana said casually, "Hey, did you ever try that new Indian place in the Square? Chiya Café?"

Marnie blinked slowly. "Indian? All those creamy sauces? I'm trying to lose weight."

"It's not like that. They have real food. We have to try it."

They went to Chiya for dinner and sat at a table this time. There was a new server, a boy in a knit cap. Diana got the *saag-paneer*, and Marnie sniffed cautiously at the *balti* bowl, but pronounced it delicious.

"This is how you ate in India? How come you're so skinny?"

Diana chuckled. "This is party food. Most Indians can't afford this stuff. They eat rice, lentils, and *chapati*. They use a dab of mango pickle to flavor a whole plate full of rice."

"You were always so adventurous. Me, I'm happy with a hamburger."

"I *thought* I was adventurous." Diana gazed around the café. "But really, I missed Chicago." She smiled brightly. "I met a guy today. He asked me out."

"A guy?" Marnie frowned. "You're back one day, and you're dating?"

"Not dating. We exchanged numbers, that's all."

"Things are so easy for you, Dee. You've always had your pick. Nice guys, too. Remember that guy, what was his name, the Spanish guy? He was a dreamboat. What happened to him?"

"Fernando? He was too clingy."

"Yeah. Of course. If a guy falls in love with you, he's finished. You always—"

Diana frowned. "Come on, I was a kid back then. I'm different now."

"You have no idea how tough it is out there." Marnie sighed. "I want to meet someone, but the doctors at the hospital won't even look at us. There's some cute Indian interns, though."

"Indian guys are tough. Very opinionated. They're little princes. Their mothers spoil them."

Diana thought of Rahul making tea, naked. His tight, round butt. The look of concentration on his face as he turned around and walked back to the bed holding two cups, careful not to spill a drop.

"Well," she continued. "Some dessert? They have *gulab-jamun*. No? Okay, next time. Hey, I forgot, I have a small present for you. Here."

Marnie slowly unwrapped the small package wrapped in newspaper. It was a wooden statue of Ganesh, the pot-bellied elephant god.

"It's a travel Ganesh. You can keep him in your locker at work. He's supposed to remove obstacles. It's made of sandalwood, and if you rub it, it'll smell good, and . . . Hey."

Tears were rolling down Marnie's round cheeks.

"Sorry, sorry. It's just that, I was so worried, Dee. Every time I read about India—a new disease, a stampede, a landslide—I prayed that you hadn't been hurt. I even took out Mom's old rosary and said prayers for you. I thought you weren't coming back."

"Hey, hey, hey. Why would you think that, Marn?"

"I don't know. You're the smart one, you're the one with the PhD, you're always doing new stuff. Me, I'm happy here, but it's lonely with Mom gone . . . Please don't go away again, Dee. Please."

Diana went around the table, hugged her sister, and then sat down again. "I'm back for good. We'll hang out, okay? We'll have dinner every week." She had to change the topic. "You know what I'm looking forward to? Unpacking my stuff. Putting it all back in the right places."

"That's you, Dee. Always organized. I'm sorry, I didn't mean to . . ." Marnie blew her nose in a crumpled tissue. "So tell me about this guy you met. Is he handsome?"

Diana mumbled something vague, and they returned to the apartment. Marnie went straight to bed, but Diana was wide awake: It was already morning in Delhi, and her body was obeying its old routine. She watched some inane sitcom on her laptop, and by midnight she was hungry.

She opened the refrigerator and saw, sitting in the back, the mesh bag of lychees. In Delhi, they had been a deep, blushing pink, but now the shells had turned gray. She tested one with her fingernail. It was still firm, but she did not feel like eating it. She found a bag of stale Oreos that Marnie had hidden in a cabinet and ate those instead.

⁓

The next afternoon, Diana stood in the living room of her apartment in Hyde Park. Her tenant had taken good care of it: the wood floors were unscratched, the built-in wooden cabinets shone, and the old gas stove was meticulously clean. It even smelled the same: of dust, lemon-scented wood polish, and the musty sweetness of old buildings. It was a gracious, 1920s two-bedroom, close to the University of Chicago; she'd bought it with her share of the inheritance from her mother, and thank god she had. Despite Marnie's worries, the area had gentrified fast, and real-estate prices were now sky-high.

She'd imagined this place many times, her tenth-floor aerie with three huge windows looking out onto the lake, always bright, even when there was no sun. It was empty now, but in a few hours, her storage container would arrive, and she'd get her things back. The high-backed Victorian couch would fill the spot by the fireplace, facing the battered old leather trunk that she used as a coffee table. The built-in bookshelves would hold her books: her marked-up copies of Malinowski and Lévi-Strauss and Geertz over there; her poetry collection on two shelves; her art books, Matisse, Giacometti, and Modigliani, away from the light, in the corner. On the wide, polished mantel over the fireplace, she'd put the porcelain figurines of ballet dancers that she'd inherited from her Cuban grandmother.

This was her aesthetic, the aesthetic of Chicago, a mix of old and new, and Rahul could never understand it. Like most Indians, he liked brand-new things. *You Westerners are hung up on old stuff, but in India we need to get rid of all this colonial crap. Build a new world. No, listen to me. You know why you're so stuck in the past? Because you guys have no gods. Ours are alive and well. See that guy, walking down the street? See that tilak on his forehead, that orange mark? He prayed to his gods this morning. He's in harmony with them. You think that keeping old stuff around will anchor you? Everything changes. That's the nature of life.*

Bullshit. What had this attitude done to Delhi? It used to be a beautiful colonial city, but now it was a choking, polluted mess of half-modern people who thought that owning a washing machine and a television was a worthwhile goal for their lives. People who saw the street kids as inhuman, as failed karma, as criminals.

Diana's phone beeped. It was a text from Christian, the guy from Chiya Café. He was coming on kind of strong: he had already sent her information about some cultural events that he planned to attend this month: a table read of an experimental play, a free performance of an opera, an upcoming puppetry festival.

Today's text was an invitation to a launch of a new novel that evening. It was about AIDS and had been well reviewed everywhere, Christian said. It was a big, important book. The City Lit bookstore was a few blocks from Marnie's apartment, an easy walk, even in the cold, and it would be nice to go to a real bookstore and browse.

Diana texted back, *Okay, I'll try to be there.*

His reply was instantaneous: *I'll save you a seat.*

Diana's phone rang right then. She answered it, and a male voice said that her storage container had arrived. She looked down into the street, into the spot where she had taped up *No Parking* signs, and there was a huge truck, with a ramp that must have had a built-in conveyor belt, because two guys in orange uniforms were guiding down a metal storage cube, also painted bright orange.

From up here it seemed too small to hold all her things, but she remembered how carefully she had packed it, eighteen months ago, methodically filling every square inch with boxes and furniture swathed in bubble wrap.

Diana took the elevator down to meet the men, who stared at her as she approached. She realized that she had been fooled by the bright sunlight and had forgotten to wear her parka. She gestured to them to wait and ran back to get it.

⁓

Diana did not go to the reading that evening. Poor Christian must have saved her a seat, must have waited for her to arrive, but she never showed up. Instead, she returned to Marnie's apartment and spent hours on the phone with the UPod Storage company, first with the local office, and then the corporate headquarters, who were two hours behind, in California. Each time, a calm-sounding woman said, "Thank you for your call. Please give me your manifest number, and I will help you."

Each time, Diana exploded. "You guys sent me the wrong container! This is not my stuff."

Each time the woman at the other end said, "Madam, the container number matches your manifest number. What is the problem?"

"You sent me a container full of some other guy's stuff! Tennis rackets, size thirteen sneakers, dumb bells! Two boxes full of VHS porn! You think I watch porn? Where the hell is my stuff?"

Each time, the calm woman said, "Please hold. I will check this for you."

Each time Diana sat for twenty, thirty minutes, listening to Muzak on a loop, till she threw the phone across the room. It was a nightmare. It was like talking to a bunch of amnesiacs.

Marnie said, "Dee, give it a rest. Try in the morning. Go down to the place, sort it out in person."

Diana said, "Do you think they've lost my stuff? Where is it? Why can't they find it?"

"I'm sure it's just a mix-up. Now, I'm going to bed. I have an early start. I suggest you do the same."

Marnie changed into her shapeless nightgown and vanished into her bedroom. Diana decided to make one last call. It was close to one A.M.

Just then her phone beeped. A new text from Christian. He'd sent her increasingly irate messages all evening, and this one just said: *????* She ignored it. What did he want from her? Why were all men such assholes?

She dialed the UPod corporate number. She knew the menu by heart now and punched in *one, one, two*, and got an operator.

"Hello." It was another calm woman. "UPod Storage. This is Lucy. How may I help you?"

Diana was exhausted. She was in a trance of hopelessness, and this time she actually listened. The woman on the phone had said, *This is Looo-seee*, pronouncing it strangely.

"I have an inquiry about my storage pod. The wrong one was delivered, and . . . Hey, may I ask you a question? Where are you located?"

"We are in Reno, Nevada, ma'am. Our corporate headquarters are in San Diego, California, but their lines are closed, so we are taking the calls now."

Something about the woman's cadence was very familiar.

Diana took a tremendous risk and switched to Hindi. *"Aap kaha hai? India mai, zaroor. Apka asli naam kya hai?"*

Where are you, really? I think you're in India. What is your real name?

There was a silence. Diana could hear breathing. The woman said slowly, in Hindi. "Oh. You are Indian?"

"*Hanh.*" Diana continued in Hindi. "I was just in Delhi. In Vasant Vihar."

"We are in Gurgaon. Outside Delhi. But we are not supposed to say that. We are supposed to say, Reno, Nevada."

"What is your real name?"

"Lakshmi, madam. But here I am Lucy."

"Is it still hot, Lakshmi? The rains haven't broken? I know Gurgaon very well. A friend of mine lives there, you may have heard his name. Rahul Kapoor. He is getting married next month. He is an industrialist's son."

There was a pause, and the woman, Lakshmi, said, "No, I have not heard of him. Sorry madam. I do not read newspapers, I just work here, eighteen-hour shifts. Then I sleep."

"That's okay. Hey, this guy, you know, he proposed marriage to me? I said no."

"Oh. Why? You are a different caste?" There was a flicker of interest in the woman's voice. "Your parents didn't like him?"

"Something like that. Yes, we're from different castes."

Rahul, naked, making tea in her tiny apartment. All the meals they'd eaten there, getting takeout from the Punjabi *dhaba* down the road. All the times they'd sneaked out to Rahul's farmhouse in the hills. He had been engaged to Indira the whole time. He had said, *Dee, we don't have to hide. Say the word, and I'll break it off. I want you, Dee, not her.*

Diana had said, *This isn't real. You know that. This is temporary. My life is in Chicago. My sister is there, she's all alone. Besides, I have my apartment, my stuff.*

He'd said, *We can make a home here. Together.*

She'd said, *You don't understand. Chicago is my home.*

"Madam?" Lakshmi's voice came over the phone. "Are you still there? Sorry, there are time limits on our calls."

Diana paused. "Do you think I made a mistake? Turning this boy down?"

"Madam," Lakshmi, whispered in Hindi. "My supervisor is coming, if he hears me, I will be in trouble. I'm switching to English. I will be Lucy. Tell me how can I help you."

They talked, in English, for another few minutes. Lakshmi looked up the manifest number and, within minutes, figured it all out: Diana's stuff had got mixed up with some other guy's stuff. That guy hadn't paid his monthly storage bill, so UPod had broken open the container and auctioned off the contents: Diana's furniture had been sold, and the rest of her stuff had been trashed. Diana could file a claim, but UPod's liability was only three thousand dollars

There was a small silence. Then Diana switched over to Hindi.

She said, "Thank you, Lakshmi, for being honest. You have helped me tremendously."

"Madam, you are very welcome." Lakshmi replied in English. "Thank you for choosing UPod Storage. For further information, please check our website."

The phone went dead. There was only the empty silence of Marnie's apartment.

Three thousand dollars in compensation: For Diana's Victorian couch, upholstered in faded blue velvet, for her old leather trunk. For all her books, collected over many years. For her vintage 50s dresses, her photograph albums with pictures of Mami and Papi. Diana felt dizzy with the loss, and unreal too, because she could clearly see all these things: she felt as though she could reach out and touch them.

The clock on the wall said it was nearly two in the morning, but she was not tired. Her body was ready for a new day, but outside the street was dark. She saw her own reflection in the windowpane: face tanned from the hot sun, gold nose ring, long dark hair, which she wore the way Indian women did, pulled back in the middle with a big plastic clip.

Who was she, now? She felt a sudden rush of vertigo, so acute that she had to sit on the couch. There was just one person who knew her, but unfortunately, she had just dumped him. If she called Rahul, what would happen? Would he turn on his haughty British accent and say, *Why are you phoning me, Dee? Are you trying to make my life a living hell? You know I'm getting married in a week, don't you?*

Would he say, *I can't live without you, Dee. Catch the next plane back. Don't worry about Indira.*

Or would he just hang up?

She checked her watch; Rahul started the day late. He would just be leaving his family's house in his chauffeur-driven Land Rover. In thirty minutes he'd arrive at work, sit at his glass desk and glance through the *Financial Times*. She always called him on his landline at work because they could talk freely. She'd even visited his office, sat in his chair, and looked out at the parched red earth, at the tombs of the old Mughal emperors looming in the distance.

In thirty minutes, depending on traffic, Rahul would be available to her. All of a sudden, this seemed like an eternity.

Diana realized she was very hungry and remembered the lychees; she could taste their sweetness on her tongue.

She checked the fridge, but they were gone, and then she remembered it was trash day tomorrow; Marnie had cleaned out the fridge earlier that evening, methodically sniffing at food, and had filled a trash bag with discards.

Diana went out onto the back porch and, yes, there was the trash bag. She rooted around and found the mesh bag of lychees at the bottom. The fruit were moldy and sodden, but a few at the bottom were still fresh-looking. She washed them and made a pile on the kitchen table.

Ten lychees seemed edible. She set them in a row and stared at them: Ten fat lychees, the pink blush of their thick skins faded, almost gray. Rahul had plucked them from the dusty trees in his orchard in the hills and brought them to her at the airport. He'd handed them to her and said, *For the flight. They're pretty ripe.* He'd looked at her, expecting a reaction, but all she'd said, very coolly, was, *Thank you. How thoughtful.*

Now, she cracked a lychee open and sniffed it: It was aromatic and juicy. She ate it, stuffing her mouth with its crisp, sweet flesh, and spit out the hard seed. She gobbled down another, and another.

Seven lychees left. She told herself that when they were finished, she would make a decision. Till then, nothing would change. Till then she would sit here eating lychees, and her future would be exactly where she'd left it.

THE GOD OF DATAMATICS

By midsummer, the sun set very late, nearly ten o' clock. The earth grew shadowy, but the sky still held the fading light, which seemed to last forever, morphing imperceptibly from bloodred to dull pink, and when darkness came, it seemed a natural extension of the day. People were out late, and no one thought it unusual that an Indian man and his eleven-year-old daughter sat in their rusty Buick, parked across the street from the Datamatics Corporation of Englewood, New Jersey.

The father and daughter waited silently. They did not speak because they were tired of sitting in the car, which was filled with the father's sour, unwashed odor. They did not speak, because there was nothing to be said. This was simply their routine, and they'd been doing it for months now: driving over to Datamatics late in the evening and waiting till all its employees left.

The father was small and bony, with thick, smudged glasses. Finally, he broke the silence. He pointed to the squat concrete Datamatics building and said, "Just a few more minutes, Shonali. Thompson will have to leave soon. That arrogant bastard!"

Shonali just nodded and said, "Yes, Baba," though the cracked leather seat chafed her thighs and her stomach rumbled with hunger.

She stared at the lit window on the third floor and prayed that Thompson would go home. He was the director of Datamatics, a hawk-faced man who wore a creaking metal brace on one leg. Shonali knew this because Baba used to work at Datamatics, and Thompson was his boss. Baba had toiled away in a windowless office, writing complex computer programs that predicted the sales of consumer products— pork bellies, umbrellas, pineapples, you name it—and the jovial white salesmen there had given Baba a nickname, had even written it on his office door, in thick black Sharpie: THE GOD OF DATAMATICS. Baba had been a god till Thompson abruptly fired him, three months ago. He still had his key, though, and they had returned to Datamatics many times, at night. Baba snooped around the office, while Shonali stood guard in the elevator lobby. Lately it had become harder to enter Datamatics, because Thompson worked late every night.

Shonali's stomach growled. She wanted to go home and eat a grilled-cheese sandwich and a can of Campbell's tomato soup, if there was any. Ever since her mother left, meals were erratic.

"Baba," Shonali whispered, "can we please leave? I'm very hungry."

"You're a good girl," Baba said absently. Then he grunted. "Aha. Thompson's light went off. Let's go. *Cholo, cholo.*"

Baba hitched up his too-big pants—he'd lost a lot of weight recently—and started off across the street, his worn leather sandals slapping against the asphalt. Shonali hesitated, and Baba waved to her impatiently. *They didn't take away his key*, she thought. *So technically, he can still go in there. Right?*

She hurried after Baba and followed him through the back door, into the dark lobby which smelled of paper and metal polish and respectability.

⌁

Many years later—when Shonali was an adult and married and had a daughter of her own—she thought back to that last evening. What if she had said, *No, Baba, this isn't right! Stop right now! Let's go home!* What if she'd used the same stern tone that Ma had used? Would Baba have come to his senses? Or were they at the end of a long chain of events that had started in India, long before Shonali's birth?

Ma had told Shonali the story of their courtship many times. They talked after dinner on Sundays, when Ma ironed her pastel-colored business suits. She was a real-estate agent, and during the week she drove all round Bergen County, showing her clients houses with sunrooms and granite countertops and three-car garages. She was very busy.

Sunday evenings were Ma's only time off, and she relaxed by ironing. Shonali loved to watch her mother's slim arms deftly pressing the steam iron into the cloth, her pale, round face damp with perspiration.

Ma said, "I fell in love with your father because of his glasses. His big, thick, ugly glasses."

She, Joya Mitra, met him when she was doing a degree in English at Presidency College in Calcutta and wore chiffon *saris* and thick eye makeup. At the Coffee House on College Street, she always saw Gautam Sen sitting at his table in the corner, his hair disheveled, hands ink-stained, working on an endless mathematical proof. All of Presidency College knew that Gautam Sen was a genius and that he had been offered a fully funded PhD at MIT, in America. Joya, comfortably upper-class, didn't care for America, and she certainly did not care for the grubby Gautam Sen, who slurped tea from his saucer. She made witty, cutting remarks about him to her friends, but one day he took off his glasses—he held them between the thumb and forefinger of his left hand, even as he continued to scribble with his right—and Joya noticed his perfect eyebrows and heavy-lidded poet's eyes. Now Gautam Sen's ink-stained hands and unkempt hair became proof of an intense inner life. To her surprise, he was charming, and chatted with her about T.S. Eliot and Ezra Pound because his genius was not just restricted to mathematics.

Before Gautam Sen left for MIT, he married Joya and she proudly accompanied him to Boston.

Ma told Shonali this story as she ironed her realtor's clothes in the basement of their ranch house in Teaneck, New Jersey. She talked slowly, her face suffused with nostalgia, because things had changed so much: She'd discovered a gift for selling real estate and now earned three times more than her husband. She'd replaced her *saris* with smart suits and high heels, while Baba wore the same clothes he'd bought years ago in India: polyester shirts with ink-stains on the pockets and dark, shapeless slacks.

Where had things had gone wrong for Baba? It was hard to say. He had done brilliantly at MIT and moved on to research jobs at Xerox PARC and IBM, but when he finished his PhD he was thirty-three years old, and it was too late to conform to the rhythms of an office job. Baba skipped work, missed deadlines, and was always fired. After an insurance company in Connecticut and a brokerage house in New York City, he finally landed at Datamatics, where Thompson let him keep his own hours.

The real-estate market in New Jersey was booming, and Joya celebrated the sale of multi-million-dollar estates with fancy dinners, from which she returned a little tipsy, smelling of cigar smoke and brandy. She insisted on being called *Joy*, not Joya. She began to put her money into a separate bank account, and six months ago, she moved to San Diego. She said that her real-estate agency needed her to head up a new office there.

At the airport Ma had hugged Shonali. "I can't take you with me," she said, "because I need to find a house, research schools, etcetera. You'll join me in California as soon as I'm settled."

Shonali nodded, but she did not trust her mother's immaculate red lipstick and her bright, breathless realtor's way of talking.

Ma flew away. Baba lay on the couch, took off his glasses, and rubbed his fists into his eyes.

"I should have seen this coming," he said. "It's this damn country. Her head has been filled with all sorts of nonsense."

Shonali put her arm around his shoulders and felt how thin he'd become.

"It's okay, Baba. She'll be back. She's just angry right now."

But Ma showed no sign of coming back to New Jersey. Instead, she sent Shonali brightly colored postcards from California, featuring palm trees and beaches and surfers. Baba received only a thick manila envelope with divorce papers, and he signed them with tears in his eyes. Just like that, their family was dissolved.

Without Ma there to regulate Baba, he never made it to work on time. He stayed up all night working on a new computer program that he said would revolutionize the consumer data industry. He said it would make Datamatics

rich—but instead Thompson fired him. The God of
Datamatics now spent his days lying on the couch, his eyes
tightly closed. He looked as though he was trying to solve a
knotty mathematical problem, one with many variables: the
abrupt loss of his job, his wife's disappearance, the extent
of Shonali's loyalty to him.

It was then that Baba started making his unofficial visits
to Datamatics, with Shonali as his accomplice.

That last evening, as they walked into Datamatics, everything
followed a familiar pattern. The elevator whined up to the
third floor, and they walked through the lobby, past a huge,
dusty rubber plant and the secretary's empty desk. Valeria
was Russian, tall and angular, with cropped, platinum-blonde
hair, and reminded Shonali of an evil stepmother from a
fairy tale. She was married but spent her time making
flirtatious eyes at Thompson.

Baba and Shonali entered the main office, a warren of
cubicles covered in beige fabric, onto which the salesmen
had pinned memos and newspaper cuttings. As they walked
in, they must have stirred up a breeze, because the papers
rustled. In the corner of each blank computer screen, a green
login symbol blinked, and the computers exuded the menace
of a sleeper who might wake at any moment.

Baba went directly into Thompson's glassed-in office
and started rifling through the memos stacked on the desk.
What was he looking for? Shonali assumed he wanted to
know how the company was doing without him; he was
probably searching for evidence of their failure. She walked
over to a row of photographs on the wall and stared at them.
Unlike the salesmen, Thompson did not have pictures of
his wife and children, but snapshots of himself in the

Vietnamese jungle, standing in the midst of a group of soldiers, all wearing green camouflage uniforms, their faces blackened, holding long-nosed sniper rifles. Something bad had happened over there, because in later photographs Thompson wore an elaborate metal brace clasped around his right leg.

Despite his injury, Thompson always wore dark, double-breasted suits and bright silk ties, and fancied himself a lady's man. Shonali knew all this because whenever Ma visited Datamatics—dressed in her realtor's pastel suit—Thompson would be sitting on the edge of Valeria's desk, talking softly to her, and the woman's face would be deep pink with pleasure. Seeing Ma, Thompson would swing himself off the desk and stand, his metal brace creaking, and make small talk. He was interested in finding a larger, fancier office for Datamatics, and he'd even ridden around with Ma for a few months, looking at commercial spaces. Nothing had worked out, but after their time together, there was an awkward intimacy between them.

When Ma walked away, toward Baba's small, windowless office in the back, Shonali would catch Thompson staring at Ma's retreating back, and then he would glance at Valeria and raise an eyebrow, and she would raise her bony shoulders in a small shrug, as if saying, *People are strange*, and Shonali realized that they pitied Ma for being married to Baba.

That last evening, Baba rummaged around Thompson's in-box, reading memos, glancing at invoices. Then he suddenly grunted, as though he'd been punched in the stomach. He turned to Shonali, with a strange, baffled expression on his face.

"What the hell are you doing in here?" he barked. "Go to the lobby. Stand guard in case someone comes! *Cholo, cholo!*"

Shonali stomped back down the corridor, but she was too hurt to comply with Baba's command. As soon as she was out of sight, she wandered defiantly in the opposite direction, deeper into the forest of cubicles, stopping to steal a few colored Post-It notes. She found herself at the back, in front of Baba's old, windowless office. It was exactly as he'd left it, with his handwritten DO NOT DISTURB ME sign taped to the door, and below it, printed in thick black marker, THE GOD OF DATAMATICS. Shonali was about to leave, when she heard, from inside the room, muffled words, interspersed with heavy breathing. Someone was in there.

Baba's replacement? She pushed the door, and it must have not latched, because it swung open a few inches. She angled her head, glanced inside, and confusion flooded through her mind. She quickly looked away and thought to herself, *You stupid fool, why did you come here? Stupid, stupid, stupid.*

She turned and ran, moving silently on the thick, springy carpeting, all the way back to Thompson's office. Baba was sitting there, his head held in his hands, a bright piece of paper spread in front of him.

"We have to go," Shonali gasped. "Right now. Someone is back there."

Baba didn't seem to hear her. She shook his shoulder, hard, and he suddenly understood, and they sprinted to the fire stair at the center of the office. The raw concrete stairwell went on forever—Shonali was gasping for air by when they emerged—but she gripped Baba's hand and pulled him across the street, all the way back to the car.

The Buick coughed into life; Baba drove down the street and merged onto Route Four. His face was strangely blank, and it frightened Shonali.

"Are you okay?" she said.

He didn't reply, so she tried again. "Baba, I'm starving, and there's probably no food at home. Can we go to the diner? Please?"

It was nearly eleven now, but the Jackson Hole Diner was open twenty-four hours. It was huge, with red leatherette booths and chrome trim, and always crowded. Shonali ordered tomato soup and grilled cheese for herself, and Baba requested a huge plate of french fries. These days, it was all he ate.

The food arrived quickly. Baba came out of his reverie and thrust a steaming french fry into his mouth. "Who was at the back of the office? The cleaning people?"

Shonali didn't reply. Baba stopped eating and stared at her. "Was it one of the salesmen?"

"I don't know, exactly."

"What?" Baba's face turned red. "I give you an important job, and this is all you can say? Are you lying? Did you just want to leave and eat dinner?"

Shonali refused to look at him. Baba reached across the table, and her head jerked back—he had slapped her, hard, across the face, but she was too stunned to even yelp. Baba sat back and closed his eyes and began to mutter to himself. Shonali slid out of the booth and ran out of the diner to the car. She sat in the darkness, lit only by the bright orange neon sign of the Jackson Hole Diner, the headlights of cars passing by on Route Four, and the occasional tracking lights of a plane flying low to Newark Airport.

Baba emerged a few minutes later, the food packed neatly into takeout boxes. He reached across and touched Shonali's cheek, but she flinched, and he withdrew his hand and began to mutter in Bengali. Shonali did not speak the language, but she understood it, and it seemed that Baba was carrying out a long complaint against women who ran around the countryside and could not attend to home and hearth, and how such women could not raise daughters, and how there was no respect in the world anymore. And more of the same.

Fragments of Bengali ran through Shonali's head, phrases that her mother would shout out when she fought with Baba:

Amar matha bathah korchay, My head is hurting.

Aamme moray jabo, are toomey janbe na, I will die, and you won't even notice.

Tomar matha kharab, You are not right in the head.

Ma was right. She was absolutely right. Shonali muttered, "Stupid, stupid, stupid," and Baba said, "What did you say?" And Shonali said, "Nothing."

They drove down Route Four and down Teaneck Road and then turned onto Cranford Place, and there was their house, faded blue siding, the lawn burned brown, the bushes grown so tall that they nearly covered the front windows.

Baba turned off the engine and said, "Shonali, I didn't mean to hit you . . . It's just that, now I have to go back again. To find more evidence."

"Evidence? What are you talking about?

"You are a young girl, you should be shielded from these things, but okay, I will tell you. Joya had an affair with Thompson. You know what *affair* is? All that driving around together, and then she left."

Shonali was too stunned to speak.

"You think I'm crazy? Look—I found it on Thompson's desk."

Baba thrust a tourist brochure at her printed with images that were familiar to her from Ma's postcards: surfers, palm trees, white pristine beaches. What did Thompson's vacation brochure have to do with Ma?

Baba smelled worse than usual, the sour odor of his unwashed clothes mixing with dense body odor. When he picked her up from school, he sat in the Buick and listened to wailing Bengali film music and tapped out rhythms on his steering wheel. Her classmates called him *Freaky Freak*.

Shonali turned her face away from him. "I want to go to San Diego," she said. "I want to live with Ma."

Baba gasped and reached out blindly. "Please forgive me. I've never raised my hand before . . . It's just that...This country, what it's done to me. That bastard Thompson, he has taken everything from me, my work, my wife, my honor, and—"

Shonali slid out of the car. She walked into the house and locked the door to her bedroom. Baba stood on the other side and pleaded with her in rapid Bengali, and when she remained silent, he stormed out of the house and drove off somewhere. Shonali crept out and dialed her mother and said, "I've had enough, Ma. Buy me a plane ticket."

Her mother said, "Oh sweetie."

Shonali left for San Diego three days later.

Before she departed, she washed all of her clothes, so that Ma would be impressed. She moved aside a pile of Baba's filthy clothes lying next to the washing machine and something fell out of his pants: the brightly colored travel brochure he had taken from Thompson's desk. It wasn't even for San Diego but for Los Angeles.

She crumpled it up and threw it away.

Baba drove her to Newark Airport. He tried to speak to her, but she turned away and stared out of the window.

The last time she ever saw Baba was at the airport: he was waving his arms and arguing loudly with a cop because he had parked in the bus lane.

~

Ma's pink stucco bungalow in San Diego had only one bedroom, and Shonali had to sleep on a fold-out couch in the living room. All the bird-of-paradise flowers in the backyard had turned brown and withered because Ma never watered them; she was busier than usual, because in California, everyone thought she was Hispanic, and that opened up a whole different market. Ma already spoke some Spanish—on the phone she was always saying, *Claro, claro*—and had cut her hair short and drove a new silver Mercedes. The kids at Shonali's new school mimicked her New Jersey accent, the way she said *chawk-litt* for chocolate and *cawfee* and *yous guys*. She missed home terribly: the hum of traffic on Route Four, going to Hot Bagels for an everything-bagel-with-a-schmear, listening to *Mike and the Mad Dog* on 1010 Wins, she even missed the burned taste of grilled cheese sandwiches. She wanted to call Baba and say that she had made a mistake, but she waited too long.

One sunny November day Ma got a call from a lawyer in New Jersey who said that Baba had been arrested. He had returned to Datamatics and been discovered there by Thompson, who was working late. There had been an altercation, and Baba threw a fax machine at Thompson's head; even though Baba missed, he was charged with burglary and assault. The police examined his papers and found that his green card had expired and that he had never bothered to renew it. After he served a short prison sentence, he would be deported to India.

Ma told Shonali all this as they sat on the hot patio, surrounded by the tall, blackened stalks of bird-of-paradise flowers.

Shonali burst into tears, and Ma said, "It was bound to happen. That man is self-destructive. He's crazy."

Shonali felt the hot sunlight on the back of her neck and could not stop sobbing. She could have saved Baba. If only she'd told him what she had seen that night, he would never have returned to Datamatics. But she was only eleven years old, and it was impossible for her to put it into words.

⌇

Many years later, Shonali returned to New Jersey and married a man from Englewood and had a daughter of her own. She ended up driving up and down Route Four a lot—which had changed, they had built townhouses on all the open fields—and she would always pass the Jackson Hole Diner. It was still there, with its orange neon sign, but she would never stop, never go in. Every time she went past, she remembered her last visit there with Baba, and she would have a hard time breathing.

The memory was burned into her brain: They had run out of Datamatics to the car. Baba had driven the old Buick, and she sat on the front seat beside him. They nosed through the thick traffic on Route Four, and soon the orange neon of the Jackson Hole Diner had appeared out of the darkness.

Baba had parked badly and then reversed and parked again, with marginal improvement. He got out without locking the car, and she had not reminded him—who would want to steal a rusty old Buick? They had walked together into the warm fug of the diner, which smelled, as always, of french fries and strawberry milkshakes. They slid into an overstuffed red leatherette booth and stared at huge, plastic-coated menus. They had pretended to look at the endless lists of items—barbeque burgers, waffle fries, Philly cheesesteak sandwiches, Mexican rice and beans, blue plate specials—and then Shonali ordered what she always did: a grilled cheese sandwich and a bowl of tomato soup, and Baba had asked for a large plate of french fries, extra-crispy.

Sitting in the booth, Shonali had tried not to think about what she has seen in Baba's office, behind the door marked GOD OF DATAMATICS, but fragments had arisen in her mind: Valeria, the secretary, bent across the metal desk, her platinum-blonde hair in disarray, her dress hiked up to her waist, and Thompson thrusting into her from behind, his pale face beaded with sweat, his metal leg brace creaking rhythmically. She was not sure what they were doing, but she knew that it was shameful and deeply private; she knew it was dangerous.

Sitting in the Jackson Hole Diner that night, she had felt a tremendous sense of relief because she had saved Baba from a terrible fate. The waitress walked toward them, holding aloft a tray, and Shonali had smelled the thick, rich odor of tomato soup, the salty tang of french fries and felt deeply reassured.

She had looked across the table at Baba, and she had seen him clearly, as if for the first time: his white polyester shirt with black ink stains on the pocket. His odd, high-waisted slacks with built-in side elastic expanders. His leather sandals, worn and scuffed. Surrounded by big, loud Americans, Baba had looked like a small, shabby alien, and she knew then that it was her job to protect him. In that moment—a minute before he slapped her—she had realized that she loved this strange man, her father, and that she forgave him for everything, and this realization had flooded her heart with a tidal surge of love.

THE ARCHITECTURE OF DESIRE

As a general rule, a single person should not live with a couple—it is a recipe for heartbreak—but back in those days, the three architecture students did not know that. They found a cavernous apartment in Cambridge, near the university, and moved in together. It was a dump. A fourth-floor walk-up, barely any heat, horsehair insulation in the walls, but it was ridiculously cheap—six hundred dollars a month—and the windows faced south, flooding the apartment with golden light.

Ali chose the bedroom in the front, overlooking Massachusetts Avenue, since he was from India and did not mind the street noise. Miles and Philomena had separate rooms along the dark hallway, but they slept together in Philomena's room and had noisy sex every night. When Ali imagined them, Miles was always on top, his pale legs scissoring into Philomena's brown flesh, because she was always so passive. They were a striking couple: Miles was blond and bearded, a carpenter, a Jesus figure, while Philomena was from the war-torn island of Sri Lanka; she had hair down to her waist, and she always wore it twisted into a demure braid.

Ali tried to stay out of their way, but he couldn't help noticing things: Miles talked to Philomena in an offhand, had been demolished, leaving empty lots, and only the Necco confectionery factory was still functional. Its tall smokestack belched out clouds of peppermint-smelling smoke which mixed with Ali's own raw panic and made it hard to breathe.

Still asleep on the living room couch, Philomena began to mumble in Sinhala, and it sounded as though she was pleading with someone. Ali went and woke Miles, who stumbled out, smelling of raw sleep and ganja. He carried Philomena back to bed and kicked the door shut. Philomena's confused mumble was followed by Miles's calm voice and then the sound of one body slithering over another. The frantic creaking of the bedsprings began, getting louder; it was as though Philomena wanted to be obliterated.

It was all too much for Ali. He gathered up his things, left the apartment, and headed for the overheated architecture studio at the university.

~

A week later, Ali came back from the studio late at night to find Miles sprawled on the battered pink couch in the living room, still wearing his tool belt. He had a part-time job building stages for rock concerts, and that night his bonus was the fragrant plastic baggie he waved under Ali's nose. Philomena didn't like them smoking in the house, so they walked out onto the back porch.

"It's getting out of control, man," Miles said ruminatively, lighting up a joint. "It's getting crazy."

"What do you mean?" Ali took a drag and passed it back.

"She's sleepwalking, man. Every night."

Sleepwalking. That explained everything. Why hadn't he figured that out?

"I mean," Miles continued, "last night, she was trying to open the front door. What's gonna happen if she sleepwalks

down Massachusetts Avenue? It's all the stuff she's seen in
Sri Lanka . . . the civil war and stuff . . . fucks you up, man."

Miles always talked very slowly, as though puzzling out
the meaning of each word.

"She has this nightmare, that she's walking home through
the city. They're pulling people out of their cars, pouring
kerosene over them, and setting them on fire. That's when
she starts sleepwalking. Weirdest thing is, she won't tell me
if it's just a dream, or if it really happened."

Ali remembered the tart smell of kerosene from childhood
in India. They'd fill lanterns with it during blackouts, and
it burned fiercely, leaving dark rings of soot on the ceiling.

"Now she sleeps with the light on. The whole fucking
night. It's driving me crazy, man. What am I gonna do?"

"What can you do? Hopefully it'll stop."

"Yeah, but when? This is getting too heavy."

"Miles? Why are you two whispering? It's late, Miles."

Philomena slipped in between them, smelling of
toothpaste. She took a drag of the joint, and the three of
them stood silently, linked by wraiths of smoke. A few
minutes later Philomena whimpered and leaned into Miles,
high already. The Necco confectionery factory let out a plume
of smoke, and suddenly the air smelled of sickly sweet
peppermint.

"Shit," Miles said, "I'm an ice-cube. The joint is all yours,
man."

Ali thanked him. He watched the two of them walk
through the lit kitchen and down the long hallway; looking
along the outside face of the building he saw Philomena's
arms pulling down their window shade.

Ali finished the joint and flicked the butt away, and its
glowing tip arced through the darkness, creating a trail of
light. Vapors of peppermint, thin and high, filled his nostrils,

and the constriction in his chest returned. He told himself that it would pass. He went back inside, climbed into his icy bed, and pulled two comforters and a sleeping bag over himself.

⸏

Something cold woke him.

When he opened his eyes, he was standing barefoot in the dark hallway, his hand on the brass doorknob to Philomena's room. Through the door he heard her shallow breathing and Miles's slow voice.

"Yeah? What's up?"

Another few steps and Ali would have walked through the door. What then? Would he have slipped into bed with Philomena, searching for her mouth with his? This is where the logic of his dream was headed.

The door opened and Miles looked out, his blue eyes naked and unfocussed.

"Yeah? "

"I'm sorry man," Ali said, copying Miles's whisper. "I must still be stoned. I thought this was the bathroom."

Miles nodded slowly. He'd seen stranger things.

"Hey," he said, "Can I use the head first? I've gotta piss real bad."

Ali leaned against the cold wall, listening to the hard spatter of urine. When Miles finished, he went back into their bedroom, muttered "Fuck it," and the light clicked off.

In the bathroom mirror, Ali saw his pale, exhausted face. Four hours of sleep a night, six cups of coffee a day, and still his design assignments weren't complete. Had his exhaustion, plus the weed, led him to sleepwalk?

The lock on Ali's bedroom door was broken, so he wedged a chair under the doorknob and balanced a tall pile of books on the seat. If the chair was moved, the sound of falling books would wake him.

It took him a long time to fall asleep. Sometime close to dawn, he heard the soft slither of Philomena's bare feet, and next morning, there she was, lying on the pink couch, saliva dribbling from her mouth and puddling into the cushion. Ali covered her up, went into the kitchen and stared at the handout for the next design assignment. This one said:

THRESHOLDS: We will interrogate and deconstruct an architectural element that is ubiquitous yet invisible: the threshold, and particularly, the door. We will look at practical considerations (connection, disconnection) as well as symbolic uses (access, denial). Your exploration of the door should choose from one of these programs: embassy/checkpoint; educational institution; hospital/mental asylum.

Ali stared at the words, but all he could think about was Philomena lying on the couch next door, her long eyelashes fluttering as she dreamed.

⌐○⌐

A month passed. It was deep winter now, and the world was stark black-and-white. Early one morning Ali stood in the kitchen, peered into the refrigerator, and started swearing.

"That's it," he said to himself, "I'm moving out. I can't take this."

Now, along with her sleepwalking, Philomena was cooking incessantly. The goddamn fridge was full of plastic boxes of food: cashew-nut curry, jackfruit, string hoppers; there was no place for Ali to put the eggs and bread that he had just bought. Philomena's food taunted him through the clear plastic, and he desperately wanted a plateful of hot curry and rice, but instead he scrambled some eggs in a skillet and ate straight from it.

Ever since his stoned sleepwalking episode, he'd spent his nights working in the studio and returned to the apartment early in the morning, when it was silent as a tomb. He hadn't seen Philomena in days; the only trace of her was the cooking pots she left soaking in the sink.

That morning, though, Philomena and Miles were awake: he heard them arguing in the bedroom. When Philomena walked into the kitchen, Ali looked up—it was her skillet, and she didn't like him eating directly from it—but that day she didn't seem to notice.

She made a soft-boiled egg, placed it in an eggcup, and ate like a cat, licking bits of yolk from deep within the fractured shell. That morning her hair was shiny, and a black ribbon was woven through her plait; even the dark semicircles underneath her eyes enhanced her beauty. As usual, she plunged right into the middle of a conversation.

"Best way to cook a soft-boiled egg," she said, "How? Come on, I taught you this before."

"*Ummm*, six minutes?"

"Wrong. Three and a half. Start in cold water or boiling water?"

Cold, boiling, what did it matter? Ali was happy to just sit with her. He shrugged.

Miles walked yawning into the kitchen and yanked open the fridge. He noticed Philomena eating and spoke slowly and reasonably.

"Hey. They said don't eat anything, okay? It's probably not a good idea, eggs and stuff, okay? They said, an empty stomach."

Philomena rose, opened the lid of the trashcan and threw the half-eaten egg into it. She turned and glared at Miles.

"Satisfied?"

The fetid, rotten smell of garbage filled the room.

Ali said, "Oops, I forgot to empty the can. It's my turn, I know, sorry," and got up to leave.

Miles said, "No, man, you'd better stay."

Shit. Now Miles was going to bring up Ali's sleepwalking episode; he was going to say that he was tired of Ali sniffing around Philomena, that he had to leave. Ali started to assemble an explanation: *It only happened once. I was stoned. It will never happen again. I swear, I promise.*

Miles spoke woodenly while looking out of the window.

"I'm moving out, man. It's where we're at right now. Best thing for us. I'll find you guys another roommate."

Ali was stunned. *Another roommate? He was the damn roommate!* Miles was the one who'd fixed up the apartment: he'd dragged in the pink couch, painted the walls canary yellow, built the shelves for Philomena's spices. This was his kitchen table, his dishes. Even Philomena was his.

Miles read Ali's mind and waved his hand around the kitchen.

"You guys keep all the stuff, okay?"

Right then, Ali thought only of Miles's generosity and felt guilty, as though all this was all his fault.

Philomena sat listening, dry eyed, and looked steadily at Miles. Then she said, "Let's go, we can't be late for the appointment."

She put on her olive-drab army coat and long scarf, and they left. Ali went to the window and watched them in the parking lot, sitting side by side in Miles's old Volkswagen van. Its engine caught and died, then ground into life.

Philomena's dark head looked straight ahead, and her hands lay lifeless in her lap.

⌒

Miles moved out to a place across the river. Philomena spent hours inside her room, talking on the phone with him and crying. She stopped cooking and became very thin.

The academic year ground on to its end. Ali survived, but just barely, with many incomplete design assignments that he had to finish over the summer; instead of flying home to India, he stayed in the apartment and got a brainless job at the architecture library. Miles found a gig in upstate Vermont, building houses with a bunch of ponytailed guys, and left town. Philomena decided to accelerate her time at the university and finish her thesis over the summer; she was developing a prototype for a tropical skyscraper.

She set up shop in the living room, and one evening Ali came home to find every light burning and Philomena pecking miserably at her electric typewriter. He moved his new Apple II computer into the living room and spent an evening teaching her how to switch it on, how to put in a disc, how to cut and paste. He grabbed her long-fingered hand and taught her to double-click the mouse.

To thank him, she said that she would make him chicken curry the next day, and he came home early to help her. Before she started, she twisted her hair up into a bun, the glossy bundle too heavy for her slim neck. Her hands moved deftly, plucking bottles of spices from the shelf.

"These are cloves," she said, sticking a handful under his nose. "You know cloves?"

She said, "This is how you break cinnamon sticks. This is how you float curry leaves."

Seeing his incomprehension, she wrinkled up her snub nose at him.

"*Chee*, you don't know how to cook anything? You left India when you were too young, you had too many useless American girlfriends, that's the trouble. Don't worry, I'll fix you up. You'll be a hot catch when I'm done teaching you to cook."

Ali turned away and hid his face in the steam rising from the rice.

The kitchen was too hot, so they took their food out onto the back porch and ate while the setting sun burnished the smokestacks of the Necco factory. With Miles gone, Philomena could make the chicken curry as spicy as she liked; Ali's tongue burned, but he urged her to make it spicier the next time.

After dinner, Philomena said she would help him with his unfinished assignments. They stood at the kitchen table together and read an assignment that had stumped Ali for weeks. It said:

> SHELTER: For our final project, each student must choose a marginal site in Cambridge. Concentrate on liminal spaces: alleys, rooftops, sheds, ruined/ abandoned buildings. Design a space for you to live. Project your life decades into the future to accommodate any additional needs that may arise. Concentrate on the practical, but remember, architecture always satisfies multiple human needs: Do not sacrifice beauty.

Ali frowned. "I have no idea what my life is going to be like. How do I even start?"

Philomena crossed her arms and stared at him. "Well, what do you want from life?"

"Fuck if I know. Survive architecture school?"

Ali walked down Massachusetts Avenue, which was deserted at this time, except for a curious trail of conical paper cups strewn down the sidewalk. He followed them and came upon a van serving lemonade to men who wore black jackets with bumblebee yellow stripes; it took him a second to realize that they were firemen. Further down the Avenue, fire engines were skewed across the street, obscuring his view, and the sky was bright orange.

Their apartment building was ancient, dry as tinder, and Philomena always ignored the fire alarm. Ali sprinted down the street and saw that the building directly across the street from theirs—a five story walk up—was burning fiercely. It was the same vintage as their own apartment building, from the 1880s, with an ornate copper cornice and bands of patterned brickwork. Now its stunned inhabitants stood on the street, clad in pajamas, and watched tendrils of flame reach out from deep inside, soundlessly shattering windows.

Ali ran up the stairs to their apartment. The living room was empty, and he found Philomena standing at the bay window in his bedroom, looking across the street at the conflagration.

He said her name and she jumped.

"Hellava thing, no?" she said quietly. "It's been burning for an hour."

"It's a four-alarm fire, for sure. Jesus. How did it start?"

"Must have been some fuel inside. Look at the way it is burning. Varnish, maybe, from the furniture store downstairs."

He stood next to her and watched the show: Firemen on ladders fed water into the blaze, while others stood behind the fire engines and gulped lemonade, as though at a picnic.

Philomena's voice came from far away.

"That's the best way to set a fire, you know. Heap up any old thing, soak it with petrol, and set it alight. The walls burn first. Then the floors collapse. When air comes in from the roof, there's no stopping it."

Philomena shivered and her eyes were unnaturally bright.

"Hey," Ali said, "hey, it's okay. We're safe here. They have it under control."

She squeezed her eyes shut, and he realized she was crying. He held her shoulders—she was as yielding as a child—and pulled her into his chest, amazed at what he was doing.

"You're freezing," he said, "get into my bed."

She lay down on his futon, and he covered her with blankets, hesitated for a moment, and then slid in next to her. She did not resist his embrace, but somehow, she was absent.

They lay listening to the crackle of the flames. She spoke softly, her breath warm in his ear.

"Gas cylinders go *boom*," she said. "But if you've hidden ammunition inside your house, that goes *pop, pop, pop*. During the war they'd burn your house and then listen to the noise. Easier than searching the whole place. *Pop, pop, pop*; if it's ammunition, they make you kneel and shoot you in the head."

She laughed soundlessly.

"Not very elegant, no? But quite effective. When they burned our house, they lined us up facing it. My father, my mother, my brother, and me. I was calculating in my head, okay, the beams will take one hour to burn through, the tile roof will collapse then, it will be over. I told my mother, *Ma, don't worry, nothing to be afraid of*. But then I remembered something. You know what it was?"

Ali shook his head, *No*.

"My father's soda decanters. Cut glass and pressurized. I kept thinking, why can't the old fool drink his soda from a bottle? But no, he had to have decanters! If those blew up, one by one, *pop, pop, pop,* then we were dead."

She leaned forward and hugged her knees.

"Our house took five hours to burn. The beams were thick teak wood. Luckily the men got bored. They let us go, and they set fire to the house next door. Bloody decanters, man!"

"Hey," Ali said, "that was years ago. It's all over now."

Philomena must have seen the worried expression on his face because she turned to him, her face illuminated by the firelight.

"Don't worry," she said, "I'll be fine. You've been very good to me, but I'm not your responsibility. Miles knows how to handle me. He just got freaked out, that's all—the procedure was too much for him. He'll be back."

Ali looked confused, and she continued, "I thought you knew about it. That morning, when he didn't want me to eat the egg—I had an abortion."

Philomena gently removed Ali's arm from around her shoulders. She stood up, walked out of his room, and shut the door gently behind her.

Ali remained in bed. Across the street, the fire burned on in muffled silence, as though the flames had eaten all the sound. He sat for hours, staring at the firelight flickering on the walls. He must have dozed off, because when he woke the fire was out, and it was curiously quiet. In the silence, he heard a shuffling noise.

He opened his door: It was Philomena, walking down the hallway in her faded blue cotton nightgown, her eyes open, but completely blank, mumbling something in Sinhala.

He did not go to her that night. Philomena's bare feet slithered endlessly over the worn linoleum, till, finally, at dawn, she clambered onto the battered pink couch and fell asleep. When the apartment was completely silent, Ali scrabbled under the corner of his mattress; the postcard from Miles was still there, a Vermont phone number written in Miles' careless scrawl.

Ali pulled the phone in from the hallway, careful not to tangle its long cord, and punched in the numbers, expecting to hear Miles' slow, careful voice, but the number rang and rang, then disconnected. No matter. Miles would wake at some point and answer the phone. He'd drive down from Vermont in his battered Volkswagen van, and arrive, smelling of sawdust and cold air. The door to their room would shut, and the rusty, rhythmic creaking of the bedsprings would resume.

Ali tried not to think about it. He got out of bed and walked to the window. The top two floors of the building across the street had burned away completely, and as the sun rose, the golden light, unobstructed, poured into Ali's room, burnishing every surface, illuminating the dark corners.

Everything looked different and very strange.

MUMMY

Every evening, after work, Karim wandered for hours through the vast grid of Washington, DC, taking random rights and lefts, till he was completely lost. The lack of physical coordinates mirrored the disorientation he felt inside himself.

Nobody at work monitored Karim—he was a lowly research assistant at a think tank—and so he began leaving early and expanded his wanderings. He discovered a Chinese place called *Full Yum* in Northeast DC. He stood outside the high walls of the Uzbekistan Embassy and heard the tinkling of wineglasses. He stumbled across the National Greenhouse and sat inside, amidst the giant ferns. Soon he was familiar with the most obscure corners of the city, and the opportunities to get lost diminished. He would have to find some other way to fill the evenings.

Still, he persisted. One Wednesday evening he found himself at a strange intersection in Upper Northwest and briefly felt hope, but then he recognized a bronze statue—a Civil War general on horseback, in full gallop, with his saber extended—and realized that he'd been there before. Following the line of the general's saber, he saw that there *was* something new across the road: a yoga studio called *The Circle of Life*. Outside it was a handwritten sign. It said:

ARE YOU PRESENT IN YOUR LIFE? All human suffering arises from the inability to be present in the moment. We will discuss this at our next Monday night meditation workshop. Open to all.

The words addressed Karim directly: a month ago, his wife, Sakeena, ran across six lanes of traffic on Connecticut Avenue and was hit by a delivery truck. She died on the spot. After the initial busyness—Karim had to arrange for her cremation, scatter her ashes in the Potomac, and donate her clothes—he'd been unable to sleep. Each night he lay patiently in bed, but sleep never came. Now his days had the grainy quality of a badly exposed photograph.

Karim and Sakeena had been married for just four months when she died. The whole episode felt unreal, and now Karim was adrift, lost in time. He decided that he would attend the next meditation session. After all, it was just ten bucks.

⁓

Karim had been raised by an aunt in Connecticut, and she had decided, when he was twenty-six, that it was time for him to have a wife. She'd even found a suitable candidate back home in India: Sakeena was an only child, a qualified accountant, and, judging from her photographs, pretty in a plump sort of way, with a round, guileless face. After a *nikkah* and a sumptuous wedding reception in Mumbai, Karim and Sakeena had flown back to Washington. They were shy and courteous with each other, in the manner of strangers, but in the privacy of Karim's one-bedroom apartment, they began to loosen up. It turned out that Sakeena was cheerful and funny and that she found Karim very handsome; he, in turn, shed the stony loneliness of his bachelor years and was transported back to some earlier, simpler time.

Everything had gone well for two months, till Sakeena made lamb curry for dinner. The meat was perfectly cooked, redolent with saffron, and Karim had stopped talking and eaten his way through two helpings. When he finally looked up, he was shocked to find his mother-in-law staring at him from Mumbai, eight thousand miles away.

Sakeena had activated a video-chat program on her smart phone and was talking to her mother's two-inch image. With her wings of dyed black hair, sharp nose, and dark, piercing eyes, Mummy resembled a crow.

"*Hanh*, Mummy, how is your back?" Sakeena was saying, "What did the doctor say? Spondylitis?"

"Doctors-shoctors, what do they know? I put some eucalyptus oil into hot water and bathed with it. Allah will take care of me. You don't need to worry. You just enjoy yourself in America."

Looking at Mummy, Karim felt the lamb he'd eaten congeal in his stomach. She was a hypochondriac, and during the wedding she had limped around, constantly popping pills from a small metal box, and described her symptoms to all the guests: asthma, rheumatism, and a mysterious affliction she described as *heavy head*. Karim had been glad to see the last of Mummy, and it upset him to see her here, in his apartment, in the middle of dinner.

Sakeena saw that Karim was staring at her and abruptly ended the conversation.

"Okay, *theek hai*, Mummy, I'm going now," she said. Clicking off the video chat, she turned to Karim. "So, how do you like my cooking?"

"The lamb curry is fantastic. It's a masterpiece, a work of art."

Karim was dubious at first, but as he breathed in, he could smell Sakeena's body and the cooking odors trapped in her hair; then the smell changed to the cold metal of the morgue. He breathed in Mummy's gasp of sorrow when she heard the awful news and then the sweet smell of bouquets that had filled the funeral hall. He inhaled all this and exhaled into an infinite dark canyon.

A gentle, reverberating gong signaled the end of the meditation session, and Karim was shocked to find that twenty minutes had passed.

All around him people wiped their eyes and slowly, painfully, came back to the present. The group discussion began, and Karim listened carefully as the plain-faced instructor talked.

"Life is just a story that we tell ourselves," she said. "We trap ourselves into a narrative. There is no concrete reality, just a web of stories." She paused to let the thought sink in. "If we can only let go of our rigid narratives and be in the present, we can truly be alive, whatever the circumstances."

Karim agreed intellectually with what she was saying, but he still ached for Sakeena. Stuffing ten dollars into the donation box, he resolved to return for the next Monday meditation session.

Outside the yoga studio, it had snowed, and the shapes of houses and trees and mailboxes were abstracted into a universal grammar. Walking back to his apartment, he realized that Sakeena had never seen snow. He had bought her a winter coat, a red parka with a fur-lined hood, but she never had a chance to wear it. It was the one garment he couldn't bear to get rid of, and it still hung in the back of his closet.

How could he have known that they would have only four months together?

Sakeena had cooked all the time. When Karim returned from work, Sakeena would have made dinner, not just Indian food, but lobster thermidor baked with Gruyère, salmon steaks with mango salsa, buttery Cornish game hens roasted with fresh rosemary. At first Karim was charmed, but then he began to worry about the expense. His job didn't pay much, and despite her accounting degree, Sakeena wasn't looking for work; she seemed content to spend all day cooking or watching the latest lurid Hindi movie on her laptop.

Then there was Mummy. Karim and Sakeena were taking a walk along the river in Georgetown, and Mummy suddenly materialized on Sakeena's phone: she sat cross-legged in her kitchen and shelled peas as she talked. Sakeena panned her phone to show Mummy the sluggish brown river and the planes roaring low overhead.

"*Hanh, hanh,* very nice, very nice," Mummy intoned in her brusque voice, without a flicker of interest in her eyes. "Did I tell you my arthritis is bad today? See my hands, so swollen?"

The calls lengthened, and soon Sakeena left the video chat on all the time. Sometimes Mummy would appear on the screen, but at other times there would just be an empty kitchen. In the background, Karim could hear Mumbai: the roar of traffic mixed in with the tinkling of bicycle bells and voices shouting in Marathi. Then sadness flooded through him, and he understood what Sakeena was going through; he told himself that she would eventually adjust to America, and that Mummy's appearances would stop.

One humid summer morning Karim took a cold shower and walked naked into the bedroom, and there was Sakeena's iPhone, propped up on the dresser, with Mummy's dull eyes staring at him. He ran back into the bathroom and yelled for his wife.

"Oh my god. Why didn't you wear a towel?" Sakeena said, after she'd shut down the video chat. Her face was flushed from cooking, and there was a smear of turmeric across her cheek.

"Jesus, Sakeena! Could you please give me a head's up when you're online with your mother?"

"Heads up? What do you mean, heads up?"

"I mean, it's not normal to have your mother on video chat all the time!"

"Normal? What is *normal*? I just wanted to see Mummy. And it's not like you have to talk to her or anything."

Karim paused. True, he was never pressured to join the conversation, and depending on how Sakeena angled her phone, Mummy might not even know that he was present. He was about to concede this, when Sakeena continued, her voice quivering with anger.

"Besides," she said, "you have no right to complain. I left my mother and my country, and I came to America for you. So if I want to talk to Mummy, I'll talk to her, okay?"

"Really? That's the deal?"

Her eyes flashed. "*Hanh*. That's the *deal*."

She stormed into the living room, sank into the couch, and opened her laptop.

Karim toweled off and dressed. It dawned on him that despite whatever Sakeena said, she and her mother were joined at the hip. The signs had been there all along—he'd just been too stupid to read them.

Sakeena had been a year old when her father had divorced Mummy, leaving them nearly destitute. Mummy had started sewing children's clothes, working late into the night, and she eventually grew it into a business that employed twenty women. And Sakeena had been there at every step of the way, imbibing all the stories: how her mother had begged relatives for money to start her business; how some nights Mummy had filled her stomach with water and given her share of food to Sakeena; how Mummy had defied the thugs who demanded protection money. Sakeena knew all of Mummy's medications, she knew the history of each of Mummy's ailments. They were one unit. Karim was the interloper.

When he left for work, Sakeena was sitting in the living room and streaming a Hindi movie on her laptop, huge headphones clamped over her ears. He saw that she had the ingredients for the day's cooking arrayed on the kitchen counter: chicken legs, big green leeks, and a pile of muddy sweet potatoes. But when he came home that night there was only the leftover rice and plain *daal* from the night before.

Mummy did not appear. They ate in frosty silence.

"Hey," he said, "can we talk about this?"

Sakeena's face became as dark as a thundercloud.

"Talk? What is there to talk about? *Hanh*? I am so lonely here, in this godforsaken country, and you won't even let me talk to my mother."

"It's not that, I'm just used to some privacy, and—"

"First you shout at me, now you want to talk? What next, you'll want me to go to therapy? Perhaps take antidepressants? *Hanh*? I was wrong. You are just like them."

"What are you . . . like who?"

"*Tu bahut American ban gaya.*"

It took Karim a moment to translate what she had said: *You've become so American.* So this is how she thought of him: As a stranger.

putting it off, and when he finally dialed it was early morning in Mumbai. When he told Mummy what had happened, she gasped, *Ya Allah,* and then began to cry softly. The sound of her sobbing mixed in with the cawing of the early morning crows.

Mummy finally took a deep breath, and Karim braced himself for a torrent of abuse: He was responsible for Sakeena's death. He had taken her only daughter to America and killed her.

"Karim, are you there?" Mummy's voice crackled with grief. "Listen to me. You must not, on any account blame yourself. Sakeena was the one who ran across the road. This is how life works. It is painful, but it is life."

"I'm sorry, Mummy," Karim said. "I let her down, I—"

"Stop, Karim. Listen to me. Just take it day by day. The sadness will come later. Now, just do what needs to be done."

Karim knew that Mummy was tough, but he was not prepared for her stoicism.

"You did your best with Sakeena," Mummy continued. "I know my girl, she is headstrong, stubborn, a difficult person, but you tried to make her happy. She got into the habit of fighting with me, and I think she was just continuing it with you. I talked to her yesterday, and she was ashamed of her behavior. She was going to make lamb curry for you and tell you that she was sorry.

"Also, I need you to do something for me. Sakeena didn't want to be buried, left to rot in the earth. You should cremate her, and do it quickly. I don't want her lying in a metal drawer. Her soul must be released as soon as possible."

Karim murmured his assent. When he hung up, he saw traces of Sakeena everywhere: her hair on the couch, her open laptop, a tattered book of recipes. He walked into the kitchen, the only neutral place in the apartment, and blindly opened the refrigerator, letting the cool air wash over his face. Right in front of his nose was a shiny, pink package of lamb, a new container of yogurt, and a bunch of cilantro, green and fresh and alive.

He stood with the refrigerator door open and cried till his stomach cramped. He threw all the food away, and it lay, stinking in the trash can, till his aunt arrived to console him.

_____

It was now midwinter, and by the time Karim reached the yoga studio it was already dark. This was the final class in the series, and Karim found it hard to concentrate; he wondered if Jocelyn would remember his offer from a week ago.

After the others left, they rolled up the mats together.

"I can come by this evening for the coat," Jocelyn said, smiling at him. "It's very kind of you."

"It's actually a parka. Red. If you don't mind red."

"Red is great."

They walked out together. Jocelyn's head was bare as usual, her shoulders hunched against the chill, and Karim moved a little closer.

"Can I ask you a personal question?" He took a deep breath. "Are you seeing anyone? Here?"

She laughed. "No. Not at all. In fact, the longest conversations I've had these last few months have been with you." Her breath came out in wispy clouds. "After my bad breakup in India, I thought I'd never heal . . . but somehow, I'm emerging from a dark period, you know? I know that sounds corny."

Karim nodded gravely. "Not at all. I understand perfectly."

They entered the warm, brightly lit lobby of Karim's apartment building, and the doorman, who knew about

"Hey, what happened?"

"*Umm*, I peeked into your spare bedroom, and there was an iPhone propped up there, and I thought it was a digital picture, you know? But then this old lady on the screen suddenly moved. It freaked me out . . ."

The blood drained from Karim's head. "Did she see you?" His voice was unsteady. "See you clearly?"

"No, I don't think so. It was dark, and . . . Who is that? Your Mom?"

He would have to tell her everything now: it was premature, it was not as he had planned, but she would understand.

"That was my mother-in-law, in Mumbai. I was married. My wife died, and... It's hard to explain. I was going to tell you when the time was right."

Jocelyn turned very pale. "Jesus, Karim. You were married? Are you serious?" She shook her head as if to clear it. "Wait, wait, wait. You *were* married, or you *are* married? If you're no longer married, why are you on video chat with your mother-in-law? Why are you worried that she saw me?"

"Look, I don't want to hurt her feelings, okay? I mean, if she sees me with another woman, so soon after . . ."

Jocelyn's gaze fell onto the red parka, which was lying on the kitchen table. "That's your dead wife's coat? That's what you were giving me?"

"She never even wore it. It's brand new, and you need a coat, right?"

Jocelyn pulled on her three sweaters and strode to the front door.

"Look, I'm not lying to you. I was just waiting for the right moment . . . Will you please listen to me?"

Jocelyn rushed through the front door and stood in the lobby, jabbing at the elevator button, and he followed her.

"Okay, yes, I'm in touch with my former mother-in-law, but you're taking it all wrong. You said we shouldn't get caught up in our stories, that it's just a narrative, right?"

"I just got out of one mess. I can't handle another one. I'm sorry, Karim."

The elevator door slid open. Jocelyn stepped into it, and there was a slow whirr as the elevator descended, and then silence.

What had just happened? Maybe he could run down the stairs and catch her in the lobby? But the expectant mood of the evening had evaporated, and Karim was exhausted. He went back into his apartment and shut the door.

The video chat with Mummy had started after Sakeena died. He gave away all of Sakeena's clothes, but he kept her iPhone, and even kept it charged. One night, at four in the morning, he could not sleep—the insomnia had returned, worse than ever—and he'd picked up her phone and clicked to video chat. Mummy was online, and her icon glowed green. When he called, she was in her cramped little kitchen, and she sliced potatoes as they spoke.

"*Beta*," she'd said, "This must be a hard time for you. Are you eating? Is your auntie taking care of you?"

He'd said that he was fine, that he had gone each day to the spot on Connecticut Avenue where Sakeena was killed and taped a fresh bouquet of flowers to a lamp post.

Mummy had squinted up at him and said, very gently, "You don't look well. There are dark circles under your eyes. Are you sleeping?"

When he broke down and said that he couldn't sleep, she had tsk-tsked and said, "You should drink warm milk with turmeric and massage your head with hot olive oil."

He didn't do any of those things, but just talking to Mummy had loosened the tightness that bound his chest. After he hung up, he'd closed his eyes and slept till dawn.

The next night he'd called her again, and this time, at the end of their conversation, she'd said, "You can just leave the video on. You sleep, and I will watch over you."

He'd drifted off, listening to the slap-slap of Mummy rolling *rotis*.

From then onward, that was his routine: he left the video chat on at night and fell asleep to the sound of Mummy cooking.

Now, Karim stood stock still, leaning against the front door. He imagined a scene in some coffee shop, Jocelyn in her three sweaters, arms crossed, and him, leaning forward, earnestly explaining. He realized that even if she believed him, he'd have to give up Mummy; there was no way that an American woman was going to share him with his ex-mother-in-law.

Karim walked down the hall and pulled open the door to the spare bedroom, and Mummy peered up at him from the lit screen of Sakeena's iPhone.

"Hello, son. Did you come in earlier? I thought I saw you."

Karim sighed with relief. All Mummy had seen was a silhouette, backlit by the bright hallway.

"Yes, I ducked in earlier, but . . . I had rice boiling on the stove, so I went back out to check."

"Rice? Good. You must eat hot food, *na?* None of this sandwich nonsense." Mummy peered into his face. "You look tired, son. Do you want to sleep now?"

Karim took off his sweatshirt and crawled into bed and yanked up the heavy comforter. He closed his eyes and heard Mummy's breathing and beyond that, the familiar sounds

of Mumbai: mynah birds chirping, the silvery tinkling of
bicycle bells, the faint beeping of motor scooters.

"Go to sleep," Mummy said, "sleep now, my son."

And Karim closed his eyes, and he did.

girls in the clubs—who had immaculate weaves and nails like hard, polished jewels—she was a dirty, scruffy monkey. Yet, there was something about her.

The girl opened her eyes: bright blue irises with white starbursts, the eyes of a visionary or a madwoman, and Sanjeev felt embarrassed to be caught staring.

Her upside-down lips curved into a smile. "Hey big guy, where you been? How's the livery business?"

"It sucks. I'm supposed to sit inside my car all day and wait for my client."

"That's tough. I'm Eula, by the way."

Still hanging upside down, Eula reached out a long-fingered hand, and he shook her callused palm and introduced himself.

She swung herself upwards, and blood rushed into her pale face. She gestured to the textbook in his lap. "You in school? Studying for an exam?"

"Oh, no. I'm just interested in psychology."

"Psychiatrists are all nuts. You should see my shrink. He never cashes my checks, and when I go to see him, half the time, he's double booked."

Sanjeev was pretty sure that psychologists were different from psychiatrists, but he just nodded. He was conscious of Eula's hard, lithe body under her faded clothes. She sensed this and grinned at him. "Gotta go, big guy Check out our new routine. We're calling it, *Speaking truth to power.*"

All four acrobats formed a line and raised their arms. They waved their arms gently, like tree branches caught in an imaginary breeze, and soon it turned into a gale. The acrobats swayed and leaned at impossible angles, and the hypnotic melody washed over them, the language incomprehensible, full of pain and protest.

Sanjeev wanted to watch the rest of the show, but the silent cell phone in his pocket made him feel uneasy. He threw a ten-dollar bill into their basket and hurried back to the car. The show continued behind him, the wailing music interspersed with the soft gasps of the onlookers.

That evening he told Tara about the acrobats. She sat propped up on the couch, her eyes sunken but her hair still glossy and thick.

Sanjeev described the music: the lament of the saxophone, the ponderous beat of the bass, the melancholy voice singing in French, or was it Spanish? He told Tara how the troupe had turned themselves into trees and reacted to the imaginary gale that blew at them. He could not communicate what he really felt: that they were not merely acrobats, but artists, risk-takers, that they toyed with movements verging on chaos.

Instead, all he said was, "Next time, I'll take a video."

Tara shook her head. From the way she tensed her neck, he could tell that the pain was worse.

"I like it better when you describe it. Then I can imagine it in my head."

"You'll get better soon, I promise. We'll go and see them, okay?"

Tara just smiled faintly. The conversation had worn her out, and she closed her eyes and dozed off.

He tiptoed into the kitchen and prepared a meal of rice and *daal*, cooked with some chicken stock, potatoes, and peas—this was the only food that Tara could tolerate—but she did not wake for dinner that night and moaned as she slept. He sat by her for a long time and then ate dinner alone.

Things were getting much worse, but the doctors were of no help. He did not know what to do.

⸙

The next afternoon was sunny and cloudless, but the acrobats were late. Sanjeev sat on the bench next to the plinth, and he must have dozed off, because he was startled to find Eula sitting cross-legged on the bench, inches away, wearing orange harem pants and a tiny black sports bra.

"Hey, we had a bet about you." She sat with her back erect, as though an invisible string ran out of the top of her head. "Where are you from?"

"What did you guess?"

"El Salvador? Brazil? Some place with big guys. You're pretty strong." She patted his bicep, a professional, appraising touch, not flirting like the girls at the clubs.

"I'm from India. I'm not strong like you guys. I mean, I lift weights, but . . ."

"India! We all guessed wrong. Hey, you should come over sometime. We make a lot of Indian food: rice, lentils, chickpeas. We live in a group house in Bushwick with some other people, jugglers, and a clown—not a funny clown, a physical one."

"Maybe I'll stop by."

"Good." Eula unfolded herself off the bench, and strolled toward the other acrobats, gesturing at Sanjeev and saying, "He's Indian, yo."

The others shook their heads in wonder, and one tall boy gave Sanjeev a thumbs-up. They put on their slow, hypnotic jazz and began to stretch each other out, but that day the show did not start.

A group of break-dancers in red tank tops and do-rags had set up by the marble arch in the center of the park. They assembled a crowd, exhorting the bystanders to clap in unison, and once their show started, their loud, thumping hip-hop drowned out the acrobats' lacy music.

Eula strolled over and apologetically asked a muscular man if he would turn the music down, but he just stared at her, and then turned wordlessly away. She returned to the acrobats, shrugging helplessly, and Sanjeev drew himself up to his full height.

"Eula, you want me to talk to them? They might listen to me."

She shook her head, No.

"Are you sure? I know how to handle people like that. Back home, I . . ."

"Forget it, Sanjeev. Hey, you want to help me stretch?"

He looked uncertain, but she said that he just had to stand still. She swung one leg up, balanced her foot high up on his shoulder and bent into the stretch.

"Wow. It's like you're made of rubber."

"It's just practice. You could do it, too, you're strong."

"Not like you." He felt the weight of her leg, the warmth of her body. "Well, I better get back to my car. My client might call."

"Okay. See you tomorrow?"

Sanjeev nodded, and Eula kissed him, once, a quick, darting peck on the cheek. She walked away without looking back.

Sanjeev found it hard to breathe. Was she joking? Was she serious? What did it mean? He walked past the break-dancers, who were spinning on their backs, their red tank tops now dark with sweat. One of the break-dancers went around, thrusting out a coffee can, and the spectators, mostly tourists, stuffed it with bills.

At the edge of the park, Sanjeev turned to look the acrobats. They were gathered at the base of the plinth, sharing a plastic bottle of water. They all looked so skinny and ragged, like street urchins. Did they rely on the money they earned in the park? How did Eula survive? He couldn't imagine her working as a waitress or a barista.

Just then, Sanjeev's cell phone buzzed in his chest pocket. This was the signal that the client wanted to be picked up; the man always called and then hung up when Sanjeev answered.

Sanjeev ran to the car, gunned the engine, and screeched to a stop in front of the town house. The client was standing at the top of the stairs, anxiously scanning the street, and he scowled as Sanjeev jumped out of the car and pulled open the rear door. The client clambered into the car, his face red, and Sanjeev waited for an explosion of words, but instead the man balled both hands into fists and rubbed his eyes. He had put on weight, and his belly pushed against the tight waistcoat he wore under his suit jacket.

Sanjeev drove slowly uptown. At this time of the evening, Sixth Avenue was tricky, seething with drivers, and the air was filled with aggression; after being cooped up in offices the whole of Manhattan spilled out onto the streets, pushing and jostling.

The client leaned his head back and closed his eyes. Five weeks had passed, and the man had not spoken. Not one miserable word.

～

The nights became warm and soft, the texture of velvet. Tara found the heat unbearable and sweated uncontrollably. She had bad dreams and let out small yelps of fear; Sanjeev stayed up all night, stroking her hair to calm her down.

One morning, after dropping off the client, Sanjeev wandered into Washington Square Park and took his seat on the bench by the plinth. The acrobats were not there yet, and he opened his Psych 101 textbook and began to read a chapter on PTSD—you didn't have to be in a war, you could get it from an abusive relationship or a bad job—but that day he found it hard to concentrate. Tara was in a downward spiral; the specialists had changed her medications, but it wasn't working. Closing the book, he tried to remember Tara in the old days, in her bright pastel suits and high heels, but the memories were unclear now. He buried his face in his hands.

"Are you feeling okay? Something wrong?"

It was Eula, standing over him, her head cocked to one side, her lips parted in sympathy.

Sanjeev wiped his eyes with his fists. He wanted to tell Eula about the bitter smell of the antibiotics that now clung to Tara. He wanted to say that Tara had always been the smart one, the one with a plan, and that he was now completely lost. He wanted Eula to kiss him, on the lips this time.

"I'm fine," he said. "Just not enough sleep. What's going on? When does the performance start?"

"I don't think we're performing today."

"Why not?"

As if on cue, deafeningly loud hip-hop music blasted, and he saw the troupe of red-shirted break-dancers enter the park, clapping and chanting in unison.

"That's not right." Sanjeev balled his hands into fists. "I'll fix those assholes."

"I already asked if they could turn down their music. Or if we could schedule different times. They're not interested."

"You people are too nice. What those guys understand is . . . Never mind, I'll take care of them."

"No violence." Eula put both palms flat against Sanjeev's chest, preventing him from rising. "That's not what we're about."

Her arms, pressing into him, were very strong.

"What are you going to do, then?"

"We'll do a different routine. We don't need music for it. We'll make a tower." She let her hands fall to her sides. "Just watch us. It's totally cool."

Eula walked over to the other acrobats, and they wrapped wide, black cloth bands across their waists. The two boys faced each other, legs wide apart, and leaned in, locking hands, and pressed their foreheads together, forming a base. The dark-haired girl took a deep breath, then grabbed one boy's waistband and hauled herself up like a monkey. She crouched on their shoulders, and then stood up slowly, swaying a little, her arms sticking out for balance.

A crowd began to form: A few tourists with cameras, students in mid-stride, old ladies out with their aides. As if in a dream, Sanjeev watched Eula, the thinnest, the lightest, rub her hands together, then clamber up one boy's back, and, incredibly, reach up, grab the dark-haired girl's shoulders with both hands, and flip herself up: she did a handstand on the girl's shoulders, extending the tower of bodies high into the sky.

The crowd gasped. People stopped to watch.

All four acrobats were one marvelously balanced organism, but how long could they hold this formation? The boys at the bottom of the tower gritted their teeth; up top, the muscles in Eula's arms quivered with strain.

A minute went by, then more. The noise from the break dancers fell away. There was just this straining tower of flesh and the expectant breathing of the onlookers. A dreaminess settled in, a slowing down of time. White, puffy clouds drifted slowly across the clear blue sky.

One of the boy acrobats screamed. With a sudden, myoclonic jerk, the base of the tower collapsed. The two girls tumbled down like cats, twisting in the air, landing on their feet. The crowd let out a sympathetic groan and began to disperse, shaking their heads, heading toward the loud, insistent beat of the break-dancers.

Eula and the others gathered around a boy acrobat and pressed a cold pack into his shoulder, which was twisted at an odd angle; Eula looked pale and exhausted and bit down on her lower lip to keep from crying. Right then, Sanjeev did not think. He simply took off his chauffeur's navy-blue tunic, folded it, and draped it across the back of the bench. Clad only in his white undershirt and dark trousers, he walked into the circle of acrobats.

"I'm strong," Sanjeev said. He gestured to the injured boy. "I can take his place."

The other acrobats shook their heads, but Eula spoke sharply, and they soon changed their minds. Eula showed Sanjeev how to stand, legs apart, how to brace himself against the boy acrobat.

"Imagine you're the arch of a bridge," she whispered to him, "you're made of steel, you're very, very strong." She turned to the crowd and yelled, "Don't count us out, folks! We're giving it another try! A human tower!"

Sanjeev assumed a wide stance, bent forward, and took a deep breath. He felt the heat of the other boy's forehead press into his.

"Ready?" Eula's voice was bright with excitement. "Here we go."

Hard, callused hands gripped Sanjeev's shoulders, and he felt the weight of the dark-haired girl as she climbed up onto his shoulders. She settled above him, and then whistled softly. With a rush of air, Eula jumped up, twisted in the air, and did a handstand onto the dark-haired girl's shoulders. The weight came down on Sanjeev like a hammer.

He grunted once. Remembering Eula's instructions, he gave himself over to the weight; he merged with the other acrobats, matching their breathing, breath for labored breath.

Sanjeev did not hear the buzzing of his cell phone as it rang, buttoned into the pocket of his tunic. He did not know that the client was standing on the steps of the town house, waiting anxiously to be picked up.

Ten seconds passed. Fifteen. Twenty. The tower still stood. Sanjeev was cemented into its base, sweat coursing down his face and dripping onto his chest. He was concentrating so hard that he did not hear, from the North side of the Park, the hard retort of a gunshot. He did not hear the panicked shouting, or the rippling wail of police sirens.

Right then, Sanjeev did not hear any of this.

Later, after the performance was over, he would see the missed call from the client, and immediately drove to the town house, but the road would be blocked by the police. When he tried to walk to the town house, a burly cop would tell him to back off. Sanjeev would identify himself as the client's chauffeur, and the cop would tell him that the client had been shot in the head while waiting on the townhouse steps. After taking Sanjeev's statement, the cops would let him go. For the next few months, he would scour the Internet, but he would not be able to find out the client's identity or learn why he was executed.

Right then, cemented into the base of the tower, Sanjeev did not know any of this.

He did not know that without the client's steady gig, he would go back to driving on call, and that, three months later, he would be on a run to JFK Airport when Tara died, of complications from her illness; an autopsy would reveal an acute inflammation of the heart. He did not know that he would return to Washington Square Park many times and sit on the bench and read his Psych 101 textbook, but the acrobats would never reappear. He would even drive to Bushwick, but no one would have heard of a house occupied by a group of ragged acrobats. He would never see Eula again. The months and years that followed would be the darkest period of his life.

Right then, Sanjeev did not know any of this. Right then, he was the base of the tower. He felt Eula above him, straight and strong, silhouetted against the blue sky. He felt the bodies of the others, every twitch and quiver of their muscles, as they all worked together, shifting and adjusting, holding the formation.

In that moment, years of confusion fell away. In that moment, Sanjeev forgot himself and became part of something larger. He was connected to the earth beneath and the vault of the heavens high above. He was made of iron. He was immensely strong, and he could bear anything.

BARCELONA

On that first morning in Spain, Ali awoke to the sizzle of fish frying. It was fish, he was sure of it, an odor from his childhood in India, and it evoked such intense nostalgia that he turned over to tell Amy, but there was only the cool, empty sheet where she had lain. She was gone.

Ali lay still, listening hard for Amy's morning noises: the running of the shower, the *tic-tic-tic* of her typing, the *ding* of the toaster. There was only a thick, reverberating silence, broken by the cloying smell of frying fish.

He pulled on his sticky underwear and jeans from yesterday's long flight and walked through the rooms of the shabby, unfamiliar apartment—they'd rented it, cheaply, on the internet—looking for a note from Amy, a few looping sentences written on yellow legal paper. There was no note on the tiny dining table, and her sensible walking shoes were gone, as was her messenger bag and her beige cotton jacket. Amy was a great walker, would head off in Boston for hours on her own, but she would always leave a note.

Ali took out his cell phone to check for a text message, but there was no reception. He jerked open the glass doors and walked out onto the balcony, and the stone tiles scorched his bare feet. It faced onto a stone-flagged interior courtyard and the windows on all four sides glared at him, blank and expectant. The hot sun beat down on his bare head—Jesus, it was nearly noon, later than he'd thought.

His phone was still dead. He searched for the apartment Wi-Fi network, but there wasn't one. *Calm down*, he said to himself, *you can figure this out*. He leaned his chest against the hot metal railings and looked down into the courtyard, empty except for a mangy orange cat napping in the sunlight.

Amy's conference—an international gathering of Emily Dickinson scholars—did not begin for another day. Was she angry at him for sleeping late? The night before she had quickly brushed her teeth, put on her old nightgown, and fallen sleep, but Ali had stayed awake, jazzed by the flight from Boston and the taxi ride through the strange city. He'd moved in close to Amy, wanting to feel the curve of her long, cool body, but she'd muttered in her sleep and turned away.

Now, Ali stood alone on the balcony, listening to the hot hiss of fish frying somewhere. He could almost taste the over-used, stale oil, and it made him sick to his stomach. He went back inside.

Opening a suitcase, he moved aside their passports—her slim American one and his thick Indian booklet, stamped with an American work visa—and searched for his sky-blue linen shirt. It was at the bottom of the suitcase, creased after being stored away for the Boston winter. Wearing it, he saw that at least his arms had stayed brown, unlike Amy's, whose freckled summer tan reverted quickly to a pale white, with bluish undertones. Thinking about her he felt the panic again and hurried out of the apartment.

The creaking elevator smelled of cat's piss. Ali emerged into the street and realized with a shock that Barcelona reminded him of Mumbai: There was the same feeling of languor, the same light, heavy with dust motes, and the

same squat concrete buildings, their balconies crowded with
dripping laundry.

In which direction would Amy have gone? They had
brought a guidebook and a map, but, apparently, she had
taken both. Ali did not mind. He was an architect, and he
liked buildings, cities, maps. As was his practice, he had
memorized the Barcelona street map and was fine navigating
on memory and instinct. In fact, he took voluptuous pleasure
in giving up control, an aspect of his character that irritated
Amy immensely. He decided now to head east toward Las
Ramblas, the ruler-straight tourist drag that cut through
the city. Surely Amy was there, eating a sandwich in a
backpacker coffee shop.

Ali walked confidently down one street and chose a lane
that seemed headed in the right direction, but it wound
sinuously, and he turned into another lane and another, and
soon he was completely disoriented. He passed Africans in
robes and shy veiled women. He went past a halal ice-cream
store and a butcher's shop with purple goat carcasses hanging
in the windows. This was Spain? Where the hell was he?

Ali and Amy were visiting Barcelona because of a
compromise. They had been dating for three years, but when
Ali said they should visit India and meet his family, Amy
wrinkled up her long nose.

"Oh, come on, Ali. They'll hate me. I'm sure they want
you to marry a nice Muslim girl."

"But you have a degree from Harvard," he'd said, smiling.
"Harvard trumps everything."

"I like *you*," she'd said. "I'm just not that *interested* in
India."

Each time Ali pressed her for reasons, she would retreat
into her work, a feminist re-evaluation of Emily Dickinson.
She was turning her PhD thesis into a book, and from what

Ali understood, the analysis had little to do with Dickinson's poems, but instead was a deconstruction of the way that *other* literary scholars had responded to the poems. Dickinson's books lay all over their apartment, and sometimes Ali would pick one up and read a short poem, full of words like *funeral* and *numb* and *drum*.

When Amy felt stuck with her work, Ali would drive her north to Amherst, to Dickinson's boxy old homestead, and they would watch the sun reflecting off its blank, lead glass windows. Ali began to associate Amy's refusal to go to India with those snowy drives up to Amherst and Dickinson's short, stabbing words. He grew sick of Amy's project, of Boston, and when Amy was invited to this conference in Barcelona, Ali was the one who pushed her to accept. "At least it'll be hot," he said. "It'll be different."

Now, he walked on, past shops selling bunches of overripe bananas and baskets of persimmons, past dark bars that smelled sourly of alcohol, past wailing Arabic music and shouts in languages he did not understand.

He was irrevocably lost. He stopped a man carrying a burlap sack and asked him where Las Ramblas was, but the man did not seem to understand, and so Ali repeated the word, Ram*blas*, *Ram*blas, a different pronunciation each time, till finally the man smiled broadly and pointed a definitive finger down a lane that curved out of sight, no different from all the other lanes, but with a higher density of pedestrians.

Following the man's directions, Ali came to a long open-air mall lined with benches and trees. At one end was an enormous brass sculpture of a cat, enlarged to the size of a small elephant, and Ali recognized the rounded curves as the work of Fernando Botero, the famous Colombian artist. This identification pleased him, located him, and he walked

confidently down what he thought was Las Ramblas, sure
now of being on track; when he heard the sharp crack of
wood hitting a cork ball, he stopped abruptly.

He thought that he was dreaming—surely he had mixed
up Mumbai with Barcelona—for beyond the cat sculpture
a cricket match was taking place. It was just like the street
cricket games of his childhood in Mumbai: two teams of
boys and men, untucked, half-sleeved shirts billowing as
they bowled and batted in dead earnest.

The cricket game was in full flight, the players shouting
to each other in Hindi and Urdu, cursing, saying *Sisterfucker*
and *You bowl like a pregnant elephant, yaar.* Ali walked
closer, the mechanics of the game instantly intelligible to
him after many years in America. There was only one other
spectator sitting on a bench, a young brown-skinned man,
Indian or Pakistani, his lanky body bent forward in
concentration. He was absorbed in the game, following the
flight of the red ball as it arced high in the air and slipped
through the hands of a negligent fielder.

Ali sat down next to the man. "He could have caught
that," he said, and the man started at him with liquid brown
eyes.

"Qué?" The man grinned at Ali. He was roughly Ali's age,
late twenties, wearing polyester trousers and a white long-
sleeved shirt, the collar and cuffs buttoned. Despite the
cheap clothes the man's high-browed, neatly shaven face
radiated an amused intelligence, and he was smiling faintly
as he studied Ali, taking in the linen shirt, the jeans, the
expensive American sandals.

Ali repeated his statement in clumsy Mumbai Hindi.
The man smiled in relief and replied in fluent Pakistani
Urdu, the two languages similar enough for them to
communicate.

"Oh yes, he should have caught that ball, but he's too fat and too stupid." The man smiled broadly. "My name is Ali Zaheer. I am from Lahore. You are from where?"

Ali was stunned at the coincidence. He'd forgotten that Ali was a common Muslim name; he had been proud of his uniqueness when surrounded by white guys named Joe, Bob, and Matt.

"My name is Ali, too. Ali Azeem. From Mumbai, but now I live in America."

The man laughed heartily, as though at the punch line of a hilarious joke. "Well, then, we are brothers. *Salaam alikum,* Ali *bhai.*"

"*Waalekum-as-salaam.* I didn't know there were Pakistanis in Barcelona."

"We are everywhere now, *bhai.* The situation back home is so bad—half my village from Pakistan is here. And it seems there are only two names that our elders know: Ali and Mohammad. Tell you what—I will call you Ali Ameriki, and you can call me Ali Isfahani, and there will be no confusion. Good idea, no?"

"It's a deal."

They shook hands. There was a lull in the cricket game as the batters changed and one player handed his splintered, taped-up bat to another, who swung it experimentally.

"So, Ali Ameriki. How do you like our Barcelona? Nice, no?"

"I haven't really seen much. We just got in last night, my girlfriend and I. She's here for a conference, I'm just tagging along."

"Girlfriend? Not a Muslim girl?"

"No, she's American, we met there—"

"*Aaare!* You have an American girlfriend! She has yellow hair? White skin?"

Ali was disarmed by the man's toothy smile, taking the sting out of his words. He remembered that this was the way they used to talk, back in Mumbai, when white women were an abstraction, their milky skin and pink lips driving the boys to flights of ecstasy.

"Yeah, Amy is blonde, and she's pretty pale." Ali wondered where Amy was, wondered if the sun in Barcelona would burn her skin. In summer she always had a spray of freckles across her nose and high cheekbones.

"You are a lucky man, Ali Ameriki. What do you do in America? Does your girlfriend also work?"

"I'm an architect. Amy's an adjunct at Harvard. She teaches poetry."

"Poetry? That's a subject?"

"Amy's an expert on Emily Dickinson, a very famous poet in America . . ." Half-remembered words flashed into Ali's mind: *pain* and *blank* and *time*.

Ali Isfahani was looking at him in frank disbelief—how was it possible to earn a living by teaching poetry?

Ali quickly changed the topic. "And you, Ali Isfahani, what do you do here?"

"Oh, me, I have a certificate in computer programming from Lahore University. I have a very good job, in a bank, in fact . . . Actually, I have to go to work soon. But I would like to talk to you more about America. About visas and so forth. I'm told that a sponsorship letter is required? Let's meet again. I'm always on this bench in the morning."

Ali Isfahani stood up and meticulously realigned the cuffs of his white shirt, revealing fine, small stitches where the torn buttonholes had been mended.

"Sure, sure, of course *bhai*," Ali said. He knew that he'd never return to this bench, would never talk to this man about visas. He felt his stomach growl and realized he was quite hungry. "Can you tell me, is there a good place around here for some food? Or even some *chai*?"

Ali Isfahani beamed. "A place for *chai*? Of course, we have a place for *chai*. And food too, the best kabobs in Europe. It is on my way. Come, I will show you."

The two Alis walked down the dusty mall, and crossed into a dingier section of the old town. Brightly made-up European women stood in the gloomy stone doorways, some of them very young, their age masked by bouffant hairdos and high spike heels. They all seemed to know Ali Isfahani and exchanged greetings with him in rapid Spanish.

"Russian girls," Ali Isfahani said, "Very expensive. But white, very white."

They went into a small bar, undistinguishable from all the others, with its smudged plate glass window and metal door. The moment Ali entered, he smelled the sharp, comforting tang of *chai*, and the rich smells of rice and roasting meat. The television was playing a soap opera in Urdu, and the faces that lined the wooden tables were all Pakistani, their dark heads bent over plates loaded with rice. Ali Isfahani whispered something to the proprietor, then lifted his arm in farewell and said that he was late for work.

"We will meet again, *Inshallah*," he said, and his lanky frame was silhouetted for an instant in the bright doorway before he disappeared.

Ali sat down at a table and drank a cup of excellent *chai* before ordering a plate of rice and lamb kabobs. Soon a few men drifted over, and Ali engaged in conversation with them. Ali's Hindi was barely a match for their rapid-fire Urdu, but the men smiled fondly at his stumbling sentences and treated him like a favorite nephew.

Nobody seemed to be in a hurry. A few men drifted in and out of the bar, but a core remained, and Ali heard their stories: Most of them had knocked around Europe, busking in London and working construction in Ireland, before settling in Barcelona, and they all agreed that it was the best city, with friendly people and good weather. In turn, the men asked Ali detailed questions about America. He told them that he had a job as a designer at an architecture firm in Boston, that he owned a car, an old red Honda, and the men sighed longingly, like penitents denied entry to the promised land.

When Ali finally looked at this watch, he was shocked to see that the afternoon had slipped away. He took out his wallet to pay, rifling through the odd-sized euro notes, when he caught sight of some folded yellow legal paper. Why the hell had Amy put a note in his wallet, and not somewhere he could have seen it? The note said that Amy had waited for him to awake, but that he'd slept on, and not wanting to waste the day, she had decided to go by herself to Gaudí's Parc Güell. Since she had taken the guidebook, she had written down detailed directions on how to get to the Plaça Catalunya, and asked him to meet her there at three-thirty.

Good old Amy. Ali felt a massive weight lift off his chest and even chuckled at the fears that had been plaguing him all day. Then he realized it was already past three, and that even if he hurried, he would be late meeting her.

He tried to pay the proprietor, urgently thrusting banknotes at him, but the money was gently turned away.

"*Nahi, nahi, nahi.* The other Ali has paid for you. He said you were his guest. He said you were like a brother to him."

Ali remembered Ali Isfahani's old, mended shirt, and wanted to leave some cash, but the proprietor's face darkened, and Ali realized that it was a matter of honor. He put his wallet away and asked directions to the nearest metro and was surprised to hear that he was nowhere near the real Las Ramblas. The site of the cricket game had been Rambla del Raval, an entirely different place from the tourist street he had tried to find.

Ali emerged into the sunlight and headed, as directed, toward the real Ramblas and found it easily, a broad river of people, with backpacking tourists and the sound of English everywhere. It was like another country. He thought of what the men had said: "We Pakistanis do not really live in Barcelona, *bhai*. We call our neighborhood Pakcelona."

He was, of course, late meeting Amy at the Plaça Catalunya. She was standing under a statue of a rearing horse, tall and slender, wearing jeans and a white tank top, and the dark line of a camera strap bisected her torso. The Spanish men who walked by stared frankly at her, and Ali could tell from her reddened face that she was irritated by the attention.

Ali got closer and apologized breathlessly, but she did not rebuke him in any way, just stooped a little to hear him above the hum of traffic. He told her how India had emerged, unbidden, here of all places, and an abstracted expression came over her face. Not knowing what to do, he kept on talking, feeling the inches of air between them.

". . . these guys have been calling me Ali Ameriki all afternoon. I think I like it. It's like a title or something."

There was a silence as Amy took out a pair of sleek oval sunglasses and slipped them on.

"Well. How interesting," she said. "Shall we get something to eat?"

"There's this great place, the Plaça Reial, I read about it in the guidebook," Ali said eagerly, "I think you'll like it. Gaudí designed the lampposts there."

He took her cool hand in his, and they walked back to
the metro from which he had just emerged. As they descended
the stairs—Ali was burbling on about how the metro stations
were so modern here, unlike Boston's peeling, leaky caverns—
Amy leaned in and sniffed at him with her long nose but
did not say anything.

"What is it?" he said.

"Oh, nothing," she replied and hurried down the steep
stairs.

Before he could help it, Ali spoke. "I didn't shower today,
is that it?"

His tone was harsh. He knew he was making things
worse, but he couldn't help it; he hated the way she blurred
things together, then left him to guess at his offenses. Why
couldn't they just fight like normal people and get it over
with?

They pushed through the turnstiles and reached the
echoing metro platform, and Amy stood looking at a route
map. From the back, her long neck exposed, she looked so
vulnerable. Ali's anger evaporated, but it was too late. They
did not talk the rest of the way.

⁓

The moment they sat down at a table within the shadowy
arcade of the Plaça Reial, Ali realized that he had made a
huge mistake. The vast public square was crawling with
tourists, drinking and eating noisily at the cheap tapas
restaurants that lined the arcades. They attracted immigrant
men who tried to sell them things, long flaps of postcards,
neon glow sticks, and cellophane-wrapped roses. Ali should
have taken Amy to a small restaurant in the Barri Gòtic,
some shadowed, intimate space, but now it was too late; a

short, dignified waiter had arrived, a white napkin draped over his arm, and was proffering menus with a flourish.

Ali studied Amy's face carefully as she ordered for both of them in Spanish—he'd never understood why a PhD in literature required Amy to learn the language, but she excelled at it—and as she spoke, the waiter responded immediately, bowing and backing away.

They waited for their food. Ali wondered what she had ordered, for she hadn't consulted him. Amy's eyes remained hidden behind sunglasses, and her face took on a distracted air. He feared the worst but then glanced behind his shoulder and realized that she was eavesdropping on the table next to theirs. A group of round-shouldered American girls were loudly discussing the joys of barhopping in Barcelona.

The food and wine arrived quickly. There was a whole grilled fish, its blank eyes staring up at them. Amy detached the head with one swift motion and put a flaky sliver of fish on Ali's plate, and he felt a sudden, uncomplicated rush of affection.

"Amy . . ." he said and was interrupted by a Rastafarian with a guitar who approached their table and started clanging out a Bob Marley tune. Ali gave the man two euros and he backed away.

Amy paused, a forkful of fish on the way to her lips.

". . . this morning, I didn't find your note till later, and I thought you had . . . just taken off."

Her tone was amused. "You thought I had left you? Here, in Barcelona?"

"I know, it was stupid of me, but yes. Listen, can we just stop?"

"Stop what?"

"Being mean to each other. I mean, we're here..." Amy filled her glass of white wine with an unsteady hand and moisture dripped off the bottle and seeped darkly into her white cotton tank top. "It was wrong of me to insist on going to India. It's just that I haven't been back for so long."

"Oh Ali," Amy said and sat back and took off her dark glasses. She stared at him, her glasses clutched in her hand.

"After dinner we could take the cable-car up to Montjuïc. The view is supposed to be stunning."

"Okay," she said, breathing out the word. "Okay." She reached across the table and gave his hand a quick squeeze.

She bent her head and ate. Ali was still full from his lunch at the Pakistani restaurant, and he picked at the fish and potato croquettes. Amy put away two more glasses of white wine, but Ali was not in a drinking mood. She began to talk, and Ali listened, feeling as though something dark and dangerous had been averted.

Amy said that Parc Güell had been so crowded that she could barely see Gaudí's famous mosaic-covered lizard. There had been people taking pictures of people taking pictures, the whole experience thoroughly postmodern.

". . . nothing is authentic anymore," she said. "Nobody is really *looking* at anything. For something to be real, people have to be photographed in front of it. It's all *commentaries* on *commentaries*."

This was her PhD voice, and for a second, Ali was worried that she would begin talking about Dickinson. Words from the poems—*death* and *marble* and *autumn*—came into his mind, and he tried to push them away.

The moment passed. Amy poured herself a fourth glass of wine. The early evening light turned golden, and the lemon-yellow façades of the buildings around the plaza glowed softly. A few balcony doors were open, and he saw an old woman looking contemplatively down into the square. What it would be like to live here, in this light? What would it be like to have sex on a mattress on the floor and afterward stand at one of those balconies, feeling the warm evening breeze on his skin?

Amy sat back in her chair and made fun of the other tourists: The Germans in their socks and sandals, the Americans with popped collars, the French girls in tiny shorts and Mickey-Mouse T-shirts. The crowd was drunk and happy, and the immigrant men selling their wares thrust postcards and glow sticks at them with great desperation, hoping that alcohol would fuel a sale. Few tourists bought anything though, and the men wandered disconsolately from table to table like lost children.

Amy put down her glass. "The thing is, those guys selling stuff are desperate, and desperation is so unattractive. But look at that guy," Amy said, pointing to a rose seller at the far side of the square. "He's good. He's got technique."

They both shaded their eyes and watched as a lanky man approached a table where a young couple sat. He carried sheaves of cellophane-wrapped roses and walked softly on the balls of his feet, with cat-like grace, and when he was close to the table, he bowed and said something. The girl at the table blushed—Ali sensed the blush from the way that she looked down—and then she laughed, and her eyes sparkled. Her boyfriend laughed too and reached into his baggy cargo shorts and paid for a bunch of roses. The rose seller turned and left their table with a courtly bow, and the girl at the table put the flowers down and kissed the boy. It lasted a long time.

Amy nodded again. "Yep. That guy really knows how to talk to women."

The rose seller now approached a long table of German tourists, thick-bodied men and women whose wide backs made a wall, blocking him out. The rose-seller bowed and knelt next to a middle-aged blonde matron in a tie-dye shirt, talking to her and gesturing with long, slender fingers. The other Germans must have been listening too, because suddenly they all snorted into their beers and turned red with merriment. Roses were bought all around, and the women at the table clutched the thorny flowers to their breasts as though bearing arms. The rose seller departed softly, tiptoeing away, and tucked the money into his trouser pocket.

"This guy is a pro. He never gives them change, and they never ask for it. I want to see how he does it," Amy said, slurring a little.

She half stood, raised her arm, and waved imperiously at the man.

The rose seller saw the wave, mimed surprise, looked around as if to say, *Who, me?* then stepped lightly toward them, a few roses still resting in the crook of his arm.

"I think I've got some euro coins, somewhere . . ."

Amy bent her head and scrabbled inside her handbag, but Ali stared at the approaching rose seller, at his dark trousers and white shirt. The front of his shirt was soaked from the moisture of the roses and the buttonholes of the cuffs had been mended with neat meticulous stitches. The man recognized Ali and stopped dead.

Ali Isfahani turned abruptly and loped away, and the roses tilted head down and left a trail of bruised petals.

"What the hell? Where's he going?" Amy pointed at the retreating figure, her fist full of coins.

Ali's face was hot with embarrassment and shame. He knew he would ruin everything if he spoke, but then he found himself speaking. "You humiliated him."

Amy looked askance. "I did *what*?"

"You humiliated that man. You beckoned to him as though he was a servant. These poor people only have their pride." Ali gripped the table with both hands and stood up. "You don't understand anything. You never have."

He ran after the trail of rose petals, but the Plaça was crowded, and by the time he reached the arcade on the far side, Ali Isfahani was gone. Ali stood in the shadowy arcade, breathing in its musty, bat-scented odor, thinking about the crestfallen, panicked look on Ali Isfahani's face as he fled, his honor in tatters.

Ali tried to shake the image from his head. He was being unfair to Amy; how could she have known that this man was his friend? But really, why the hell did she have to wave like that? He saw again Amy half-rising, the drunken, imperious swoop of her arm as she beckoned to the man.

Ali walked slowly back to their table. Amy was still sitting there, staring into the distance, and the waiter, sensing the end of the meal, hurried up with a bill on a plate. Amy slammed down her credit card, and when the receipt came, she signed it with a slash. They left the Plaça together and entered the crush of the Ramblas. It was very crowded, and Ali stepped aside to let Amy walk in front of him; she passed him without a word, stiff-backed with anger. They walked past the human statues on their pedestals, past the portrait artists, past the crowded sidewalk cafés.

At the upper reaches of the Ramblas the crowds thinned out, but they remained apart. They walked on through the endless evening, through the honey-colored light, neither slowly nor quickly, careful not to touch each other.

THE SECOND LADY

It was August, Congress was in recess, and Washington, DC, lay stunned under the merciless summer sun. That weekend, everyone had gone to the shore, but Omar stayed behind. He planned to go to the Bethesda Country Club and play a game of squash—at forty-two, he was very fit, beating men half his age—but instead he stayed home and had tepid sex with Annalisa, a girl he'd met at the Italian Embassy. Afterward, they ate a brunch of bagels, lox, and scrambled eggs.

While Annalisa showered, Omar lay in bed, feeling bloated and disgusted with himself. Without thinking, he clicked on the television, and there was the former First Lady, giving a speech somewhere, tall and elegantly dressed, and Omar felt a pang of nostalgia—she had famously said, "When they go low, we go high," and where had that gotten us? Standing behind the former First Lady was a young Pakistani-American woman, strangely familiar, and Omar looked harder, and it was Laila, his ex-wife.

It was unmistakably Laila—tall and bony, with lilac circles of tiredness under her dark eyes—but instead of her usual *salwar kameez*, she wore a dark blue business suit with brass buttons, and her deferential air had been replaced by a steely hardness, as abrupt as unsheathing a knife. Omar stared at the screen: Where was she? Istanbul? Jakarta? Mexico City? He pulled out his phone, frantically googled Laila, and found out that she was now the former First Lady's personal assistant, and that they were on a ten-country tour to promote women's rights.

The shower turned off. Omar quickly clicked off the television, and Annalisa emerged from the bathroom, clad in an absurdly large bath towel, dripping water all over the carpet, and usually, the sight of her blue-black hair and smooth, youthful thighs would have pleased Omar, but today he felt a surge of irritation. Why couldn't she dry off in the bathroom, like a normal person?

Annalisa spoke in a lilting Italian accent. "Something bothering you, *caro mio*?"

"Tough week at work, that's all."

She leaned down and kissed Omar's forehead with rough tenderness. "Want to come out tonight? We're going dancing."

"I'm kind of beat. If I change my mind, I'll text you. Have fun."

Omar wasn't really tired, but he had lost his taste for nightclubs and pounding techno. It didn't help that Annalisa and all her friends were in their twenties and treated Omar with elaborate, forced courtesy.

Annalisa didn't try to convince him to join them, a bad sign, and Omar wondered if she was tiring of him. She dressed quickly in a silk T-shirt and tightly fitted jeans and blew him a distracted kiss. Soon the front door clicked shut, and he heard her humming as she waited for the elevator.

Omar threw on a robe and walked through the enormous living room, past the imitation Louis XV furniture, the murals painted on the walls, and the absurd crystal chandelier. The vast Watergate apartment had once belonged to a Saudi prince and was meant to be temporary, a place for Laila and him to live for a few years before buying a house in the suburbs; after the divorce, three years ago, Omar had just stayed on, barely noticing where he was.

He made a cup of black tea, pulled open the sliding glass doors and sat out on the curved balcony. Across the road, the Potomac River flowed past, brown and sluggish, thick with débris.

Many evenings, Laila had sat here with him, her dark eyes fixed on his face, and Omar had done all the talking: long riffs about his brilliant prospects at the International Monetary Fund, about the sons Laila would give birth to, about the future. Omar and Laila had both been born and raised in Pakistan, but it was now a failed nation-state run by third-rate generals; only here, in America, was a fresh start possible. The first Black president had broken all the barriers. Why couldn't Omar's son be a senator? Why not the first Muslim president?

Now all that seemed absurd. The administrations had changed, and that orange-faced madman had taken power; in any case, Omar had no sons, only a five-year-old daughter, Saadiya. She had been a chubby baby when they got divorced, but now she resembled Omar's father: she had the same thick eyebrows and large, accusing eyes, and that increased the pain Omar felt on the rare occasions that he met her.

He sipped his tea. It was a rare, first-flush Darjeeling, prepared strong and hot. Annalisa teased him about drinking hot tea in the heat, but Omar wasn't about to change; summer or winter, he sat outside and drank his tea. He had inherited this habit from his father—Papa liked to sit out on the lawn in Lahore, and drink leisurely cups of tea. For years, Omar and Papa had tea together every evening; especially after Omar's mother died—he was fourteen at the time—this ritual held them together.

Now Papa, too, was dead. The garden in Lahore was gone, paved over. That stolid old colonial world had vanished, replaced with . . . What exactly? Chaos? Some new, inchoate form of existence, where modernity blended with medieval norms?

Out on the balcony, Omar breathed in the fetid air. It grew dark, but he remained seated, sipping his tea, sweating copiously, as if enduring a punishment. The brake lights of cars glowed red. Airliners roared overhead, their blue and white lights blinking. Still Omar sat, invisible in the gloom, and the same question haunted him: How had his life gone so terribly wrong? How had he made so many mistakes?

The first time Omar met Laila, he was on his annual vacation to Pakistan. It had been raining for a week, and Omar was tired of being stuck in the crumbling old bungalow with Papa, who had taken to sneering at him and saying, "Your America" and "Your invasion of Afghanistan." When Omar's favorite female cousin stopped by with a friend, he had been overjoyed.

Both women were soaked, and the bottoms of their baggy *salwars* were stained with mud. They demanded towels and hot tea. They kicked off their heeled slippers and sat on the sofa, legs tucked under them. The rain hammered so loudly on the tin roof that conversation was almost impossible. Omar just stared at Laila's bony face—her large eyes were shadowed with dark rings of exhaustion. She won over haughty Abdul, their old servant, by praising the delicacy of the *chai* he had prepared, but Omar could sense that she was making a tremendous effort; beneath the surface, her vulnerability pulsed like a badly concealed wound.

The rain let up and Omar found himself telling her about Washington: Its tribal ways, its intrigues and feuds, its long memory, the outsiders who arrived seeking connections to power, not understanding that there were no systems, no prescribed pathways, only history to be patiently gleaned and used to one's advantage.

"Sounds like a medieval court," Laila said quietly. "There are ceremonies and rituals, but all the work is done behind the scenes."

"Exactly. Are you a student of history?"

"My degree was in English. But my mother could teach Machiavelli a thing or two."

Omar laughed in delight, and his cousin watched in mild alarm; she was no fool and she could sense the chemistry between her gawky friend and her playboy cousin, a bit old to be unmarried, but still fit and boyishly handsome

Well, not exactly a playboy anymore. After Omar's fun times at Yale, and then a PhD from Cornell, he had risen quickly at the International Monetary Fund in Washington. He was already playing squash with the boss-man, smart enough not to lose on purpose, but to make the boss-man run and sweat, so that, being competitive, he always wanted a rematch. This was how the man had come to respect Omar's drive and focus.

Omar told Laila about all this on that first evening, and she listened carefully.

"It's a good strategy," she said, "but competition only works with men. Women operate differently. Tact and delicacy, not brute force, is what we value."

Omar nodded in pleased agreement and yelled for Abdul to make more *samosas*.

That night, at dinner, Omar was in a rare good mood. Papa, sensing this, decided to act perversely.

"So I see that the Mamdani girl has made quite an impact on you? Is it so?"

Omar bent his head and tucked into his lamb *biryani*, which Abdul had made from Omar's dead mother's recipe. It was very good, but there was something missing, some spice that Omar couldn't pinpoint.

Papa pressed on. "I saw her sitting out there, pretending to be shy. She's a *character*, that one."

"Why?" Omar stopped eating. Being a *character*, in Papa's book, was a very bad thing. "Because she has a brain? Because she dared to voice an opinion, unlike all those idiotic friends' daughters that you're always introducing me to?"

"Hmmpf." Papa beckoned to Abdul and was served a steaming second helping of rice and lamb. "That Mamdani girl was engaged to a very nice boy, nephew of a friend of mine, solid boy, going to inherit the family business. He got cancer, and she broke off the engagement. Made up some story about him being abusive, slapping her around, calling her a gold digger, etcetera."

Papa paused before delivering the punch line. "The correct course of action, of course, would have been to marry the boy. See him out, inherit his estates, be his widow. An engagement is an engagement. You can't just go around breaking things off."

"That's absurd." Omar pushed his plate away. "That's medieval thinking. Was Laila supposed to sacrifice her life for a dying man?"

"Just telling you the facts." Papa stuffed more *biryani* into his mouth. He had put on a lot of weight in the years since Omar's mother died. "That girl is no fool. You have to be careful with women like that. She's damaged."

"Thanks for that gem of wisdom, Papa."

"Go ahead, Omar, be the white knight. Just like an American, bringing your outrage and morality to a situation you don't understand."

Omar got up from the table, but Papa wouldn't stop.

"You always want to save sad, abandoned things. Remember that damn dog? That didn't work out so well for you, did it? She reverted to her true nature and ran away."

Papa's bitter laughter followed Omar as he walked out into the sodden, overgrown garden. Here and there a twisted rose bush produced a bloom, but his mother's flower beds had been overrun with weeds. Jesus, the old man was impossible. Why had he brought up Rani, after all these years?

The puppy had wandered into their compound a few months after Omar's mother died. She was dung-colored, and one ear was shorter than the other, which gave her a comical, vulnerable look. Omar had pleaded with Papa to keep her, but Papa, enraged with grief, had forbidden it.

Omar hid the puppy in the servant's quarters and named her Rani. He fed her twice a day, bathed her with delousing powder, and bought her a broad leather collar. Under his care, Rani stopped snarling and instead became a fearless watchdog. She barked ferociously at the bearded Afghan refugees who had camped out on a patch of waste ground next door, tall, scowling men who wore the baggy *shalwars* and tall turbans of their mountainous home. Abdul, the old servant, said that they were all thieves and murderers. Even Papa feared them, and that was why he relented and let Rani stay on as a guard dog.

Back then, Omar and Papa would drink tea in the garden together every evening and argue about the same thing. Omar wanted to apply to college in America—he wanted to get away from Papa's bitter rage—but Papa insisted that he stay, attend Punjab University, and take over the family's garment business. Eventually Papa would grow red in the face and shout, "Okay, fine, leave. Let everything I have worked for go to ruin!"

As they argued, the sky would darken, and hundreds of black crows would settle into the mango trees, cawing hoarsely. Rani would run in endless circles around the trees, till she grew dizzy and staggered to a stop.

Papa would yell, "*Yaar*, stop that racket!" but Rani would refuse to obey. Papa would shake his grizzled head and laugh and say, "Crazy dog, *yaar!*"

Omar would laugh, too, and their enmity would be forgotten, and they would talk openly. Then Rani disappeared from the house, the week before Omar left for Yale, and Omar stopped talking to Papa.

Now, Omar stood in the overgrown garden and dismissed the past with a shake of his head. It was over. Rani was gone. Papa was eating himself into a heart attack. Omar's future was in America. He turned, walked back to the house, telephoned Laila, and asked if she would join him for lunch at the Gymkhana Club the next day. She instantly accepted.

⁓

Omar and Laila were married in Lahore and a few months later they moved to Washington, DC, to the vast Watergate apartment with its crystal chandelier. Omar worked very late at the IMF, but those first two years were good ones.

Laila knew Omar's aversion to cold food and always had a steaming hot dinner of rice and kebabs when he returned. She sat at the kitchen table while he ate, wearing her faded blue cotton nightie, her feet tucked up under her, big, dark eyes fixed on his face, listening intently. When she spoke, her comments were remarkably perceptive; having grown up in a huge family, she was used to reading the signs of an ecosystem in constant flux.

Laila got pregnant, and in their third year together they had a child. Saadiya was a colicky newborn; Omar complained that he wasn't getting enough rest and took to sleeping alone in the guest room. When he returned late from work, the apartment was dark—there were no more late nights sitting and talking at the dining table—and he began to behave like a bachelor. He ate alone, in front of the television, a glass of scotch at his elbow, then headed blearily to an empty bed, shedding his clothes along the way.

One winter, when Saadiya was two years old, Omar, because of his position at the IMF, was invited to the White House Christmas party. The evening of the party, he had a slight temperature, enough to malinger in bed and enjoy an evening free of Saadiya's incessant crying.

"I think my body is breaking down," he said to Laila. "The work is killing me. And after Papa's death . . ."

Laila turned to him in concern. Papa had had died a month ago, in his sleep, of a massive myocardial infarction. Omar had flown down to Lahore for the funeral and spent a week cleaning out the huge bungalow. He'd sold the house, given away Papa's old furniture, and brought back only a few photograph albums.

"You poor thing," Laila said. "The White House Christmas party doesn't matter. You're still grieving for Papa."

Papa had always disliked Laila, always referred to her as *that Mamdani girl*, but Laila had never reacted. Even when Papa visited Washington and made outrageous demands, Laila always performed the role of the dutiful daughter-in-law.

"No, no." Omar smiled bravely. "You and Saadiya go to the party. You're on the guest list, and I've called a limo. Besides, you've been looking forward to it so much."

"You're sure? Is it okay for a wife to go without her husband?"

Laila stared at Omar. Even without makeup, her eyelids were violet, and those dark eyes in that pale, bony face had an erotic pull for Omar; he felt it in his groin, even while he lied to her.

"Of course! But don't get your hopes up. You might get a few seconds to talk to the First Lady, but the President, forget about it. Besides, that Afghan girl will be there, the one whose nose they cut off. You're always talking about her."

Laila had recently become interested in Afghan women's rights and started volunteering at Global Village, a non-profit that advocated for the education of Afghan girls.

"Though personally," Omar continued, "I think it's a waste of time. We had an Afghan squatter encampment next to our house. Those people are incorrigible. All they've known, for generations, is war. You're never going to convince them to stop killing each other, even if you have a Nobel Peace Prize."

"Fahran Yusufzai. That's who you mean. She's already done so much."

Laila hadn't liked his sarcastic tone. She pulled out the ironing board, turned on the iron, and tested it by spitting on it, an old habit from Pakistan. She began to iron her new lilac *salwar kameez* in large, awkward strokes.

Why was she doing this, when they had a maid? Laila had been raised in a crumbling apartment in the Lohari Bazaar area with no servants; she was so meek to everyone, so self-effacing, and it drove Omar crazy.

Laila stepped out of her jeans, pulled off her T-shirt, and went over to the dresser to apply deodorant. He glimpsed her long, brown body, her surprisingly full chest, the dark shadows under her armpits. She slipped on the crisp, still-warm *salwar kameez* in one graceful movement.

Omar should have said that he was feeling better. He should have gotten out of bed, shaved—there was still time—pulled on a suit, and walked into the White House Christmas party with his wife and daughter. Instead, he did not move.

This was his first, fatal mistake, but he did not realize it.

After they left, the massive apartment took on a silent brooding air. Omar opened a bottle of craft beer, sat in the living room, and flipped through a photograph album that he'd brought back from Papa's house. Black-and-white photos were mounted with gold corner squares on thick black paper, and the album even smelled of the old house, of dust, neglect, and mold.

There were pictures of Mama, young and dark haired, holding Omar as a pudgy, naked baby. Pictures of a slim Papa, in a dark suit, throwing Omar in the air. Behind him, the lawn was immaculate, and the flower beds were surrounded by neat borders of brick. How affectionate the old man had been when Omar was young, grabbing him in a headlock, kissing his sweaty head and murmuring, "My son, oh my son." When had all that stopped? After Ma's death?

Omar turned to the end of the album, and there, unmounted, were several faded color pictures: Rani, his old dog, sat on the lawn, grinning up at him with her lopsided ears, young and full of life. In another picture, she was just a dark streak running across the lawn.

Omar felt a pang, because Rani had vanished one particularly bad monsoon day. Papa said she had run away, had returned to her old life on the streets, but Omar was sure that she'd never do that. He'd driven around the neighborhood, calling out, "Rani, here, girl."

He thought he saw a dung-colored dog run into the patch of waste ground occupied by the Afghan refugees, and he stopped the car and got out, but then the Afghans came out of their squalid tents and stared silently at him, and one man, with a hennaed beard and tall turban, stepped forward, one hand resting on a curved dagger in his belt. Omar scuttled back to his car and drove away. Back home, he told Abdul, their old servant, what he'd seen, and Abdul had shaken his grizzled head and said, "Those Afghans eat dogs, you know. They're savages. They need meat." Omar hadn't believed Abdul, who was given to flights of fancy, but he never saw Rani again.

Omar slammed the photograph album shut. Forget about lost dogs. Forget about lost gardens. Forget about Papa. He cracked another beer. He turned on the television set and let the roar of a Lakers basketball game flood his mind.

⁓

When Laila returned, three hours later, Omar was slightly drunk and irritable—the Lakers had lost horribly. He barely listened as Laila chattered on about the White House party.

That Afghan celebrity girl had been there and was also wearing a *salwar kameez*. She had been thrilled to meet Laila and cooed over Saadiya and introduced them both to the President and First Lady. Laila even had a souvenir photograph with the first couple, but Omar barely glanced at it. It was just a frameable memento, ubiquitous in Washington.

Omar thought nothing of his absence from the photograph, even when Laila posted it on Facebook and garnered many likes. One of Omar's aunts, blunt as usual, asked, *But where is Omar?*, and Laila replied that he had been sick, adding a sad emoticon.

A few weeks later, Laila was invited to a private lunch by the Afghan celebrity girl to talk about expanding the mission of Global Village. The First Lady happened to be having lunch at the same trendy downtown restaurant, and, in a tremendous breach of protocol, dropped by their table. The three women ended up talking for over fifteen minutes.

The First Lady was a highly experienced corporate lawyer, widely rumored to be more intelligent than her husband. Clearly chafing at her constricted life, she had become deeply involved in women's rights, and something about the two bright-eyed, voluble, South Asian women appealed to her; maybe she shared their aversion for the traditional roles they were forced to play.

Whatever it was, a week later an assistant from the White House called Laila. This time, she had lunch alone with the First Lady, in another downtown restaurant that served overpriced interpretations of Indian food. Laila later told Omar that the two women sat in the back, separated from the other customers by a wall of tall, dark-suited secret-service agents. When the meal ended, Laila left by the front door, but the First Lady was whisked away via a service corridor in the back.

Omar was amused by this sudden connection between his awkward wife and the First Lady, and it gave him a certain prestige around the office; he sensed a frisson every time he walked into a meeting, his calfskin portfolio case tucked under his arm. Because of Laila, he was unexpectedly connected to real power. He took it all lightly, with an amused, sarcastic smile.

This was his second mistake.

⸺

That summer, an envelope arrived by courier. The invitation inside was on formal White House stationery. Laila was invited to a weekend at Camp David—the presidential retreat, set deep in the woods of rural Maryland—but Omar was not.

"I know it's awkward," Laila said soothingly as she packed her suitcase, choosing each garment with great deliberation. "But even if you were invited, what would you do? I spend my time with the First Lady, and the President, he's off somewhere else. It's not like being friends with a normal couple."

Omar sat on the edge of their bed. He tried to disguise his hurt by studying his fingernails. "What do you talk about, anyway?"

"Girl stuff. She likes to hear my stories about Lahore. She says it reminds her of her family in Chicago . . . She's lonely, Omar, she needs some company. Can you imagine what her life is like?"

But Omar was imagining himself at Camp David, walking along a leafy, winding path with the President, who would ask Omar for his opinion on the economic situation in South Asia.

Omar kept silent till a black Escalade came to collect Laila and Saadiya; there was apparently a staff of caregivers at Camp David. Just as Laila picked up her bags, he spoke.

"Leave Saadiya with me. I can easily take care of her for the weekend."

Laila just laughed, with the infant sitting astride her hip.

"Really, Omar, the things you say. You haven't even made it through one night, and anyway, I've given the maid the weekend off. We'll be back before you know it."

⁓

Omar moped around for the rest of the weekend, and when Laila came back from Camp David, he watched her anxiously; she seemed strangely distant, and there were no juicy details about the First Family. Laila talked instead about the many walks she had taken, the way that deer came out to graze right by the windows, the night when Indian food was served, and the President asked her opinion about its authenticity.

It was clear that she had spent a lot of time with the First Lady, who had offered her thoughts on Saadiya's prospective education. They must have talked about more intimate things too, because sometimes Laila slipped and referred to the First Lady by her first name.

"So," Omar pushed, "is it true? She's the brains behind the operation? How do they seem, together?"

"Omar, I can't give you any details. I promised the First Lady I'd respect her privacy."

"Are you serious? I'm your husband! You can't talk to me?"

Laila looked away as she spoke. "She said that all men are weak. That they trap us with their needs. That one should never give up one's identity for a man."

"Really? So now the First Lady is giving you marital advice?"

"She wasn't talking about you—she was making a general comment. See, I shouldn't have told you anything."

He tried to bait Laila some more, but she lay down to sleep, pulling a mask over her eyes.

When Laila was asleep, Omar went through her suitcase, but there were just her dirty clothes, nothing to indicate that his wife had just spent forty-eight hours with the most powerful couple on earth.

He went into the living room and stared at the large color photograph taken at the White House Christmas party. It was curiously arranged: The President and First Lady should have been in the center, with Laila next to them, holding Saadiya in her arm. Two couples, two groupings, maintaining the implicit power disparity, but instead, Laila was in the *center* of the photograph, flanked by the President and the First Lady, who was holding Saadiya protectively in her arms. It seemed as though the first couple were doting parents and that Laila was their daughter and Saadiya their granddaughter.

Omar dismissed the queasy feeling in his stomach. This is what powerful people did, he told himself. They took on playthings, but they ultimately got bored. The First Lady's mind would soon wander off to another cause, and Laila would be dropped. Then Omar and Laila would revert to their old selves. She would be waiting for him when he returned from work, and they'd sit at the kitchen table and talk, like old times.

⁓

As summer turned to fall, Laila went out a lot. Washington, it seemed, had a huge number of think tanks working on women and poverty, and the recent outrages against Afghan women drew everyone's attention. Farhan Yusufzai, the Afghan celebrity, always talked up the revolutionary work done by Global Village, and Laila began to receive invitations to conferences about the fate of Afghanistan. She often took Saadiya with her; the two of them were an act, it seemed, dark-eyed mother and daughter, dressed in their colorful Pakistani clothes.

When Laila attended a state reception for the Afghan president, Karzai—that crook came to beg for more American aid—she caught the attention of the Washington press corps. They photographed her wearing an orange *salwar kameez* and identified her as "A women's rights activist and close personal friend of the First Lady."

Close personal friend? After one weekend at Camp David? Really?

Things were different at Omar's office, too. Somehow word had gone out that he hadn't been invited to Camp David, that he was not a power player. When he arrived late at meetings, he had the sense of conversations being suspended, of jokes being made at his expense. He ran the meetings fiercely, cudgeling his subordinates with his superior intellect, but it wasn't enough.

⁓

One evening, six months later, Laila appeared unexpectedly, wearing her customary blue cotton nightgown. She padded barefoot across the living room carpet and sat next to Omar on the couch. He continued watching basketball on television—the Thunder were playing the Warriors—but secretly, he was glad. He wanted to share some good news with Laila: he was about to get a giant promotion at the IMF—which meant a lot more money, which meant a fancy house in the suburbs—but before he could speak, Laila cleared her throat.

"Omar, can we talk? Could you turn off the television, please?"

He muted the sound but left the picture on. He took a gulp of scotch and nodded to indicate he was listening.

"I want to run something by you." Laila sat very straight, her hands in her lap. "A job offer. After the First Lady leaves the White House, she's going to focus on her foundation, and she wants me to advise her on women's rights. It's a paid position. I'll have an office and some staff."

"You? What do you know about politics?"

"Nothing much." Laila tucked her feet up under her, and he was suddenly reminded of the afternoon they'd met. "I've just placed over three thousand Afghan girls in schools and negotiated with warlords and convinced Karzai to back our health initiative to reduce infanticide."

He clicked off the television and pretended to give her his full attention.

"It's not a good idea to take on more responsibility. Who will take care of the baby?"

Laila shook her head slowly.

"This is so predictable. I get an amazing job offer, and you . . . Never mind. I'm going to take the job. It would be nice to have your support, but I don't need it."

Laila spoke in the calm voice of a politician, emulating the First Lady, and Omar found himself shouting.

"The fucking Afghans are a bunch of thugs! No matter what you try to do, they'll keep on killing each other and screwing their cousins!"

Laila's voice was still mild. "Really? I didn't know you had such strong feelings."

"I know those bastards well. There was an Afghan refugee camp right down the lane from our house. My dog, Rani, she wandered into it. Those bastards killed her and ate her."

"What on earth are you talking about? That's crazy. Muslims don't eat dogs, Omar."

Laila laughed out loud. He tried to interrupt her, but she held up her hand.

"All these years, I've been making excuses for you: *His mother died when he was a teenager. He was raised by that rough old man. He's not arrogant, he's just insecure.* But really, this bit about the dog? Do you know how absurd you sound?"

Laila stood up and walked down the long hallway. He screamed after her.

"You're not taking that job. Do you hear me? You belong at home!"

Laila's bedroom door clicked shut. Omar gulped down the rest of the scotch and glimpsed his reflection in the blank television set. His hair was disheveled, his eyes wide and staring.

Why had he blurted out that stuff about the dog? He'd sounded petulant, childlike, irrational. This time, he knew that he'd made a crucial mistake. This time, everything had changed. He knew it in his bones and could not deny it. And yet . . . the moment had seemed eerily familiar—he had experienced something like it before, but when? He reached for his glass of scotch, swallowed a burning gulp, and tried to remember.

Two scotches later, he lay half-drunk on the couch, and it finally hit him. Yes—that last evening he'd spent with Papa, before leaving for college in America.

The sun was setting. They sat on cane chairs on the lawn, side by side, drinking tea. Flights of crows flapped through the sky and settled into the trees, cawing and croaking.

Papa and Omar did not talk. Rani had disappeared, and without her frantic antics, there was nothing to break the silence between them. Omar drank his tea defiantly, in a white ceramic mug that Yale had sent him; Papa slurped his tea from a Wedgwood cup, the saucer rattling with his fury.

On that last evening, why hadn't he reached out and kissed the old man's grizzled cheek and said gently, *Papa, I am not leaving you, I just want to live my own life. Please let me go.* But Omar was pumped full of youthful arrogance, and he sipped his cold, bitter tea and did not speak.

Soon all the light had left the earth, and Omar couldn't see the house. He couldn't see the lawn or the flower beds or Papa's face. Soon there was just the raucous screeching of the crows, and everything else was swallowed up by darkness.

THE PALMVIEW HOTEL

Anil Sharma trudged out onto the beach of the Palmview Hotel in Barbados and stared at the view: the blue-green ocean shimmered, coconut palms rustled overhead, and blond tourists lay on deck chairs, sodden with pleasure. Anil thought of his beloved brother here, on this very beach, and hot tears filled his eyes. He turned and hurried back to the hotel. He was still dressed for a New York winter in baggy, wide-wale corduroys and a long-sleeved shirt, and by the time he reached the hotel lobby he was sweating heavily.

A smiling Palmview employee in an orange T-shirt approached Anil and gestured to a spray bottle full of cold water. "Some spray, sir?"

"Spray? Why on earth?"

"For relief, sir, relief."

Anil felt as though the boy had seen into his soul, and he nodded, and the boy spritzed Anil's face and hair with icy water. For a second, he did feel better, but then the cloying grief returned.

The manager appeared behind the counter, a slim young Bajan woman in a white blouse and a dark-blue, old-fashioned skirt, almost like a school uniform.

"Rajesh Sharma was my older brother," Anil said, ignoring her smile. "I'm here for a short while to clear things up. I believe that you have his personal effects?"

The woman trundled out a sleek aluminum rolling suitcase and left it for Anil, the handle raised like an invitation.

"It's unlocked." she said. "Why did your brother go swimming here? The current here is the worst. A riptide. That's why we have a red flag. See?" She pointed through the dim lobby to a red cloth flag snapping in the breeze.

"My brother was a strong swimmer," Anil said. "Maybe he saw it as a challenge."

The manager stared blankly, and Anil realized that he had to do better.

"It doesn't make sense. Rajesh would never kill himself."

"You . . . you look like him," the manager said, peering into his face. "I see the resemblance. Not as tall, but still, a resemblance. You are a novelist, yes? He mentioned you."

Anil was stunned. He'd given Rajesh a copy of his novel, *Mumbai Babylon*, two years ago, just before it disappeared into oblivion. Rajesh had texted back—*Thanks for the book, bro, will get to it*—but there was not a word about the novel in all the scattered conversations that followed.

"He told you about my book?"

"Yes, yes, he was reading it by the pool. He told me you wrote it." She saw the pain in Anil's eyes and elaborated. "He read it the entire week he was here. A lovely man. Always so polite, respectful."

"People always liked Rajesh. Yes. Well, thank you."

"So sorry for you," the woman murmured. "My name is Mrs. Braithwaite. Anything I can do, you let me know, okay?"

Anil pulled the smooth metal suitcase down the corridor and into his large ground-floor suite, the same suite that Rajesh had occupied; it had glass doors that let out onto a

shady veranda and was twice the size of Anil's cramped New
York apartment. Ordinarily, he could never have afforded
it, but the rates had dropped because any day now the dry
season would come to an end and the monsoon rains would
roll in. Of course, any trace of Rajesh was long gone from
the suite; since his death, God knows how many people had
fucked and slept here. Anil felt a surge of anger, but he told
himself to be reasonable—what was the hotel supposed to
do, turn it into a shrine?

He opened Rajesh's suitcase. On top was a gray lightweight
suit and a pink broadcloth business shirt, below that, polo
shirts in magenta, lime-green and orange, two pairs of slim-
fit khaki shorts, and dark-blue silky underwear, unlike the
sagging Jockeys that Anil wore. No sign of Rajesh's titanium
cufflinks or his Piaget wristwatch with the alligator strap.

Maybe they were in the outside pocket of the suitcase,
but instead Anil found a warped, water-stained hardcover
of his own novel, *Mumbai Babylon*. A bookmark—a boarding
pass, Frankfurt-Barbados—was jammed into it, at page
twenty-seven. Rajesh had been carrying the book all week,
and this is all he'd read? Anil scanned the final paragraph
on that page, an elegiac description of old Mumbai, of how
the monkey man would arrive at the front gate of their
bungalow with his pair of trained monkeys—moth-eaten
tiny beasts with the faces of octogenarians—and, for a few
coins, perform a wedding between the two animals, who
wore grotesque human costumes and, with jerky gestures,
approximated human behavior. The description went on for
pages and pages. Jesus Christ, why had he put that in there?
He shut the novel and thrust it angrily back into the suitcase.

He imagined Rajesh in this very room, closing the book
and walking out through these glass doors onto the veranda,
skirting the pool and then crossing the beach, the white

sand crunching under his feet. According to the Barbados police report, the sea had been rough that day, and a hotel employee had seen Rajesh diving under the crashing waves, swimming out farther and farther. After that, the police report, meticulously compiled, became speculation, because what happened next had no witnesses: Rajesh had drowned somewhere out there, and his body had washed up two days later, farther down the coast, with salt water in his lungs. Given that Rajesh was a rational man, a man who made economic calculations for a living, the Barbados police had ruled it a deliberate act, a suicide.

The police inspector who'd called Anil, a man named Lallu Hanuman, had elaborated in his mellifluous accent.

"It is not uncommon," Hanuman had said, "for foreigners to kill themselves here. Your brother, sir, is the twenty-third person this year to vanish into the ocean. It is easier to end your life in a place where the air and the ocean are the same temperature as your own blood."

Anil did not believe a word of it. Sure, Rajesh had flown to Barbados without telling anyone, not even Elsa, his wife. Sure, Rajesh lived in a non-stop world of calls and meetings and transatlantic flights, and he needed a rest. A few days alone here, sleeping, soaking in the sun, sure, that made sense, but Rajesh would never kill himself. Anil was sure of it, and he was determined to find out what had actually happened.

〜

He unpacked his own things, a few faded half-sleeve shirts and a pair of cargo shorts that still fit him. There was nothing else to do—he had a meeting two days later with Inspector Hanuman—so he stripped, wore his red swim trunks, and walked through the veranda to the pool, conscious of his round, flabby belly.

It was already dusk, warm and breezy and full of the rhythmic chirping of tree frogs. The other tourists had headed indoors, bloated with sun and alcohol, and Anil had the pool to himself. He swam lengths. It grew darker, and the underwater lights came on, illuminating the sinuous curves of the pool, and he steered a course right down the middle. The taste of the water changed as he swam—sweeter sunscreen here, more floral there—and it occurred to Anil that this very same water had flowed through many crotches and armpits and anuses; to share a pool of water, one had to participate in a mass illusion. Anil ignored the thought. Steadily—one breath for every two strokes, as Rajesh had taught him—he swam up and down.

Soothed by the constant motion, his mind drifted. Why had Rajesh chosen Barbados? When had this become the way to travel, anyway? Fly to a tropical country, strip off your clothes, lie basting in the sun, and read a mediocre novel?

These vacations were so different from their childhood holidays. Anil had written about it in *Mumbai Babylon*, changing the names. One scene—right after the mother dies—he'd plucked directly from memory.

Anil and Rajesh were on vacation with Papa, high up in the Himalayas, staying at a shabby British-era hotel, and one morning Papa had insisted that they hike to a Tibetan temple high up above the town.

A clammy fog shrouded the mountain tops, but that didn't deter Papa. He strode effortlessly up the steep path, and athletic, long-legged Rajesh easily kept up with him, but Anil lagged behind. He imagined himself falling off the path into a ravine, falling into unending darkness. Soon he was far behind, and Papa's crisp, confident voice called out, "Anil, keep up for God's sake. Stop slacking."

The Tibetan monastery had golden domes and was squat and colorful, like a birthday cake. Anil was glazed with sweat, too exhausted to circumambulate the smoky, dim interior, and he sat outside on the steps, and the prayer flags rippled and snapped above him.

Rajesh gave him a plastic bottle of water. He leaned in and whispered, "Don't worry, you're doing fine. Papa is just angry."

"Why? What did I do?"

"It's not you. He didn't get promoted to general manager."

"I hate him. He's angry all the time."

"Yes, I know."

The two brothers stared at Papa, who had now engaged a young monk in his hearty bank manager's voice and asked rapid-fire questions about the monastery, but then did not listen to the answers.

Anil said to Rajesh, "We should never be like him. Never."

Rajesh nodded, and from that day onward, their unspoken contract was that they would be different from Papa and thus defeat him.

Now, Anil swam down the length of the pool, lost in his thoughts, but found his path blocked. A group of blond, muscular men had entered the water. They stood around sipping brightly colored cocktails and shouting *Wunderbar! Es macht Spaas!*

Anil could not weave through their legs. He gave up, pulled himself out of the pool, and walked back to his veranda, conscious of the men's toned, gym-built bodies, and felt a paroxysm of hatred for his own flabbiness. Here he was, broke and alone at thirty-eight, living in a lightless basement in Brooklyn and teaching badly paid creative writing courses. If anyone should commit suicide, it was him, not Rajesh, Mr. Bigshot Business Consultant, with his partnership at McKinsey, his designer mansion right by Piedmont Park in Atlanta, and Elsa, his trophy Swedish wife with her gold nose ring.

He was thinking all this as he walked through the veranda and slid open the glass doors to his room. A thick-bodied woman in an orange T-shirt was vacuuming the living room, and she jumped back in surprise.

"So sorry," Anil said, "I didn't expect anyone in here."

The woman drew herself up. She had a snub nose and glossy hair that lay around her shoulders in lustrous, artificial curls.

"We have to clean the room. If you don't want a cleaning, then you must hang out the *No Disturb* sign."

Anil smiled weakly and sat out onto the veranda, dripping water. Then he realized that the maid might be able to help him and went back in. She was in the bedroom, pulling the bed sheets tight. Her name, *Sadie*, was engraved onto a brass bar pinned to her chest.

"Sadie, I was just wondering if you talked to my brother, Rajesh Sharma? He stayed in this room. About six weeks ago."

Sadie straightened up and stood with her hands on her hips, thinking.

"Oh Lord. Your brother, he is the man who killed himself?"

"Did you know him?"

"Know? How do you mean *know*?"

"Did you talk to him? Did he say anything?"

"Just the usual chatter. Very polite man. *Hello, thank you*, like that."

"So you do remember him. Anything else?"

"That man liked to walk. He walked every day, from here to Carlisle Bay. Now I must clean three more rooms. G' night."

Carlisle Bay? Where was that? Anil resolved to walk there the next morning.

⁓

The next day, Anil woke very late, into bright sunlight and the roaring of the ocean. By the time he set off for Carlisle Bay, it was nearly three in the afternoon. The coast road was dusty and choked with traffic, but there were a few old bungalows left, with frangipani blooming in their overgrown gardens.

The Barbadians sat outside in shack-like bars, drinking and laughing and carrying out long, melodic conversations. An old woman standing by a roadside food stall called out to Anil, "Here boy, eat sumpin', nuh, you too thin!"

"Maybe tomorrow," he shouted back.

She broke out into a big, gap-toothed smile and said, "Eat now, man, tomorrow you could be dead!"

Anil walked away, smiling. Barbados reminded him of Mumbai in the seventies, when the old colonial bungalows still existed; back then there was still the fragrance of trees and flowers, before it all vanished under asphalt. Did Rajesh come here for that reason? Did his nostalgia kill him?

It didn't make sense. Rajesh had always moved ruthlessly forward. It was Anil who had been the nostalgic one. He'd stuffed his novel so full of vanished Mumbai that one review in the *Boston Globe* had been scathing. An influential reviewer had said, ". . . a novel about a mother dying, a family falling apart, and its impact on two brothers, but the author does not deal with the pain at its core. The novel is simply a series of stylistic devices, lush prose, and a suffocating nostalgia for a childhood world that discounts the fact that 'good old days' only exist in retrospect . . ."

Other reviews had echoed this view, and within days, his novel was dead. Anil hadn't written a word since. He'd begun and abandoned many projects and driven his literary agent crazy, so that the man now refused to return his calls.

Anil was sweating heavily by the time he reached Carlisle Bay. The beach curved north to Bridgetown, and the ocean here was calm. He dug his toes into the warm, white sand and stared at the water. Dusk fell, and a booze-cruise boat appeared, steering erratically across the bay, crowded with drinkers, and the thumping bass of American hip-hop carried across the water.

Something was bothering Anil. He pulled out his phone and called Atlanta.

"Anil. How are you?"

It was Elsa, Rajesh's wife, her British-accented voice blurred by a few glasses of wine. He imagined her thin, pretty face framed by lank blonde hair; the stiff, affected way she held her wine glass, as though she were being photographed.

"I'm in Barbados, at the Palmview. Staying in Rajesh's suite."

"Oh my God. Why?"

"Rajesh was my brother. *Is* my brother. I can't just let this go."

She exhaled, a long, exasperated sound.

"Elsa, I don't mean to be out of line, but . . . was something wrong at Rajesh's job? Did he get denied a promotion or something?"

"Why would you say that?"

"You tell me. You're his wife."

She sighed, followed by the clink of the wine glass being set down. "All I know is that he had some difficult conversations at work. He didn't give me any details. You know how he compartmentalized. Work was one box. I was in another box."

That's because you don't want to know, Anil thought. *You saddled my brother with your need for a fancy house, an expensive car, but you couldn't help him when things got tough.*

"Come on, Elsa. That's not enough. Rajesh was a resilient guy."

"There is nothing else. Rajesh was a grown man; he made a choice. And I resent the implication that I had something to do with his death. If you're such a great brother, why didn't you call him more often? Ever since your book was published, you've been in a funk. A deep, self-centered funk."

"My brother is dead, damn it! And you, you—"

Elsa hung up. Anil trembled with anger and jammed the phone into his pocket. It was all her fault, it was.

He remembered his last trip to Atlanta, right after his book tanked. New York was unbearable just then; the bookstores, which had been his refuge, were now reminders of his failure. He'd sat with Elsa in the living room, waiting for Rajesh to return from work, and in her crisp British accent she'd described their travels: Berlin, Morocco, the Amalfi coast. "You haven't been? You simply must go, it's divine."

A car door slammed outside. Anil smiled apologetically at Elsa and walked outside to greet his brother. Rajesh had his back turned and stood in the bright Georgia sunlight, appraising his two-million-dollar house, and right then, Anil made three observations:

One. Rajesh was now driving a brand-new red Volvo (Papa's favorite car).

Two. He was wearing a shirt with French cuffs (Papa's preferred style).

Three. On his wrist was a slim Piaget with an alligator strap (Papa had always wanted one).

Rajesh turned, and his face lost its beatific expression. Anil saw himself through his brother's eyes: crumpled and overweight, pale from hours in dank coffee shops, writing fiction that no one wanted to read.

To retaliate, Anil pointed at Rajesh and chortled.

"Hello. What's so funny?" Rajesh frowned.

"Papa. You're him."

"What on earth are you talking about?"

"Nothing. Just a bad joke."

Rajesh's face went blank, but he had understood. Even though Anil held his tongue for the rest of the trip, the damage was done. Their conversations after that were perfunctory.

Now Anil sat in the darkness of Carlisle Bay, lost in his memories. The cruise boat chugged close to shore and hung there, engine throbbing, and a string of drunken revelers jumped off and trudged up the beach, laughing boisterously. They ignored Anil, as though he were invisible, but then one large figure waved at him.

"Mister Anil. What are you doing here?"

It was the maid, Sadie, no longer in her orange hotel T-shirt, but in a tight white tube top and faded denim skirt, her lustrous curls askew. She smelled of rich rum molasses.

"Oh, hi. Wow. The one person I know on the island."

"I have the evening off today. My cousin, it is his birthday." Sadie gestured at the whooping revelers. "Come and have a drink with us."

"No, no, I don't want to intrude. You go ahead."

"Come on, man." Sadie grinned at him. "You can't sit here all alone in the dark. There's a nice place across the road."

"Okay, sure," Anil rose and dusted the sand from his shorts. "Why not?"

"This is my boy. Come here, Roggic."

A teenaged boy turned and shook Anil's hand. It was the boy from the hotel, the one with the spray bottle. Roggic had lost his cheerful demeanor and was cool and reserved; he swaggered up the beach with a packet of cigarettes rolled into the sleeve of his T-shirt.

"I just don't know what to do with this boy," Sadie said, well within Roggic's hearing, "Eighteen years old and he's out of hand. I light candles, I beat him good, but it doesn't help."

Roggic waved a hand at his mother. "Ma, you're making too big a thing. I'll catch you later."

He turned and vanished into the darkness, and Sadie chuckled grimly.

"I don't know when I'll see him again. He runs with a bad crowd. Come on. Now I really need a drink."

They walked across the road to the "Car Park Bar." Sadie said that it was a parking lot during the day, but at night a bar was set up, and white plastic tables were scattered across the cracked asphalt. Blue fairy lights twinkled overhead, giving a deathly sheen to the faces of the Brits who sat in groups, drinking steadily.

Anil huddled at the bar, next to Sadie, swallowed up in a crush of sweaty, happy bodies. He ordered a round of beer for everyone, and they smiled and toasted him, crying out, "Cheers! Bottoms up!"

A microphone screeched, followed by a man singing. There was a karaoke machine in the corner, and a bald British man belted out "Killing Me Softly" on a microphone. Amid the applause, another burly Brit ambled up to the mic and mangled a Bob Marley tune.

Then Sadie strode over and conferred with the man who sat behind the karaoke machine, and he put an old R&B love song that Anil did not recognize, but all the Barbadians knew the tune and applauded as Sadie grabbed the microphone.

"Everybody done gone," she sang, "Gone and left me. I'm all alone, alone again."

"My heart was whole before," she sang, "and now it's broken. Broo-ken."

The recorded chorus came in sweetly, wailing, "Where do I go, where do I go from here?"

Sadie sang her heart out. When she finished, everyone clapped loudly, and even Anil had tears in his eyes. He clasped Sadie's warm hand and said, "Wow, wow," and ordered another round for the whole group.

He and Sadie chatted through a fog of alcohol. She told him about her life as a cleaner at the Palmview Hotel—the Brits were the worst, vomiting everywhere; the Germans were neater, but tried to grope her—and about the hotel management, which forced her to work twelve-hour shifts.

"That's horrible," Anil said. "That's terrible."

"What are you going to do?" Sadie shrugged her wide shoulders. "A job is a job, right?"

Soon they ran out of conversation and drank in silence. Sadie turned her wide face to Anil and gazed up at him with reddened eyes.

"I should not be telling you this, Mr. Anil, but you are a good man. And your brother was a good man, too." She took a dainty sip of beer. "They have cameras in the lobby, in the hallways. Your brother must be on the tapes."

Anil sat up, suddenly alert.

"Who has the tapes? The manager, Mrs. Braithwaite?"

Sadie shook her head, and her big, glossy curls wobbled.

"Winston is the security man for the hotel." Her voice dropped. "Winston, he went into your brother's room, before the police arrived. He took some things. I saw him go in, and he cut a look at me. That's why I kept my mouth shut."

"What did he take?"

"I dunno." Sadie looked suddenly sober. "Please don't use my name. I could lose my job. Winston, he is a vindictive man."

"Don't worry. I'll be very, very discreet. Thank you."

Anil touched Sadie's broad, warm shoulder and staggered back to the hotel. The fucking Palmview: All this time, they had security tapes, footage that would show Rajesh's every move. He was going to get to the bottom of this.

It wasn't that easy getting hold of the security man, Winston. Anil found him in the lobby, late the next afternoon. He turned out to be a tall, elegant black man, sipping daintily at a glass of ice water. He wore a sky-blue shirt and white pants so tight that Anil could see the outline of car keys in his pocket.

"Mr. Sharma. You been looking for me? Well, here I am."

Anil was polite. "Mr. Winston, I would like to ask you a favor. I noticed you have security cameras all over the hotel, and I was wondering if I could see the tapes? You see, I'm assuming my brother is on there. It could help explain what happened."

"So sorry." The ice cubes tapped against Winston's teeth as he drank. "I cannot do that."

"And why is that?"

"There are no tapes left. We wipe them every thirty-six hours, unless a crime has been committed. Your brother committed suicide. That is not a crime in our country."

Winston straddled the bar stool and calmly sipped his ice water.

Anil leaned in. "You corrupt bastard. I know what you did, okay? You went into Rajesh's room. You took his watch and his cufflinks before the police arrived. You wiped the tapes to cover your ass."

All the smugness vanished from Winston's face. He slammed down his glass and the ice cubes rattled. "I don't know what you are talking about, Mr. Sharma."

"You know *exactly* what I'm talking about. I'm going to the police."

Winston's smooth face crumpled with rage. "I would advise you not to do that."

Anil's fists were balled up. He stalked out of the hotel lobby and into the bright sunlight of the parking lot, then paused, disoriented. Winston crept up to him and whispered in his ear.

"Go ahead," he murmured, "Nobody going to believe you."

⁓

"This is a serious accusation." Inspector Hanuman spoke slowly, as if fighting a fog of tiredness. He had a chiseled profile, long sideburns, and hooded eyes.

It was four o'clock on the same day, and Anil sat across from Inspector Hanuman at the St. Lawrence Gap Police Substation. The small, whitewashed room hummed with heat, and somewhere in the station there was the clacking of a manual typewriter. Anil repeated what he'd just said.

"Someone at the hotel clearly saw Winston. He stole my brother's things, for sure."

"Someone?"

"I am not at liberty to reveal my sources."

"So, it was the maid, yes?" Inspector Hanuman massaged the bridge of his nose. "This would be Sadie, yes? Her son, Roggic, he is a member of the Outlawz gang. He is in deep trouble, indeed very deep."

"What does that have to do with anything?"

Inspector Hanuman smiled. "You are Indian, yes?"

"Originally. I'm a US citizen now."

Hanuman closed the door to his office. He sat on the edge of his desk, inches away from Anil.

"My great-great-grandparents, they were from India. We were brought here to work the sugarcane fields, after the blacks revolted. You know, the slave revolt of 1816? They shipped us here from India because we were reliable, but it didn't work. We mixed with the blacks. We all have black blood, now."

"What does this have to do—"

Hanuman raised a hand for silence.

"You need to know your history. Barbados is a small island. Everyone is connected here. Look, Mr. Sharma. I will tell you something. Indian to Indian. Okay?"

Anil felt stifled by Hanuman's proximity, but he nodded.

"Listen good. Officially, there is no crime here in Barbados. We do not tolerate it. Crime is bad for tourism, bad for business. But things happen inside the hotels, you know? They are private, we do not control them. At the Palmview, we have Winston. He is a good man, he deals with a lot of shit for us. He makes a lot of troubles disappear."

Anil started to talk, but the Inspector held out his hand again.

"So . . . on to your brother. Mister Rajesh Sharma, American national, walks into the ocean, he kills himself. I told you this on the phone; I sent you the report. Now. What did your brother leave in his room? Drugs? Pills? Something embarrassing? Maybe Winston just cleaned it up."

"That makes no sense. My brother's Piaget wristwatch is missing, his titanium cufflinks—"

Inspector Hanuman moved even closer, his breath warm in Anil's face.

"You came all the way here, for cufflinks? You got your brother's suitcase back, yes? Would you have got *anything* back in Puerto Rico? In the DR? No, you would not. So you should not complain."

"Maybe Winston destroyed a note from my brother. Explaining things—"

"Explaining? Explaining what? Your brother's actions speak loudly. The man swam straight out into the ocean, and he drowned. You need me to explain that?"

Anil gripped the arms of his chair. "This is bullshit. I demand that you investigate."

Hanuman's heavy-lidded eyes drooped even more.

"Yes. I can make a formal complaint. But then Sadie's name will go into the report. And nobody will believe her, because her son is a criminal. And Winston will find out, and Sadie will lose her job. I will have another file, and it will just gather dust. Is this what you want, Mr. Sharma? Is it?"

"No, of course not, but my brother, I want—"

"You a novelist, right? I looked you up. One novel. Nice cover. So you are a man of imagination, yes?" Inspector Hanuman leaned forward and gripped Anil's shoulders. "You go home, now, man, and write your books. There is nothing for you here. Any day now the dry season will end, the rains will come. It will pour down, boy. Go home."

"This is not acceptable. I will take this up with the American Embassy, I will petition my congressman. You have not heard the last of me."

Anil rose from his chair and walked out of the dingy police station. It was glaring hot outside, and he squinted as he walked down the dusty street, past a bus stop where two middle-aged ladies stood with parasols held over their heads.

"You need a hat, boy," one of them shouted to Anil. "You will get the heatstroke."

He ignored her and walked on. The lady spoke loudly to her friend.

"These tourists stupid. Too much sun make they brain go soft."

That evening, Anil swam in the pool and lost count at two hundred lengths; when he got out, his fingers were shriveled and prune-like. He walked back to his room, clad only in his swim trunks and a towel and saw that a large part of the building was dark now—anticipating the monsoon, many of the tourists had left. Let it rain. He was not going to leave till he found out why Rajesh died here.

He walked through the veranda and pulled open the glass sliding doors to his suite, and a skinny young girl with dreadlocks stopped vacuuming and jumped back when she saw him.

She stared at him, half naked and dripping water, and then found her voice. "Good evening, sir. I am just finishing up."

"Where is Sadie? She always cleans my room."

"Don't know. I am new, sir."

Still dripping water, Anil walked down the corridor and into the lobby. The manager was standing blankly behind the counter and examining her long red fingernails.

"Mrs. Braithwaite. Do you have a minute?"

"Mr. Sharma. You are wet."

She pointed to a sign on the counter which said: HOTEL GUESTS ARE REQUESTED NOT TO BRING WATER OR SAND INTO THE LOBBY.

"Where is Sadie? She always cleans my room." Anil leaned his elbows on the granite counter. "You fired her, didn't you? Because of Winston?"

"I'm sorry, I cannot discuss the staff roster with you."

Anil closed his eyes for a second. He opened them and spoke deliberately.

"You know that I'm from New York, and that I'm a writer, okay? I have friends there, reporters at the *New York Times* and the *Wall Street Journal*. I will tell them that your director of security stole my brother's things and destroyed evidence." He lied through his teeth. "My friends will write about it. The headline will be, 'American Tourist Dies in Mysterious Circumstances,' and the Palmview Hotel will be named . . ."

The manager's face reddened, and she backed up against a display of bright tourist brochures.

". . . and the owners of the hotel will not be pleased. They'll blame you. It will be the end of your cushy job. You'll be out on your ass."

"Sir, none of this was my idea. Winston, he makes the decisions here. I am just an employee, and—"

"Call him." Anil stepped back from the puddle he had made. "Tell Winston I'll make a deal. If Sadie gets her job back, I will leave this hotel and go home. Tell him that. Be very clear about it."

Turning on his heel, Anil stalked through the lobby. The girl with the dreadlocks was probably still cleaning his room, and he did not know what to do, so he got back into the pool.

He swam slowly at first, but soon the familiar returned to him. He heard Rajesh's voice, during that long-ago summer in Mumbai, teaching him how to swim: *Breathe, hold, palms cutting into the water. Kick harder. You can do it. That's it, you're getting it.*

Rajesh was a strong swimmer. To tire himself out, how far would he have had to swim? A mile? Two miles? How many lengths of the pool would that be? Anil had no idea.

He swam fifty lengths, but he wasn't really tired yet, since he could push off the end walls and gain some momentum; Rajesh wouldn't have had that, he would have struggled out in the open ocean, fighting the waves.

The underwater lights flickered on, and Anil swam through patches of light and darkness. He lost track of time. Maybe it was the sense that he was at the end of this trip. Maybe it was the sound of the blood pounding in his ears. Whatever it was, he found himself recalling a memory that he had stashed away, deep inside himself.

It was the day that Rajesh died. Anil had been at a hipster coffee shop in the West Village, pretending to work on a new novel, but actually yearning after the petite barista. She had huge eyes, ink-black hair, and a slow, sarcastic way of talking. He'd just managed to strike up a conversation—they were discussing the latest Almodóvar movie—when his phone rang; it was Rajesh, probably calling from some airport. He always ended his calls abruptly, saying, *Hey, they're calling my flight. Gotta go, bro, gotta go.*

Anil silenced the call. He continued chatting with the barista, but then she got busy making an elaborate coffee drink, and Anil became afraid that she was avoiding him. He waved nonchalantly, packed up his laptop, and walked through the freezing, slippery streets, headed home to his cramped, cold apartment, way up in Inwood, at the northern tip of Manhattan.

At the West Fourth Street subway station, Anil checked his phone and saw that Rajesh had called two more times but hadn't left a message. He didn't give it another thought. Rajesh only called when he had a few spare minutes; he was always distracted, always signed off in the middle of one of Anil's stories. *Gotta go, bro. Gotta go.*

As Anil waited on the platform for the A train, Rajesh was wading out into the ocean. As Anil found a seat on the jam-packed, fetid train, Rajesh swam steadily into the ocean. By the time Anil was at Fourteenth Street, Rajesh was far out, the waves as big as houses, crashing down over him, the salt water corroding his palate, choking down his throat.

Gotta go, bro. Gotta go.

Now, Anil swam up and down the pool of the Palmview Hotel, pushing himself hard, and an iron band tightened across his chest. He ignored it. Fifty more lengths, fifty-five, an eternity, but still he continued. Halfway across the deep end, his thigh muscles cramped, and he began to sink.

"Help," he shouted. "Help me!" But there was no one around.

He gulped down chlorinated water, felt it rush into his lungs. Thrashing wildly, he made his way across the pool and clung to the concrete lip, gasping and retching.

Gotta go, bro, gotta go.

He hung in the water, lacking the strength to pull himself out. He sucked in air, but it was strangely moist; while he was swimming, it had started to rain. The drops stung his back like dull needles, but he could not move.

Despite the agony in his body, Anil found himself recording it all. He knew then that he was going to write about all this: The way you can love someone, idolize them, and how they can change completely, can become unrecognizable to you. He'd start with the scene in the coffee shop, and this time he would be mercilessly honest—he would put his torment and confusion right on the page. This time, he would get it right.

He clung desperately to the edge of the pool. Lightning forked on the horizon, and in its icy-blue, electrical flash, Anil saw the roaring waves, the empty beach, the palm trees doubled over, their fronds flapping wildly. There was no doubt about it: The dry season in Barbados had come to an end.

EMERGENCY ROOM

At a dinner to celebrate his return to India, Doctor Biju Bose regales his guests with stories from the emergency room: traumatic brain injury, spinal fractures, people crushed between cars, cracked skulls, collapsed lungs, burns to sixty percent of the body. Gunshot wounds to the gut, knife injuries, and men with light bulbs in their anuses.

The guests listen raptly and nod their heads. They are surgeons and anesthesiologists, oncologists and cardiologists, portly and gray haired, but they have remained in Calcutta, and success has dulled them; having Biju back from America—how fit he looks, how sleek from playing tennis!—reminds them of their own heroic, youthful days, and they are grateful for this feeling.

Dr. Biju Bose waves his hands at the restaurant he has chosen for this celebration, the back room of the Amber Palace, with its faded velvet banquettes, its surly waiters and bright-red *tandoori* chicken.

"Look at this place! It looks exactly the same!" he says to his guests. "Remember how we used to come here, when we were residents? In seventy-six, or was it seventy-seven? The only thing we could afford was brain curry? *Hanh*? Brain curry, and two *chapatis*, that's all we ate."

"Yes, yes, we remember," the guests say. "But Biju, you have done damn well for yourself!" They turn to Dr. Bose's family. "We knew he was talented, of course, but to become the head of an emergency room in Connecticut! You must be so proud!"

Dr. Bose's two grown daughters smile faintly, but his wife, Mumtaz, is not listening. She ducks her head and fiddles compulsively with her wedding ring. Thank god she isn't humming, which she does when she's anxious.

"Mumtaz is tired, aren't you ?" Dr. Bose says. "Jet lag! It was a long trip from Hartford. Isn't that right, dear?"

Mumtaz looks up and nods absentmindedly. There are entire days when she is silent. Dr. Bose glances around, but his guests haven't noticed; they're too busy eating. He snaps his fingers and orders more *reshmi* kabab, another platter of steaming *biryani* and a dozen buttery *naans*. His guests protest, but when the food arrives, they fill their plates, and the air is thick with cries of delight.

The dinner is a great success. When it ends, Dr. Bose lags behind his family and stands outside, under the flickering neon sign of the Amber Palace. Even the dark, piss-smelling street does not bother him; it's a reminder that he has traveled far from Calcutta, the city of his birth. He is no longer Biju, lanky and hungry, subsisting on cups of cold tea and Benzedrine tablets—he is Dr. Bose, he lives on Avondale Road in West Hartford and drives a silver Jaguar. His older daughter, Hema, has completed graduate school at Yale, and she has insisted that they return to India for her wedding, so he, Dr. Biju Bose, has rented out the Taj Bengal hotel for the lavish reception. It costs a fortune, but never mind. Money is just money, and he has plenty of it.

Dr. Bose stands on the darkened street, his stomach full of hot food, and just then a young woman steps out of a dark doorway, a few yards away, and beckons to him. Maybe it's the jet lag, or maybe it's his doctor's ego—whatever the reason, Dr. Bose walks toward her, smiling faintly.

Up close, the woman wears pancake makeup and a flimsy turquoise *sari*. Her full breasts are barely contained by the straining cotton of her blouse.

"Hello, mister," she says. "You like me? Six hundred rupees. There is a place we can go."

Is Dr. Bose dreaming? No, he can smell her perfume, a smell from the past, cheap and cloying and very familiar.

He frowns. "Look, you're mistaken. I must . . . You see, my wife is waiting for me."

"Wife?" The young woman's plucked eyebrows shoot up. "Does your wife have this?" She pulls down her blouse and exposes one lolling breast.

Dr. Bose gasps and hurries away from the woman, but he can't help looking back. She is beckoning to him, the gesture contradicted by the blazing contempt in her eyes.

He dashes to the chauffeur-driven car idling at the corner and slides into the back seat, next to Hema, his long-haired, elegant elder daughter. She is hunched over her phone, texting furiously, and Mumtaz is huddled next to her. It is plump Sonu, now a sophomore at Vassar, who turns around from the front seat and stares quizzically at him.

"Credit card." Dr. Bose wipes the sweat from his eyes. "Forgot it in the restaurant. Jesus Christ, it's so hot here."

Sonu's big eyes don't leave his face. "You okay, Baba? Indigestion? I have Tums. Here."

Dr. Bose gratefully accepts three pastel-colored tablets and the familiar, chalky taste calms him. They drive down Chowringhee, and Sonu points at a spotlit marble dome.

"Baba? Hey, Baba, what's that?"

Dr. Bose peers out of the window. "That's the Victoria Memorial. Built by the British. Your mother and I used to go there, when we were courting. We used to sit on those benches. See, over there?"

Sonu's face lights up. She has an intense nostalgia for Calcutta, for a past that is not hers, and Dr. Bose loves her for it.

"You guys went there because you were poor, right? You couldn't afford restaurants?"

Dr. Bose loves to have his own stories quoted to him, and he nods.

"Moomie," he says to Mumtaz, "Look. Victoria Memorial. Look."

"Oh, no." Hema points down at her phone. "Dan has diarrhea."

Dan is Hema's fiancé, a laconic blond boy from Colorado, and he's staying in a hotel across town. They are to be married in five days.

"What?" Mumtaz snaps into focus. She is a doctor herself, a pathologist at a smaller hospital in Hartford. "Tell him to take two Imodium tablets, right away. He must drink fluids, bottled water only. And he *must not* eat the street food. There is cholera, diphtheria, dengue fever. Some of these strains are antibiotic resistant. Do you know, the CDC just released a report, and they said that you could die if you—"

"Jesus, Ma," Hema snaps. "Dan's not an idiot. He backpacked all over Asia for three years."

Dr. Bose takes Mumtaz's hand into his own and squeezes hard. His message is clear: *Don't act crazy. Not when your daughter is getting married.*

Mumtaz stops talking. She yanks her hand away and slides it beneath the cloth of her *sari*. Sonu sees this but pretends not to. Hema is texting furiously, probably complaining to Dan about Mumtaz.

Dr. Bose stares at his wife. In the half-darkness, the pouches beneath her eyes are hidden, as is her thinning hair, and her haughty profile is as sharp as a Mughal painting. Dr. Bose sees once again the desirable, young Muslim girl he married, causing a huge scandal. Back then, Hindu-Muslim weddings were rare.

We made it thirty-four years, he thinks, *we'll be okay. We'll get through this.*

⌁

It is very late by the time they get back to Mumtaz's huge, ancestral bungalow in Alipore. The whitewash on the outside is peeling, but the cool, high-ceilinged rooms inside are clean and comfortable. Dr. Bose brushes his teeth and watches Mumtaz. She sits on the bed, stares at her phone, and deep furrows appear in her forehead.

"It's starting," she whispers. "The deportations. Trump has signed the order. They're hunting down Mexicans, taking them to the border, oh my God."

"Stop reading that nonsense." Dr. Bose snatches away her phone. "The courts will stop it. Besides, those people are illegal, it's their own fault. Now, it's late, please get ready for bed."

Mumtaz enters the bathroom, and Dr. Bose quickly, efficiently, disables the wireless network on her phone. She will not know how to reconnect, and he can always blame the lousy reception here. Mumtaz does not need to absorb the toxins of the world.

Can she hold it together for another five days? Tonight, the doctor's friends suspected nothing, but that's because they remembered Mumtaz from the old days, as a stunningly good-looking, haughty, silent girl.

Mumtaz comes out of the bathroom and peels off her yellow *sari*. In her white underwear and bra, she is puffy and bloated—a side effect of her medications—but there is still something girlish about her figure. He wants to hold her, to feel her skin against his; they have not had sex for at least two years.

"Come here," he says, and she complies. He pulls her head to his chest and inhales the musky, slightly sour scent of her hair, which has always appealed to him.

"I'm worried about Dan," she whispers. "His stomach . . . do you think . . ."

Dr. Bose closes his eyes and waits for a monologue.

". . . do you think that the Imodium will work?"

"Yes, of course." He is relieved at the reasonableness of her question. "As long as he doesn't go around eating at food stalls. All his spiritual yoga nonsense won't save him from the bacteria here."

"Yes," Mumtaz nods. "He thinks he's invincible. But he's a good sort. You have to give him a chance, Biju. Get to know him."

Dr. Bose holds her closer. They had agreed, many years ago, that their children could marry anyone of their choosing, but does that include a yoga teacher like Dan? A confused, long-haired boy who seems to enjoy being bossed around by Hema?

"Our daughters are wonderful," Dr. Bose says. "We are lucky people."

Mumtaz stays in his arms for a few minutes. She takes an Ambien and slips quickly into sleep, but Dr. Bose is wide awake and stares up at the slowly turning fan. He tells himself that he has avoided coming back to Calcutta because he has nothing here: His parents are gone; his two sisters, much older than him, are dead too. Then he remembers the pale-faced prostitute from the alley, her thin, silky turquoise *sari*, the sheerness of it like an invitation. He feels an old emotion—lust mixed with shame—and quickly pushes it away.

I am Dr. Bose, he tells himself. *I am no longer that boy.*

But that boy is still inside him. The past is stirring, pushing its way into his consciousness, and he cannot stop it.

⁓

Back in the 1970s, Biju Bose was a nobody, a bright, lower-class boy who had escaped his family's auto-parts business and made it into Calcutta Medical College. With his skinny frame, cheap clothes, and downcast eyes, he was easily overlooked by the richer students. They only began to notice Biju Bose when he aced every exam; he studied eighteen hours a day, took Benzedrine tablets to stay up, had a photographic memory. For Biju, every exam was one step closer to getting out of this shithole.

His goal was America. To prepare for his new life, he bought used copies of *Life* magazine from a stall on College Street, and in moments of self-doubt, he would flip through them and examine the ads; he wanted a Pontiac Firebird, a ranch house with aluminum siding, and a wife with glistening white teeth and upswept blonde hair, just like Farrah Fawcett.

But at times those images were not enough. Biju did not drink cheap rum to relax, as the other students did; every evening, he pulled on his worn leather sandals and walked all over the city, returning exhausted and ready for sleep. It was on one of those outings that he crossed Kalighat Bridge and noticed the young girls standing at discreet intervals, their bright nylon *saris* hiding their bony country-girl bodies, their eyes glittering with fear. On an impulse, he had followed one down a narrow lane and into a room with a sour-smelling bed. She charged him twenty rupees. When he left, he felt drained, his head clear, and he studied till dawn.

He returned there every week. Because he could only afford the cheapest women, he became addicted to their meager bodies, and to their smell, of smoke, sweat, and cheap, cloying perfume. This secret made him feel superior to his fellow students. He watched the boys pursuing the girls with endless, earnest conversation, receiving at most a chaste kiss. They wasted many precious hours while he, Biju Bose, could drain the tension from his body quickly and then get back to his surgery textbooks.

Then one day he saw Mumtaz Azeem. She was waiting outside the crumbling medical college gates, a slim, poised girl with enormous eyes and fashionable short hair. She came from a rich upper-class Muslim family, and her father was a brilliant, stubborn man, a barrister at the High Court. He adored his only daughter, and every evening he picked her up from college in a chauffeured Fiat.

Biju Bose was taken with Mumtaz's self-possession; he craved her the same way he craved his red Pontiac Firebird.

"I'm going to marry that Azeem girl," Biju confided, in a moment of weakness, to his roommate, a crude Punjabi boy.

"With what money?" the roommate said. "She'll see your raggedy clothes and run a mile. Plus, she's Muslim, and you're a fucking Hindu Brahmin. Her parents will kill you."

But Biju Bose was bold. The next evening, when Mumtaz was waiting for her father, he walked up to her and scowled.

"We should study together," he said. "You could use some help in anatomy. Your marks in the last exam were not exactly stellar."

"*Stellar*?" Mumtaz looked confused. She was not used to being talked to like this. "And you are?"

"Biju Bose," he said. "You must have heard of me. I'm going to be a surgeon. I'm not like these other boys."

He expected her to laugh, but instead she regarded him with her clear, limpid eyes. He noticed her slim, fine nostrils and the scar on her forehead from a childhood case of chicken pox. She turned away without a word.

Biju Bose was not deterred. He returned the next evening and accosted Mumtaz while she waited for her father's car.

"Have you thought about my proposition?"

"*Proposition? Stellar?* Where do you learn these words?"

"From books. I'm always improving myself. It's the only way to get ahead in the world."

Mumtaz regarded him through narrowed eyes. She must have seen something in him, because she nodded abruptly.

"Fine," she said. "I'll talk to my mother. Come to my house on Thursday afternoon. Now leave, before my father sees you."

And with that, Biju's life changed. He entered into the Azeem household as a tutor and sat at their long, mahogany dining table, teaching Mumtaz the intricacies of anatomy and drinking endless cups of Darjeeling tea.

The Azeems were very well off. They had a cook, who made Western chops and soufflés, and Mumtaz even had a personal servant—a young girl drew her bath and combed her hair—but Biju pretended not to notice. He arrived every day wearing his one clean shirt and his worn leather sandals and won Mumtaz over by refusing to go away. It helped that Mumtaz's mother liked Biju's intensity and ambition and was secretly thrilled that her daughter was in a romantic entanglement.

When old Barrister Azeem died suddenly, of a heart attack, Mumtaz was heartbroken, but an insurmountable barrier disappeared: Biju could now marry Mumtaz. With the barrister's money, they could travel to America and take their recertification exams. Suddenly, Biju's future was within reach.

The morning after the dinner at the Amber Palace Restaurant, Dr. Bose wakes early, as is his custom, and does a hundred pushups. When the body falls apart, the mind follows. Most people think it's the other way around, but it isn't. He showers and puts on a fresh orange polo shirt, well-pressed chinos, and his Brooks Brothers' tasseled loafers, but he still doesn't feel like himself. He glances at his Rolex; it is late at night in Hartford, but Mary Anne will take his call.

She picks up on the first ring. "Biju? Finally. How are you?"

He can see her: lank brown hair, clear blue eyes, quick, competent hands. His right hand, the head nurse at the ER.

"I can hear India. It's noisy there, huh? So, you finally went back. What's it like?"

"Crazy. Crows, sparrows, scooters, trucks, bicycles. I can't really talk long. Just wanted to check in."

"How are you? Holding up?"

Dr. Bose knows that she is in her tiny one-bedroom apartment near the hospital—a narrow bed with a hard mattress, cracked yellow tiles in the bathroom, sagging fabric blinds. The only nice thing she has is a stainless-steel Krups coffee maker that he gave her years ago. God, he knows that apartment better than he knows his own house. He feels homesick for it now.

Mumtaz walks into the bedroom. The frown on her face means that she is looking for her reading glasses, and Dr. Bose lowers his phone.

"Over there, on the night table." He gestures to his phone. "I'm just checking in with Mary Anne. Seeing how things are at the ER." He puts the phone back to his ear. "All good over there? Dr. Patrowski managing okay?"

Mary Anne laughs. "Patrowski's an idiot. I'll try to stop him from killing too many patients, but get your ass back here soon. And bring me back something nice, okay? One of those carved elephants, maybe."

"Yeah, yeah."

Dr. Bose hangs up without saying goodbye. This is his style, and Mary Anne knows it.

Mumtaz has recovered her glasses but stands in the middle of the room, staring through the window at the overgrown garden. Today she is wearing a white *salwar kameez*, and her hair is up in a ponytail, which makes her look twenty years younger.

"You look nice." Dr. Bose says. "What's on the agenda for today?"

"Have you forgotten?" She laughs. "Now that you don't have your head nurse to remind you of your schedule? We're collecting the ring today."

Dan's family is paying for the wedding ring, but Hema has designed it, and Mumtaz has been deputized to pick it up from the jeweler. Dr. Bose nods. "Ah. Of course. The ring."

He accompanies Mumtaz to the jeweler's shop, deep within the gloomy arcades of the New Market. The wedding ring that Hema designed has two elaborate claws of gold that hold a large, sparkling diamond. Dr. Bose examines it, wondering how long the marriage will last. Hema is clearly marrying Dan as a final, rebellious act. Oh well, what can he do? She never listens to his advice.

In the car on the way back, Dr. Bose sits with his thigh pressed against Mumtaz's, feeling her fleshy warmth; he is shocked by his own arousal.

They stop at the tailor's, who assures them he is almost done with Hema's wedding *ghagra-choli,* bright pink with gold embroidery, modeled after one worn recently by a Bollywood actress. Their last stop is the air-conditioned atrium of the Taj Bengal hotel, where they consult a young hotel employee who carries a large plastic clipboard. They visit the banquet room and marvel at the lush, private garden outside; this is where the cocktails will be held.

"Remember our wedding?" Mumtaz says. "How nervous you were? How we got married in the garden of my house? How we had to chase out all the stray dogs?"

"How could I forget? The dogs, oh my god, it was like a comedy show."

They both laugh, and he notices, with a small shock, that Mumtaz's eyes are clear today.

They walk back to the car together, holding hands. Decades have miraculously fallen away, and Dr. Bose is back at the beginning of his life. This feeling does not leave him all day.

⁓

Late that night, after dinner, Mumtaz lies in bed and holds Hema's diamond ring up to the light. It throws sharp, glittering shadows onto the wall, and she plays with it like a child, twisting it to compress the shadows, then splaying them out.

"Moomie, give me that." He takes the ring from her and locks it away in the cupboard.

"Are you feeling tired?" he asks, smiling.

This question was, in the old days, a prelude to sex. If the answer was *Fine*, they would proceed.

"I'm fine. Why do you ask?" Mumtaz sits straight up in bed. "Do I look bad?"

"No, you look beautiful."

And indeed she does. She has washed her face, and her hair is still pulled back into a girlish ponytail. He touches the faint scar on her forehead, then kisses her. Her lips are dry, but she does not turn her head away, as she usually does.

"Moomie, I'll be right back. Don't go anywhere, okay?"

"Where would I go, silly?" She smiles at him, leans back, and closes her eyes.

In the bathroom, Dr. Bose brushes his teeth. From his toilet case, he takes out a small bottle of French cologne and splashes it on his cheeks. He returns to the bedroom, and Mumtaz is waiting for him. She allows him to undress her, allows access to her body, but her mind drifts away, god knows where. After he is done, she lies silently with her head on his chest

"I'm sorry," she whispers. "There is something wrong with me. You should have married someone else. Me, I'm not suited to—"

"Shhh." He pulls her head onto his shoulder. "Shhh. It's fine. Everything is fine."

He hides his disappointment and strokes her hair, letting each fine strand fall through his fingers. She cries for a while. He gives her an Ambien, and she drifts quickly into sleep. Tonight, the moon is full, and in the silver light he sees her clearly—the hollows under her deeply lashed eyes, the creases that now bracket her mouth.

Why does her brain work like this, bottling up anxiety? Was the darkness always there? Or is she just a spoiled, rich girl who could never adjust to life in America?

The last thought gives Dr. Bose some comfort: *Yes, she isn't tough like me. For years, I've tried to protect her, but this is beyond me, it really is.*

He remains awake for a very long time.

⁓

Those first years in Hartford were grim. The girls were young. They were still poor then and lived in a small apartment right by St. Joseph's Hospital. All day and all night the wail of ambulances filled the air.

One summer, the heat was ferocious; it drove the inner-city gangs out onto the streets, and a war erupted. The ER was inundated with muscled young men who were wheeled in bare-chested, compression packs already on their gunshot wounds, eyes wide and staring. The waiting room filled with stoic octogenarian grandmothers, wailing girlfriends, and pudgy toddlers; sometimes rival gang members attacked each other, and the security guards had to break it up.

All that summer, as the body count mounted, Dr. Bose returned home late, stinking of blood and death; he wanted only some rice and *daal* and mutton curry and to watch a lurid Hindi movie and forget what he had seen. Instead, there was Mumtaz, curled up in front of the television screen, watching the news reports on WVIT.

"I hate this place," she said. "I want to go home."

"Come on," Dr. Bose said. "Don't take it personally. Soon I'll be making more money. We can move to the suburbs. Is there any food?"

But Mumtaz had turned back to the television and was watching gang members throwing up signs and clowning for the television cameras.

There was never any food at home, and soon Dr. Bose began to stay late at the ER. One evening, a new nurse—he couldn't remember her name—beckoned to him and said, "Hey, Doctor B, we're going out for pizza, want to come?" Even though there was an unspoken hierarchy, and doctors did not go out with nurses, he had agreed. The nurse's name was Mary Anne, and she was both soft-spoken and bold; her lank brown hair was cut short, so that the pink tips of her ears poked out. After that, pizza together became a routine, and Dr. Bose got home late every night, after the girls had gone to bed. Only Mumtaz was awake, stoned on television and fear. He would turn off the television and make her climb into bed with him, and she lay, quivering, against his chest. Late at night he'd hear her walking around the darkened house.

That fall, he was in the ER, attending to a three-hundred-pound man who had been shot six times in the chest—his hands were covered with blood—when his beeper went off. Something was wrong with Mumtaz, but he couldn't leave the ER. It was Mary Anne who'd driven to his apartment and found the girls huddled on the couch and Mumtaz hiding under the bed, her eyes wide and staring.

Dr. Bose took Mumtaz to one of his colleagues, a psychiatrist, who listened to her family history and prescribed a raft of medications and therapy. The psychiatrist took Dr. Bose aside and talked about *inherited trauma* and *PTSD*. Dr. Bose did not believe this mumbo jumbo, but he complied. He drove Mumtaz to regular therapy sessions and made sure that she took her blue and green pills.

It felt a relief to enter the ER. He felt calm, almost happy, as he walked into the operating room, wearing a rubber cap printed with parakeets. His staff instantly arranged themselves around him and became an unthinking extension of his will; all he had to do was glance at Mary Anne, and she knew exactly what to do—she'd hand him the right tool or bark an instruction to the others.

Dr. Bose began to live at the ER. Unmonitored, Mumtaz stopped going to therapy and took her medicines only intermittently; by the end of that year, she had taken a leave of absence from her job at the pathology lab and spent her days sleeping. Dr. Bose was at his wit's end. He borrowed money from an older Indian doctor and bought a small ranch house in the suburbs, and that seemed to do the trick. Removed from the vicinity of the hospital, Mumtaz slowly recovered and even started to work again; the quiet, analytical work of pathology seemed to suit her. The years went by, and that summer of madness receded.

It came back, decades later, after the girls had grown up and left the house. In small ways at first—Mumtaz compulsively trawled the internet for new diseases—and it seemed manageable. Then, one night, Dr. Bose returned late from the hospital and shrugged off his lab coat. On the TV screen, Trump's orange face was saying some outrageous shit.

"If he wins," Mumtaz asked, her voice quivering. "What will happen to us?"

"Mumtaz, listen," Dr. Bose had said. "First of all, he's an idiot; he's not going to win. Have you seen Hillary's approval ratings?"

"Yes, but . . . if it happened? What then?"

"This is America. There are courts, procedures, laws. Plus, nothing will happen to us. I'm high up in the hospital. Is there any dinner? No? Please stop watching that nonsense."

The television stayed on. Mumtaz not only stopped cooking, she barely ate, and her monologues about insecticides became more frequent. By midsummer, Dr. Bose came home to find his wife attacking the kitchen cabinets with a Brillo pad, scraping at their polished veneer till the bare grain of wood showed through.

"What the hell? You're behaving like a madwoman!"

"I am not mad!" she had screamed. "I'm just keeping the house clean. Can't you see? He's poisoning us all!"

It quickly became unbearable. Hema, recently engaged to Dan, came up with the idea of a trip back to India. "Let's get the hell out of here, Baba," she said. "I've had enough of that asshole Trump. I want to get married in India, and Dan agrees. It's too poisonous here."

And that was why Dr. Bose had returned to Calcutta, after all these years.

Two days before the wedding, Dr. Bose wakes late. For a moment, he cannot remember where he is, and then he hears the hubbub of traffic, and he remembers: Calcutta. Hema's wedding. Almost there.

Dr. Bose has massively overslept. It is past eleven, and he normally wakes at 4:45 A.M.; his first surgeries are scheduled for 6:00, when his mind and fingers are rested. Mumtaz is gone from the bedroom, and he panics and runs downstairs, but the old servant says that Memsahib and the two girls have gone *sari* shopping. He eats breakfast, reads the papers, and waits for them to return.

It is past noon when the car pulls up outside and the girls stagger in, carrying heavy packages of clothes. Mumtaz follows, wearing a simple pale-blue *sari*. Her sadness of the last night has evaporated; does she even remember what happened? She bends down, kisses Dr. Bose on the forehead, and says, "Good morning sleepyhead. Tired from last night?"

He wants to cry with relief, but he cannot not let the girls see this. Instead, he says, "Oh, I need to find my glasses," and leaves the room to stand in the stairwell, but Mumtaz finds him there and asks, for the first time in years, "Are you okay, Biju? Is something wrong?"

"Yes, yes, I'm fine," he says. "What did you buy? Show me."

For the next hour, Dr. Bose sits in a chair and watches his daughters and wife parade back and forth, showing off their new silk *saris*. Colors that would have been gaudy in America—tangerine, peacock blue, daisy yellow—are vibrant here.

When Mumtaz goes upstairs for a nap, Dr. Bose beckons Hema and Sonu into their grandmother's old bedroom and shuts the door. The room still smells like the old lady, of Vicks VapoRub and bitter herbal pills; the house is so big that the servants have simply closed the door to this room, leaving plenty of space for life to go on.

Hema walks over to the dresser and picks up an ivory-handled hairbrush.

"Look, Nani's hair is still stuck in here. What are we going to do with all this stuff? We can't just leave it like this."

"Yes, yes," Dr. Bose says. "We will clear it out. But I asked you in here to talk about Ma. She's so much better, yes?"

Sonu sits on the bed, swinging her feet. "Yeah. She seems less nuts. Back on her meds?"

"I hope she holds it together," Hema says. "I mean, okay, she's right about surveillance and Big Data, but Jeez, it's so embarrassing when she goes on and on about it. I don't know what Dan's parents will think. They arrive today, you know."

"That's not the point." Dr. Bose is not used to talking to his daughters. "The point is—why do you think she's better? Look around you. No television. Her smart phone doesn't work here. She's being shielded from the news. Trump isn't making her crazy."

"Huh," Hema says, "I think she's paranoid. It's her, not the news. She can take anything and twist it. On the plane she refused to eat the food because she said that corporations are poisoning the soil."

"Look . . ." Dr. Bose's face turns red. He glances at Sonu— she will back him up. "What do *you* think?"

Sonu's face becomes solemn. "I agree with Baba, she seems better. It's better for her to not watch the news."

"Thank you." He wants to kiss her. "So, we're agreed, we protect Ma from the media? Okay? Don't leave your phones around."

"How long can we do this?" Hema glares up at him. "Isn't it . . . sort of dishonest? Why don't we get her to therapy?"

"She doesn't want to go. What can I do?"

"Yes, of course. What can you do? You're always so busy saving lives." Hema laughs. "Always hiding in the ER. Playing god there, with your sidekick."

"What the hell . . ." Dr. Bose is flushed with anger. "Do you know who pays the bills? Me. Do you know how I do it? By working my ass off."

"I'm going to visit Dan. Are you coming, Sonu? No? Okay."

Hema sweeps out of the room. Dr. Bose turns to his younger daughter.

"Why is your sister behaving like this?"

Sonu looks up at him with her big, empathic brown eyes. "She's stressed, okay? The wedding. Dan's stomach. Ma says wacky stuff, and it doesn't help. I better go with her. See you in a bit, okay?"

Sonu kisses him on the cheek and leaves the room too, and Dr. Bose is alone with the bitter smell of old medicines. How can Hema blame him for Mumtaz's illness? It is too much.

My daughters are spoiled, he thinks. *They have been raised with Barbie dolls and music lessons and art classes, all paid for by my hard work. Hard, grinding work that has nearly killed me: That time when a needle from an AIDS-infected patient pierced my thumb. That time a trucker, high on amphetamines, hit me in the face. I shielded them. I didn't tell them what happens in the ER, what really happens in the world.*

Dr. Bose thinks of the years when he was a medical student and owned one polyester shirt: he washed it every night and hung it out to dry when he slept. The years he ate cheap dinners at Amber Palace Restaurant, a plate of brain curry and two *chapatis.* The years that he rented *Gray's Anatomy* from the bookseller because he could not afford to own a copy.

He isn't going to tolerate any more nonsense from Hema. Wedding nerves or not, she can't talk to him like this.

⁓

They go to bed early that night. The next morning is the wedding rehearsal at the Taj Bengal hotel.

Mumtaz brushes her teeth first and slides into bed. When Dr. Bose emerges from his turn in the bathroom, Mumtaz quickly pushes her hands under the bedsheet; if he wasn't so focused on her, he would have missed the movement.

"Moomie, what's going on?"

She smiles up at him, clear eyed. "Nothing. Are you coming to bed?"

"Yes, I am." He smiles, exuding kindness, but inside him the panic creates loops and whirls.

He walks over to her side of the bed and yanks down the sheet—lying on the mattress is an old, rusted paper clip, which Mumtaz has straightened out. Clearly, she's had it for some time, because her forearms, usually covered by her long-sleeved *kameez*, are striated by deep, infected cuts.

"Moomie, what are you . . . how long have you . . ."

"It's nothing," Mumtaz says mildly and pulls the sheet up again. "Don't worry." She absentmindedly pats his face, as though he is a child in need of comforting.

"He's started," she says, calmly. "It's all started."

"What?"

She gestures at her phone. "Trump. Mexican women crying, their children being taken away. Toddlers dying in detention. Don't you know about it?"

She gestures at her phone, and it seems to be working fine, because the *New York Times* homepage is on the screen.

"How did you fix it . . ." He stops. It doesn't matter. "Moomie, why are you cutting your arms?"

"The pain," she says, matter-of-factly. "It distracts me from my thoughts. Biju, I think I'm going crazy."

He yells for Sonu, who calls their family doctor. The man arrives and gives Mumtaz a tetanus injection and bandages her wounds and prescribes a powerful sedative that sends her into a deep, trance-like sleep. Dr. Bose, the head of the ER at St. Joseph's, watches helplessly.

Out in the corridor, Hema is weeping silently, but she steps back from his embrace. Her hair is open, down to her shoulders, and she looks like a young Mumtaz, her bearing upright, her eyes blazing.

"You did this to her!" Hema pokes a long finger into his chest. "She could have been fine."

"That's absurd. Hema, I will not tolerate—"

"Back when we were kids, Ma was going to therapy, she was getting better, but you couldn't stand it, could you? You were too scared of what she'd say. That's why you stopped taking her."

Dr. Bose tries to protest, but Hema shouts over him.

"I know why you love the ER. I've seen you strutting around, I've seen the way that Mary Anne is all over you—it's disgusting. You think nobody knows?" Hema covers her face with her hands. "Everybody knows, everybody—they just pretend not to. Poor Ma, it's right in her face, and she refuses to see it, and that has made her completely nuts—and now my wedding is completely ruined, all because of you..."

Dr. Bose speaks in his detached voice, the one he uses in the ER. "Please lower your voice. It's been a tough night. But Ma will be okay, the wedding will proceed as scheduled, okay?"

Hema just stares at him. When she speaks, her voice is soft and controlled. "You're disgusting. I don't want you at the wedding. Do you hear me? You are *not* to attend."

Dr. Bose is speechless. He swallows a few times, and then he finds his voice.

"Hema, I understand, you're upset, but . . . Hey, where are you going?"

She turns on her heel and stalks down the corridor, and Dr. Bose turns to his younger daughter. "Sonu, this is crazy. Talk to Hema, please. Talk some sense into her."

Sonu meets his gaze. She follows Hema down the corridor and grabs her hand, and the sisters vanish into their bedroom and slam the door. He hears the murmur of their voices, his name mentioned, again and again: *Baba this, Baba that.* Hema's voice is thick with contempt.

This is absurd. This is madness. Dr. Bose turns on his heel and enters the darkened bedroom, shaking with anger.

He looks down at Mumtaz, sleeping so peacefully now, and he feels like shouting at her. *So, I haven't been the best husband, but our daughters don't know what it's been like, being married to you! Migraines, nightmares, craziness! Tell me, what is a man to do when his own wife can't cater to his needs? Hema blames me, but she doesn't know the first damn thing about our marriage!*

Dr. Bose lies on the bed in the darkness, and his mind goes back to that terrible summer when Mumtaz first went mad.

It had started raining in late September, and the temperature finally dropped. Like a disease that had crested, the shootings dropped off, and there were lulls in the ER. Late one night, Dr. Bose had completed a twelve-hour shift and was napping on a sagging cot in the doctor's lounge.

Mary Anne tugged at his elbow, and he woke instantly. He could read her face: from the thin, flat line of her mouth he knew that something bad was awaiting him in the ER. He didn't hurry. He took a few seconds to clear his mind, and then he trotted out into the fluorescent-lit mayhem.

The patient was in a corner cubicle, curtains drawn, his team already working on her. A young, Hispanic woman with long, beautiful dark hair; he saw from her blueish hue that she wasn't breathing.

"Cyanosis. What's the cause? Come on, people."

"Airway obstructed," someone shouted.

Dr. Bose had seen this before. He tore open a trache tube and grabbed a scalpel.

He swiftly made a horizontal incision, half an inch deep, between the Adam's apple and the cricoid artery, and he pinched the cut to open it. Just then Mary Anne grabbed his elbow.

"What?" The trache tube was in his hand, poised above the incision.

"Biju, stop. Stop!" Mary Anne pointed to a slim silver bracelet around the woman's wrist. It was engraved with the words DO NOT RESUSCITATE.

"No, she's too young. Could be a fashion thing. I can save her. Let me—"

"No Biju." Mary Anne took the trache tube from his hand. "Legal will have our ass. We can't." She pulled him outside the curtained area and grasped his hand tightly.

He heard, through the curtain, the patient's tortured wheezing. It became a choking, gargling sound, and then it stopped. The ER was quiet for an instant, one of those odd, inexplicable silences. Then it all erupted once again, phones ringing, people shouting, and someone was calling out, *Dr. Bose, Dr. Bose, over here.* He shook his head, as if to clear it. He ran, adrenalin pumping, to the next patient, with Mary Anne at his side.

They slept together that night for the first time, in Mary Anne's shabby apartment. Afterward his mind was clear, and months' worth of tension drained away. Driving home, he even listened to music on the radio. The girls were asleep, but he stood for a long time in their darkened bedroom, looking at their angelic faces. In his bedroom, Mumtaz was a crumpled ball under the covers, and he was about to slide in next to her when he caught a whiff of Mary Anne's perfume on his skin.

He took a shower, soaping himself fastidiously. He told himself that Mary Anne meant nothing; it was just a release that allowed him to function. The world was a dangerous place, and he was out there, in the ER, in the blood and noise, so that his family could remain safe and oblivious. If nobody else could understand that, so be it. He, Biju Bose, would go it alone, as he always did, and that was fine by him.

EL CABALLO AMARILLO

It is Saturday night, and the girls are out in Seville. Girls in crackling leather miniskirts and halter tops sashay through the narrow cobblestone streets by the cathedral. Girls sit on benches down by the river, sticking their tongues into their boyfriends' mouths. Girls squat and pee in alleys, leaving long, fluid trails.

These are not beautiful girls, okay? These are those ugly-sexy Spanish girls with bony faces and hoarse voices, but Kamran, Little Joey, and Ajay—three frat boys from New Jersey—want them desperately. It is their junior year abroad, and they chose Spain because they thought they could get lucky.

So, they wait. They sit on a concrete bench on the Alameda de Hércules, armed with a gallon jug of vodka and an orange Fanta chaser, waiting to start a *botellón*. The girls arrive, in groups of three or four, sweetly saying *Hola*, but after they've taken a swig of vodka, and their mouths are dyed orange from the Fanta, they glance down at their phones, start texting, and slip away, like fish from a net. Soon the vodka is finished, and all the girls are gone.

"These Spanish girls are hos, real hos," Joey says. His scalp gleams pink under his super-short buzz cut

Kamran nods his bespectacled head. "Yeah. Totally transactional."

"Yo, chill out," Ajay says. "They know that we're here for, like, nine months, and they have to *live* here. Plus, they're Catholic, they believe in original sin."

"Bullshit, Ajay." Joey snorts. "I was banging three Puerto Rican *chicas* back home. *Three.* You Indian guys wouldn't know what to do with pussy if it hit you in the face, okay?"

It's true. Kamran and Ajay don't have girlfriends back in New Jersey. The Indian girls only date white guys, the white girls think they're nerds, and they're terrified of the black girls. Whatever.

It's already midnight, but they don't want to go home yet. The whole town is out, entire families promenading through the narrow streets, taking in the cool night air. They decide to walk over to La Catedral, sit on the steps, and watch the costumed freaks. It always makes them feel better.

Tonight, the freaks are out in force: A human flowerpot. A guy dressed as a baby, babbling away in a gigantic baby carriage. An enormous, devilish goat, its hair made out of plastic streamers. Etcetera. The freaks are North Africans who have swum across the Mediterranean using inner tubes and kids' rafts and now live in the bushes down by the river. Most of them sell knockoff handbags, but a few prance around in front of La Catedral, wearing outlandish costumes, and earn a few euros by performing for the *turistas*.

The guys aren't in a sympathetic mood when a freak trots up to them. Close up, it is so obviously fake: a bright canary-yellow horse with pink polka dots. There's a wide seam visible along its back, and on each side of its head are eye slits with thick black eyelashes sewn on. Still, there is something very horse-like about it: it stands like a horse, head slightly cocked, tail swishing on hidden wires.

"Fuck off, horsey," Joey says. "Jesus, you're pathetic, okay? Why can't you sell handbags, like the other Africans?"

Ajay winces. It's not right to talk to the horse like this; many of the Africans drown crossing the Mediterranean. They eat food from the trash. Their lives suck.

"Hey horsey, horsey," Ajay says, "here's some *dinero*, okay?" He puts a note in the horse's mouth and then feels sick. "Crap. That was a ten. I thought that was, like, a one."

Joey laughs his ass off. Then he stops and points to the edge of the plaza. "Here come the cops! Run, horsey, run."

Two blue-and-white vans pull up, and a bunch of CNP cops in dark uniforms pile out. They run after the freaks, rip open the paper and plastic outfits, and drag the lanky Africans to the vans, whaling on them all the time. A bunch of asshole German tourists are laughing and videoing the whole thing.

The horse disappears around the corner. The van doors slam shut, and they drive off. Soon the plaza has the anticlimactic feeling of a theater after a performance is over. There is nothing else to do; Kamran, Little Joey, and Ajay have to go home.

They cross the San Telmo Bridge to Triana—the stone balustrades are dotted with young Spanish couples, French kissing and feeling each other up—and their collective mood darkens. They hear a rustle and see that the yellow horse is following them, clopping along with its head raised in panic. So, it got away from the cops, but what does it want from them? More money?

They walk faster, jeering at the horse, but it accompanies them down the Calle Pureza, past the empty lot where they have torn down an old house, and it stops when they do, at their *casa*. Ajay unlocks the door, and the horse makes a mournful, neighing sound, and all three of them crack up.

Okay, so it's funny, but then the horse runs through the open doorway, across the cobblestoned courtyard, and stops under the tattered palm tree in the corner, its big head drooping with tiredness.

"Haha," says Kamran. "Poor horsey. It's a homeless horsey."

"Yo, this is crazy," Ajay says. "Guys, get it out of here."

"Don't be so uptight, Ajay," Joey says. "The horse is tired. The horse needs a place to sleep. I thought you were a *nice* guy? A *thoughtful* guy?"

Joey is always ranking on Ajay, because he went to private school in New Jersey, and because he's majoring in art history. *So,* Ajay thinks, *screw it—after they finish dicking around, they'll throw the horse out, right?* He walks up the open flight of stairs to his room. When he looks down into the courtyard, Joey and Kamran are laughing and patting the horse's head.

⟶

The next morning Ajay wakes up with a hammering headache, completely panicked: What if those drunken fools have let the horse stay? They have laptops and iPhones and iPads; they have enough gear for a moon landing. All the gigabytes that make up their lives will be gone: the pictures of castles, bullrings, and churches, the snapshots of their families, their illegal MP3 downloads, their bookmarked porn sites.

But nothing is stolen, and the yellow horse is still there, lying under the stairs. They gather about it, bleary eyed, clad in T-shirts and shorts, and it nods its head and sniffles with pleasure.

Joey opens the front door and points to the street. "Go home, horsey," he says. "Go join the other freaks. Shit, maybe he only speaks African?"

Maybe the horse doesn't speak English, or maybe it has nowhere to go, because it ignores Joey and doesn't move. Despite a few hours of sleep, they are all still drunk. They decide to brew some strong coffee and then figure out how to get rid of the horse.

They drink coffee. They take turns using the shower—the hot water runs out quickly here—and by then it is early afternoon, and the yellow horse is still sitting under the stairs when the *intercambios* arrive: Maria, Cristina, and Alba, the Spanish girls who come over to practice their English. The girls really like that the guys have their own house—a living area on the ground floor, facing the courtyard, and above it, three cell-like bedrooms. The girls all share rooms with their little brothers and sisters, and they are tired of all the yelling and fighting and their mothers constantly going through their stuff. The *intercambios* like listening to R&B and hanging out and drinking beer, but one glimpse of a bedroom, of a bed, freaks them out. They are used to making out on park benches, down by the river. They are like outside cats, wary of closed doors.

That afternoon the *intercambios* see the yellow horse lying under the stairs. They gather around it in their stilettos, their booty shorts and fishnets, and gape at it.

"Where did it come from?" they ask. "What is its name?"

"It just followed us home," the guys say. "It has no name."

With its long eyelashes, the horse looks feminine, and maybe they should name it *Lucy* or *Evelyn* or some crap like that, but they think of it as just *Horse*.

Normally the girls sit in a row and speak their messed-up English, and when their mouths hurt, they get up, yank their shorts up in the back, and leave. Today they stay, because they are given horse rides. They all trot around the small courtyard, their hair flying. Maria even lets Ajay help her down from the horse, and he feels the skin on her shoulders, soft and surprisingly warm, as though she's been lying in the sun all day.

The afternoon turns into evening. The girls stay to drink vodka shots and eat Snickers bars and kiss the boys with their sticky lips. Kamran pairs up with Cristina, who looks Indian, with a long straight nose and dark hair. Joey likes Alba, who is platinum blonde. And Ajay ends up with skinny Maria, in her knitted Rasta cap and glittering nose ring; she works in a bakery, and her long, pale hands smell of vanilla.

Things progress. The girls walk up the stairs and enter the boys' tiny bedrooms; they sniff their colognes, open their dressers, even sit down on their beds. And then, one by one, the boys close their doors.

Their bedrooms are all in a row. Kamran and his girl murmur to each other. Joey is doing his *Oh-my-gawd, Oh-my-gawd* routine, and beneath Ajay lies Maria, her flat, hard chest pushing into his. Maria makes so much noise that night that Ajay hears the horse outside let out a whinny of triumph.

When the girls leave, late at night, the boys escort them out to the taxi rank in Triana and press euro notes into the hands of the cab drivers. They return home transformed by sex, transformed by Spain. Kamran and Joey want to sit around and discuss their girls' techniques, but Ajay is baffled: What the hell has changed? Why did the girls put out?

It is Kamran who speaks, waving at the courtyard, his voice thick with satisfaction. "They like the horse, man. The horse, it's a chick magnet."

"What do you mean?" Joey scratches his scalp.

"It's about belief systems," Kamran says; he's read Freud and taken Psych 101. "The girls do not think of the horse as a human being. They accept it as a horse. The Spanish are open to the miraculous, to the grotesque. So, what happens here is not reality, okay? It's like, a dream world, and anything goes."

Ajay doesn't believe this, but simple-minded Joey thinks it is a brilliant explanation.

"Hey," he says. "If the horse can get us laid, should we kick it out? I mean, look at the fucking thing."

The horse is fast asleep under the stairs, slumped into a pile of yellow and pink cloth.

"You guys are totally insane," Ajay says. "You want to keep it? Really?"

"Don't be so uptight, Ajay," Joey says. "Clearly it likes being a horse. It's got a place to live, and the police won't bother it here."

"Yeah, Ajay, relax a little, okay," Kamran adds. "We're doing a good thing. The horse is like, a refugee. We're giving it *refuge*, okay?"

Ajay knows when he is outvoted. He gives them the finger, goes to bed, and locks his door. After the African steals all their stuff and runs away, they'll wake up. Crazy fuckers.

⁓

The horse stays. It does not eat or sleep like a human being, but always behaves like a horse. Somehow its yellow cloth coat stays clean and fresh, though it lives out in the grimy courtyard. When they go to class, they leave it apples, candy bars, and carrots, which are gone by the time they return. There is stuff missing from their kitchen—bread, bananas, cheese, ketchup—but the horse never drinks their beer, or opens their canned food. During the night, it sleeps under the stairs.

Maria, Cristina, and Alba return and bring along their friends, who all squeal with joy when they see the horse. It gallops mightily around the courtyard, giving them rides, and when the other girls leave, the *intercambios* stay behind.

Ajay has to admit that he was wrong: The horse is working out.

They tell another of their Alpha Delta Psi brothers about it. Danny is a rich prep-school kid from Manhattan who wears corduroys and V-necked sweaters; his Spanish is pretty good because he grew up with a Colombian nanny or some crap. It is Danny's idea to throw regular Friday parties.

On one side of the courtyard, they set up a plank on two trestles, loaded with jugs of Rushkinoff vodka, flat sesame crackers, and serrano ham and olives. They string twinkling Christmas lights across the courtyard and crank techno from these huge speakers that Danny brings over. Crowds of *intercambios* get hammered and gallop the horse around the courtyard, clasping its flanks with their strong young thighs, shouting *Vamos! Más rápido!*

Danny scoops up the best-looking one—a leggy brunette with a red paper flower in her hair—but there are plenty left over. Kamran trades in his Indian-looking girlfriend for a new Indian-looking one, and Joey switches his blonde for a loud-mouthed, plump girl with tats. Ajay sticks with Maria; her tongue is pierced, a hard metal knob in the midst of the slippery muscle, and kissing becomes a new experience. Besides, she always brings him leftover chocolate-chip cookies from the bakery where she works.

On Maria's days off, she wanders with Ajay through the stone-flagged rooms and shady patios of the Museo de Bellas Artes, looking at the Baroque art. They both like the sculptures of the emaciated saints with their ropy muscles and dripping wounds, their radiant eyes rolling toward the heavens: San Jerónimo, San Bruno, and San Juan Bautista. All that suffering really turns them on, and sometimes they have to hurry back to the house.

A month passes, and then another. It becomes colder, and the morning chill lingers later into the day. Thanksgiving slips by, unmarked, and Christmas markets spring up all over the streets, selling *belén*, nativity figures: fat little baby Jesus and pale Virgin Mary and horses and mangers.

A new crop of freaks is out by the cathedral: a giant yellow SpongeBob, a dancing dog, a clown on stilts. They prance and whimper and beg, and there are always crowds of *turistas* who cluster around, cell phones raised, laughing. Ajay thought Europeans were supposed to be sophisticated, but in his experience, they are simpleminded fucks. Still, none of the guys want to return to the United States for the winter break; they are scared that during their separation the *intercambios* will get a taste of their final, inevitable departure.

In the days before they leave Seville, they look at the city with fresh eyes: The cloudless azure sky, the ochre-colored buildings, the deathless hush of siesta, the taste of fresh *churros* and thick hot chocolate. And it is during this reevaluation that they notice the condition of the horse: its usually immaculate yellow coat is grimy, and it lies wheezing under the stairs, its big head resting on the cobblestones. They leave it Tylenol and multivitamins, but it doesn't get better.

Before they depart for the States, they discuss the horse. Ajay wants to leave the living room unlocked for it, but Joey and Kamran have stashed all their leftover vodka behind the couch, and besides, they are worried about Danny's state-of-the-art speakers. They outvote Ajay, and so the horse stays outside, but they come up with a clever solution: they ask Danny to check in on the horse every few days and make sure it has food and medicine.

The flight back to the States is at dawn. They pull their suitcases across the dark, cobblestoned courtyard and head to the cab parked outside. The horse watches them from under the stairs, motionless, reduced to a crumpled silhouette.

"Get better, horse," they say loudly. "Take the Tylenol, three times a day. There's a bottle of Robitussin, too. We'll be back in three weeks, but don't worry. Danny will look in on you—he's reliable. He's an Alpha Delta Psi, like us."

They wave to the horse, lock their front door, and get into the cab. Ajay feels uneasy about leaving the horse alone, but then, in the departures lounge of the airport, he sees an image on television: A dead African, washed up on a beach in southern Spain, drowned while trying to cross the Mediterranean. He lies face down, half buried in the sand, while Spaniards in swimsuits picnic around him, behaving as though he is a piece of driftwood.

At least the horse is safe inside their house, Ajay thinks. He'll be okay.

⁓

The winter break finally ends. They fly back to Seville, and it is still Christmas over here; the Spanish have an extra week till the three kings show up. Strings of winking Christmas lights are still up over Calle Sierpes and Calle Tetuán and it feels like they've never been away. Only the vacant lot next door has changed; all the crap that filled it—old tires, mattresses, and discarded iron bed frames—has been hauled away, and it looks like construction is going to start soon.

When they walk into their house, the space under the stairs is empty. The bread and cheese and apples they left are thick with mold, so the horse probably ran away right after they left.

Joey's scalp, under his fresh buzz cut, turns pink with anger.

"We give that fucker a place to live, we feed it—and it takes off. No fucking loyalty. How did it get out? We locked the courtyard door."

Kamran peers around. "Maybe it climbed over the wall. Hey, maybe it will see the lights on and come back."

Ajay is not surprised that the horse left—he wouldn't want to stay alone under the cold, dark stairs for three whole weeks. Something else is bothering him, too. Their frat brother, Danny, was supposed to look in on the horse and post status updates on Facebook, but he hadn't, and that pisses Ajay off. But Danny is hardly in town; he uses Seville as a base for jaunts to Paris, Prague, and Dublin.

A week later, Ajay sees Danny in a sidewalk café on Calle Betis, wearing Raybans, the collar of his camel-hair overcoat turned up, drinking coffee and looking across the river, not a care in the world, as though he is a fucking tourist.

Ajay sits down across from Danny and stares at him with dagger eyes.

"Shit, Ajay," Danny says. "What's your problem?"

"My *problem* is that you promised to check in on the horse. You're a fellow Delt—you're supposed to keep your promises. So, what happened?"

Danny shrugs, his eyes hidden by those stupid hipster sunglasses.

"I checked in on the horse. Okay, not right away, but, like, a week after you guys left. It was gone, man."

"Gone, where?"

"How am I supposed to know? It was not in the courtyard. I dropped the ball. Mea culpa, okay?"

"Thanks for nothing."

Ajay walks away, mad at Danny, but also feeling crappy. They should have let the horse stay in the living room. It wasn't well, for fuck's sake.

When Maria shows up at their house the next day, Ajay tells her that the horse was ill and left. Her face twists into a scowl, and she says something in Spanish, fast. He tells her to slow down, his brain has been polluted by English, but he gets the gist of it: Maria says that they are *hijos descuidados*, careless children, that they treat the horse like a toy. He eventually calms her down, and they go to see the statues of the Baroque saints, but now they seem lifeless.

The next week Maria stops coming over. Ajay is sure that she will call and say that she has been to visit her mother in Valencia or some shit, but she never does. He stops by her bakery, but the Moroccan manager tells him to stop bothering Maria and makes a gesture, drawing his thumb across his throat.

Maria has dumped him, just like that.

Things change among the three of them, too. Without the horse, they no longer have parties. Joey starts hanging out in the wild, working-class nightclubs of Triana; he gets into fights, and his face and arms are often covered with dark bruises. Kamran's Indian-looking girlfriend has a fit of Catholic guilt, and now all he gets is the occasional hand-job in a bathroom stall at the Alameda Theater.

Ajay prefers to be alone. Using his art-history textbook, he visits every museum in Seville, every monastery, every convent and church, even the ugly concrete ones out in the new suburbs. He eats tapas alone in neighborhood bars. He watches the *tursitas* pouring out of their busses and taking endless photographs of the freaks. He's always on the lookout for a canary-yellow horse with pink polka dots, but he never sees it.

⟋⟍

Months pass and the winter chill fades away. It is time for *Semana Santa*, the Holy Week leading up to Easter. Every night the narrow, winding streets are crammed with religious floats heading to the cathedral. Each float is devoted to a neighborhood saint, weighs over a ton, and is carried by forty men crouched underneath.

On the fourth evening of the festival, Ajay is down in the Macarena neighborhood, waiting for the famous Virgin to go by. He hasn't eaten dinner and ducks into a small neighborhood bar. The walls are decorated with the stuffed heads of black bulls with ferocious, flaring nostrils, and it is crammed with drunken Spanish men in dark church suits. A young couple in the corner stand out: A slender man in a white linen suit is French-kissing a baby-faced girl with mocha skin and short, tousled dark hair. Ajay gets closer and sees Danny, clearly about to score.

Danny spots him, too. Ajay has no choice but to walk over, a stiff smile on his face. They shake hands.

"This is Lori," Danny says in his superior, bored voice. "She was at Dalton with me. She's visiting for a few days. She wants to see the Macarena Virgin, so we stopped by."

"Good choice," Ajay says. "They say the Macarena Virgin statue is ancient, but actually it was created by a gay hairdresser in the 1930s. For the real thing, you have to see the *Cristo de la Buena Muerte*, it's sixteenth century, carved by Juan de Mesa."

"Hey, I'm writing a paper on Borges and the Baroque. You like this stuff?" A silver ring pierces Lori's lower lip, accentuating its plump softness.

"The Mueso de Bellas Artes has all these crazy Baroque sculptures—you should check it out. One of my friends, Kamran, he has this theory about the Spanish and the surreal . . . well, I don't want to bore you."

"No, no, on the contrary, what you're saying is fascinating. Go on."

Danny looks pissed off and goes to get them some sherry.

Ajay has been alone for too long. He's fired up by Lori's angelic face and finds himself telling her about the yellow horse and its disappearance. She listens with shining eyes, and when he is done, she laughs and punches him hard on his bicep.

"You're full of shit! A yellow horse with pink polka dots? And it lived in your house for, what, three months?"

"I'm not kidding. It's true, it happened."

In the faint light from outside, her silver lip ring glistens with saliva.

"You're fucking crazy," she said, laughing. "I like you, Ajay."

Danny comes back with three glasses of sherry, a mean smile on his face.

"It was super crowded at the bar," he says. "So, what have you two been talking about?"

"Your friend here is quite the storyteller," Lori says. "He's been telling me about a yellow horse with pink polka dots. Very Borges." She looks into the distance with unfocused eyes. "I gotta pee. Where's the restroom? Hope they have some toilet paper. How do Spanish girls wipe themselves?"

She lurches away, and Ajay is left alone with Danny, who downs his glass of sherry in one angry gulp and leans in.

"Shit, Ajay. Why are you telling her about the fucking horse? What's your problem?"

"My problem is that you were supposed to look after it. We trusted you."

"You're such a loser, Ajay. Get on with your life."

"And you're an asshole, Danny. A total asshole."

Ajay starts walking away, but Danny grabs his wrist. His eyes are bright, his breath thick with sweet sherry.

"I wasn't going to tell you this, but fine, okay. I did look in on the horse. It wasn't a pretty sight, okay?"

"Yeah, it was sick. That's why we asked you to—"

"Shut up and listen. The horse was dead, man. Stiff as a board. But I took care of it, okay? You know the empty lot next door? They were cleaning it up, they had a dumpster in there, full of old mattresses and shit, and I dumped the horse in there. What I did is way above and beyond, okay? I saved your sorry ass. So shut the fuck up, and stop hitting on Lori. I've been showing her around for three days, and I'm going to get some tonight."

Lori staggers back to their table, her face wet with water.

"No toilet paper," she says breathlessly. "How do Spanish girls—"

"We're leaving. Say goodbye to Ajay."

Danny pulls her out into the street. Lori gives Ajay a drunken, amused look, and then they both vanish into the crowd.

"Hey, Danny, wait up. Are you serious? Hey—"

Ajay runs after them, pushing his way through the crowd, using his elbows, saying, *Pardon, pardon,* but he cannot spot Danny's white linen suit anywhere.

A chant begins all around him: *La Macarena, La Macarena!* The float from the church of the Macarena heaves into view. It is topped with a statue of the Virgin Mary dressed in white lace, surrounded by a thicket of flickering white candles.

The crowd is too dense. Ajay is trapped between two old Spanish ladies crying into their handkerchiefs, and somewhere high up on a balcony, a sweet, high voice is singing a *saeta*, a lament.

The float shimmers past Ajay. He feels the heat of the candles, smells melting wax, sees the Vaseline tears glistening on the Virgin's face. He waits till the float passes and then shoves his way to the other side of the street. The crowd is thinner on this side, but Danny and Lori have vanished. He cannot find them anywhere.

⟶

The next morning, he tells the others what Danny said.

Kamran takes off his glasses and rubs his eyes, but Joey just laughs.

"Yeah, right. Look, I know Danny, okay. He's full of shit. He told this one chick that he would take her on his family's yacht. His dad's a surgeon on Park Avenue, but he doesn't have a yacht, okay?"

Kamran puts his glasses back on. "I tend to agree with Joey. Danny likes to see himself in a heroic light. But there's one way to know for sure. We go down to the cathedral, and we look for the horse."

"Yeah, well, I already did that."

"Ajay, Ajay, Ajay." Kamran blinks rapidly. "Think, brother—use your brain. The horse's costume was all messed up. It probably got a new one."

"So how are we going to recognize it?"

"I'm disappointed in you, brother. It'll recognize *us*. Of course, it will. So, we just wait for a reaction." Ajay starts to protest, but Kamran cuts him off. "It'll work, man—don't worry."

That night they—Kamran and Little Joey and Ajay—find themselves sitting on the stone stairs of the cathedral. It is a hot night, and the warmth has released the smell of Seville that was locked up all winter: a dull, brown odor, composed of drains and dust, a smell that they've found on the necks of their girls, in the hollows behind their knees, on the insides of their thighs. It makes Ajay queasy and simultaneously sick with nostalgia.

"You guys smell that?" Ajay asks, but Joey and Kamran shake their heads, *no.*

Joey takes a hit from a tall bottle of vodka and passes it to Kamran, who takes a big gulp. Ajay waves it away. He needs to keep a clear head.

"Come on, Ajay," Joey says. "Take a hit man."

"I quit drinking," Ajay says.

"Since when?"

"Since right now, okay?"

"Suit yourself, man. Suit yourself." Joey leans back and squints down at the freaks. "It'll show up, for sure. Just relax."

"Yeah, yeah, yeah."

The freaks are out in force this evening: The goat with the plastic hair. The human flowerpot. An angel with white gossamer wings.

The streetlights come on. The freaks spin and mewl and squeak. Joey and Kamran pass the bottle of vodka to each other and say *Aaah.* They finish the entire bottle and lie back on the stairs, and soon they are snoring softly.

Only Ajay stays awake. He's sweating, barely able to breathe.

On the periphery of the plaza the streetlights snap on. The *turistas* thin out. The freaks stand around dejectedly, jerking into life now and then.

Ajay stares into the darkness. He remembers the time that the cops chased the freaks across the plaza and tore open their costumes and yanked them out. One dark-skinned man, clad only in a soiled T-shirt and shorts, had tumbled out, and lay on the cobblestones, knees pulled up to his chest, as though he was being born. How insubstantial the man had seemed, a collection of long, flat bones, his dark skin less a casing and more a bag for the bones. Who would miss such a body? Who would mourn for him?

A few of the freaks wander away. Soon only the goat with the plastic hair is left, wandering disconsolately in a circle, uttering an occasional *baa-aaah*.

Ajay says, "Come on, Horse, where are you?"

He says, "Is that you, Horse? Come on, give me a sign."

He closes his eyes and prays. He prays for the freak to recognize him, to save him from what, now, is surely to come.

ROSETTA STONE

Mumbai was an assault on the senses: a fug of diesel fumes and cooking smells, overlaid with beeping car horns and blaring Hindi music. Kavita had grown up in the ample silence of suburban Boston, and she craved quiet, so she started waking before dawn. She made a pot of tea and sat out on the veranda of their fourteenth-floor apartment, relishing the sound of her own breathing. Normally the stillness gave her space to think, but on that day, it filled her with dread. It was the twenty-third of October.

Every year she hoped this day would not arrive. For a long time, it didn't, but then time sped up, and the night before, she couldn't sleep. The day arrived, and every year she fell into it like a crevasse, a fissure in time. *Breathe*, she thought, *just breathe. It's been three years. It'll get easier. It's not just you, it happens to a lot of women.*

Kavita stared out of the veranda—as the sun rose, the water of the Arabian Sea brightened, taking on the texture of wrinkled skin. Crows flapped through the lightening sky, ripping the silence with their cawing, and then the first double-decker busses roared through the streets, followed by the raucous cries of the wandering tradesmen, fruit sellers, key makers, and brass polishers. For once, Kavita was glad. Out in the world, life went on.

To distract herself, she opened her laptop, and clicked on Rosetta Stone, an interactive language-learning program. A young Indian woman with ruby-red lips appeared, hands joined in the *namaste* greeting. "*Roti*," the woman said, "*Bread. Roti is bread. Roti.*"

"*Roti*," Kavita whispered, "I know that. Let me try something harder."

She went up two levels. Anand was always teasing her because her Hindi was awful, but it wasn't her fault; her parents had emigrated from India to Boston in the 1980s, and hadn't taught her the language. Anand was born here, a Mumbai boy, and he spoke crude Mumbai Hindi with relish.

Today, Kavita couldn't concentrate. She wished Anand was here with her, but he was still asleep; he'd had a conference call at midnight with his team in Boston. She decided to get into bed with him, cuddle up and inhale his warm, sleeping smell; it always made her feel better. She finished her tea and walked through the vast, marble-floored apartment, a luxury in Mumbai, where real estate was more expensive than New York or Tokyo.

Anand lay sprawled on the crumpled sheets, the fan turning ineffectually above him, and his thick black hair was soaked with sweat. He had fine eyebrows and dark eyelashes, and each hand was curled into a tight fist, battling even in his sleep.

She'd met him at Harvard. Back then he'd been a gangly, shy boy, straight from India, lost among the reticent New Englanders and the ancient brick buildings of Harvard Yard. Back then, she had been the confident one, the American, but she gradually realized the depth of his ambitions. Harvard was just the first step, and he had it all planned out: Stanford for intellectual property law, partnership in a big-five firm, then a triumphant return to Mumbai. His dark eyes shone with this vision, and Kavita had signed onto it, content to exist in his slipstream.

Now she sat down carefully on the edge of their bed. Anand must have sensed her presence, because his eyes fluttered open. He stared at the digital alarm clock and groaned. "Kavi. What time is it?"

"Too early. Sleep some more. I'll get in with you." She rested her hand on his warm shoulder.

"Crap. It's six. I'm going to be late for the call to Singapore."

"Can't you take it at home?"

"It's video-conferencing. The whole team will be waiting at the office." He stumbled out of bed, and she felt the warmth of his body as he passed her. Didn't he remember what day it was? Kavita wanted to say something, but just then the doorbell rang.

She undid the three deadbolts and pulled open the heavy front door. It was Reshma, their maid, a tiny, dark woman in a crushed cotton *sari*. She glanced at Kavita with worried eyes, left her worn rubber slippers right by the door, and rushed into the kitchen to wash the dirty plates from the night before.

Anand showered in their bathroom, and Kavita walked over to the guest suite and brushed her teeth there. In their tiny apartment in Boston, she and Anand had lived on top of each other, but here, in Mumbai, they had spread out. Anand took over the master bath and had his own study; Kavita moved her things to the guest bath, and she'd colonized the veranda.

She showered quickly, avoiding the sight of her own naked body. Drying off, she noticed a few new strands of wiry gray in her hair; unfair, so unfair that Anand's hair remained glossy and black as a raven's wing. She pulled on a new blue *salwar kameez*, even though she'd rather have worn a backless summer dress; she didn't want to look like a clueless American expat. She wanted to be Indian, to blend in.

Kavita was the first to arrive at the mahogany dining table. She wanted another cup of tea but decided to wait till Reshma brought out the porcelain teapot and cups, laid out on a silver tray. She'd told Reshma not to bother with all that, but the woman wouldn't listen; she had spent her life working at Anand's mother's house, across town, and refused to change the way she did things.

Anand walked in, threw his gray suit jacket over a chair, and quickly crunched through two pieces of buttered toast. He had put on weight, but he wore it well, his boyish intensity now replaced with the calm, measured gravitas of a successful lawyer.

"Reshma," he shouted, and the maid appeared in the doorway, her head covered with the *pallu* of her *sari*.

Her refusal to enter the dining room irritated Anand, and he spoke to her in Hindi in a clipped, distant voice, ordering the food for the day. After three months of teaching herself Hindi, Kavita could understand some words, but she remained silent.

Reshma hung her head and said "*Hanh*, Sahib," before scuttling back into the kitchen.

Later, in the chauffeured car—Kavita would get dropped off first at the Bombay International School, where she taught English, and Anand would go on to his office—she waited for Anand to speak, to acknowledge the importance of the day, but he remained distant, lost in his thoughts.

Instead, she said, "Why were you so rude to Reshma?"

"What?" Anand didn't bother to hide his irritation, a new development. "It's good to maintain a distance from the servants. These people are desperately poor, and if you get too familiar, they'll take advantage of you."

"What do you mean, *these people*? How are they different from us?"

Anand pointed out of the window: The car was passing the slum where Reshma lived, clustered at the base of Malabar Hill. From high up on their verandah, it looked like an abstraction of rusted browns, but now Kavita could see individual shacks, roofed with corrugated metal, and the open drains that ran between them, thick with sewage. Women walked down the narrow lanes, carrying brass pots of water, bare-chested children ran and shrieked in the dust, and men brushed their teeth in open doorways.

The silence inside the car lengthened, and Anand took her hand and squeezed it. She felt a surge of relief. Surely now he would address what they were both thinking.

"Kavi, listen, I might be late at the office tonight. I'll have her call you." *Her* meant Leela, his assistant, a slim Mumbai girl who wore bright silk blouses and pencil skirts. "Why don't you go to the club after school? Get in a swim?"

Was this his way of acknowledging that she should not be alone today? But really, the Breach Candy Club? It was full of bikini-wearing Brits and Swedes, who sunned themselves by the pool, blithely ignoring the chaos swirling outside.

"I don't want to go to the club. I haven't seen you for three evenings in a row . . ."

"I'm really sorry. We'll get away this weekend, maybe go up to the hills? It's cooler up there, you'll like it. It'll be *fun*." He smiled brightly to emphasize the last word.

Anand was quoting her. On their first date they'd gone to an Indian restaurant in Harvard Square, and Anand had been upset by the mediocre, tasteless food. To placate him, she'd said, "Well, it's a cute place, and it was really fun." He'd stared at her and said, "*Fun?* What the hell does that mean?" From then onward, she'd teased him, saying that Indians had no sense of *fun*.

Anand leaned in and fixed her with his dark eyes. "You'll love the hills, Kavi. We used to drive up to this old British club in Mahabaleshwar. They have strawberries and cream for tea, and there's this beautiful lake—" His cell phone rang, and he stared at it. "Sorry, I have to take this."

He turned away, and his forehead furrowed in concentration.

She looked out of the window at the stalled traffic. If it weren't for the heat, it would have been faster to walk. Their car trundled by a tea shop at the entrance to the slum, little more than a shack with a charcoal stove. The tea-shop owner sat cross-legged behind his boiling cauldron and looked into the car with sharp, curious eyes.

Kavita quickly looked away. It was amazing how, in a city of this size, her presence was noted and filed away. Even after three months, she couldn't get used to it.

⁓

She returned from school late in the afternoon, and Reshma was gone. She went into the kitchen, lit the gas stove, and waited for the teakettle to boil. Being in the kitchen always upset her; the granite counters were chipped, the pea-green walls smudged with years of handprints, and Reshma piled all the old newspapers along one wall, along with rusty tins and empty glass bottles, and these often housed small, glittering cockroaches.

Kavita made tea and retreated to the veranda. She turned on her laptop but just stared at the screen. During her first month here, she had written long, detailed emails to her mother in Boston and to her college friends in Brooklyn. She was determined to show all of them that the move to Mumbai was having its desired effect. She had recovered. She was no longer depressed. She was getting on with her life.

In her emails she had described the Bombay International School, an old colonial bungalow high on Malabar Hill with wide eaves and high ceilings, its immaculate lawns surrounded by red-flowering *gulmohar* trees. The third graders she taught were polite and well behaved, so unlike the rowdy kids she'd taught back in Boston. There were fair-haired diplomats' children and also plenty of Indian kids, with big heads and large, liquid eyes. She had written that they were all spoiled, having grown up in a world of chauffeurs and *ayahs*, nannies who accompanied the children to school and sat all day under the trees, waiting to pick them up.

The weeks passed, and she found her emails getting shorter. Soon she just wrote disjointed fragments and saved them in a file on her computer.

"Servant," she wrote today, *what a peculiar word. I feel strange anytime Anand uses it. They seem a race apart— smaller, darker, almost invisible. Anand's mother has a live-in maid who doesn't have a room. She rolls out a straw mat and sleeps in the corridor. All her possessions are kept in a small cloth bag, stashed somewhere under a bed. Imagine, living your entire adult life without even a room to call your own . . .*

She tried to remember the details of Reshma's face, but she could only visualize a small woman in a crumpled *sari*. All her entries were like this, stalling beyond a few paragraphs. In college she had read about Napoleon's troops invading Egypt: They were fascinated by the royal harems but were denied access to them, so they produced detailed drawings of the doors, down to the elaborately made locks.

Kavita's cell phone rang, a jarring Hindi film tune. It was Leela from the office. Kavita could imagine her shiny shoulder-length hair, the way she swiveled slightly in her ergonomic work chair, her slim ankles crossed.

"Mrs. Shah?" Leela's voice was perfectly modulated, with that slight British accent that upper-class Indians affected. "Mr. Shah said to tell you he will be a *little* late tonight."

"How late is a 'little'?" Kavita was still Kavita Sen, but she was used to being addressed in India solely as Anand's wife.

"That's all he said. A *little* late."

"All right. Tell him I'll wait for him."

Kavita hung up. Anand could be half-an-hour late, or he could stroll in at midnight; despite the glass-walled conference room and the ergonomic chairs, Anand's office still ran according to an Indian sense of time.

Kavita clicked open Rosetta Stone and began a lesson, "*Mai Hindustan se hoon,*" she said. I am from India.

"*Aap ka naam kya hai?*" she said. What is your name?

"*Aap koan ho?*" she said. Who are you?

The sun began to set, dyeing the ocean a bright orange. Kavita worked her way through the vocabulary list till it grew dark. The outlines of the tall apartment buildings around her dissolved and became grids of light.

⁓

Anand came home a few minutes past ten. She heard the rumble of the elevator and rushed to open the front door. She took his briefcase, its handle warm and sticky, and he kissed her, his breath thick with whiskey.

"Sorry, Kavi, the damn client insisted we go out for a drink," he said, walking over to the drinks cabinet to pour himself a scotch. This client, she knew, was a big exporter of *basmati* rice and had hired Anand's firm to protect his product from American imitations.

Anand sat out in the veranda, sipping his scotch, and she heated up dinner in the microwave: oily mutton curry, yellow *daal*, sticky white rice, and okra fried to a crisp, all made by Reshma, who cooked the way she had been taught by Anand's mother. Anand ate the food of his childhood with gusto, taking swigs of scotch between mouthfuls of rice. He ate with his fingers, Indian style, and they became stained with yellow turmeric.

Apparently, the meeting with the client had gone well. Anand was in a good mood and talked about the client: The man had transformed himself from a bazaar trader into an international exporter of *basmati* rice, and although he lacked a formal education, he was very shrewd and instantly understood the intricacies of intellectual property law.

When Anand finished, Kavita started to tell him about her day at school.

"Today, at school, some of my kids—" She saw him flinch when she said *my kids* and stopped abruptly.

"Go on, I'm listening."

"No, it was nothing," she said. She tried to hide her hurt and changed the topic. "You know, I'm thinking about redoing the kitchen here. It's so dingy. We should get Reshma some bins for her piles of newspaper and her empty bottles. I mean, it's great she recycles, but—"

"Kavi, really. Recycling." Anand smirked. "Reshma doesn't give a damn about the environment. Haven't you heard the rag-and-bone men shouting from downstairs? The servants rush down with whatever they've gathered and sell it. That's how they make a few extra bucks."

"Oh." She felt stupid.

She looked out through the living room at the brightly lit high-rises. Entire families were jammed into one-room apartments, eating and bickering together, and here they were, just Anand and her, in this enormous place.

She stood up and pulled shut the thick, dusty curtains, blocking out the view. She sat down, breathing heavily. Anand scrutinized her with his dark eyes, suddenly worried.

"Kavi, did I do something? Are you upset?"

"Do you know what day it is? It's October, right?"

"Oh." Anand sat back and stopped eating. "Of course, I remembered. I just didn't want to bring it up. I thought it might upset you. Was I wrong, Kavi?"

He leaned in and took her hand, but she wouldn't meet his eyes.

"Don't bullshit me. Did you remember?"

"Kavi, please. Let's not start this. You're doing so well. The move has been good for you, for us. It's been three years. We have to move on."

He had made this about her mental health. If she pushed it, she would be the crazy one, the depressed one, the unreasonable one. She pretended to be reassured, but she wasn't. Anand had become such a good liar. He did it all the time, for work—she'd heard him on the phone, reassuring a client. How had he changed so much?

⌒⌒

The monsoon arrived a few days later, and Kavita had to abandon the veranda. Now she drank her tea in the living room, and rain pounded against the closed glass doors. The streets below turned into brown, swollen rivers; tree branches floated by, and white plastic bags, and once she saw the bloated carcass of a dog.

For the third morning in a row, the phone rang early, part of a telephone chain. Kavita listened to the voice on the other end, and then dialed five other numbers, giving each of them the message: School was cancelled. In the background, she heard children whooping with delight. In Boston, cancelling school would have been a hardship on the parents, but here, there were plenty of maids and *ayahs* to look after the children.

Anand said that their Mitsubishi Pajero could easily brave the flooded streets, and he insisted on going to work.

"Look how hard it's raining," she said. "It's like the deluge. I'll never see you again."

"Don't be silly," he said. "It's just the monsoon. Standard."

She wasn't being silly. Every day in the papers she read about people being drowned or electrocuted, trains that fell into swollen rivers. The country was one big sodden disaster area, with no help in sight.

After Anand left, she took her laptop out and started up Rosetta Stone. The Indian woman appeared on her screen, joined her hands in a *namaste*, and started to speak.

"*Paisa,*" the woman said slowly. "*Paisa.* Money. *Paisa. Mere pass kutch paisa nahin hai.* I do not have any money."

"*Mere pass,*" Kavita said slowly, "*kutch paisa nahi hai . . .*"

She'd nearly finished the lesson when the doorbell rang. It was noon, and Reshma stood at the door, her *sari* soaked through, her legs covered with mud. She was carrying her son on her hip, a tiny, wizened child with a dark mark drawn on his forehead to keep away evil spirits. He saw Kavita and let out a wail, and Reshma, red-faced with embarrassment, hustled him into the kitchen.

The child's clothes were soaked, and he could easily catch a chill. Kavita went into the guest bedroom and rummaged through a cardboard box that the previous inhabitants—American diplomats—had left behind. She found a pair of child's shorts and a purple T-shirt that said, JAKARTA FIELD DAY. They would be too big for Reshma's boy, but it was better than his soaked clothes. She gathered them up, along with a pair of canvas shoes and a handful of plastic toy cars.

When Kavita entered the kitchen, Reshma was vigorously cleaning plates, and the little boy sat passively on the floor, staring into space. He had the resigned, lined face of a very old man.

"Please, Madam," Reshma said, frowning hard to get the English words out of her mouth. "No tell Anand Sahib. That I bring my boy."

"You speak English?" Kavita couldn't conceal her surprise.

"Little, little only . . ."

"Your boy is sweet. What's his name?"

"I have two . . . boy. One bigger one, Ramesh, eight years. This one is Raju."

"Well, these are for Raju." Kavita thrust the pile of clothes and toys into Reshma's arms, and the woman's eyes widened in surprise. Before Kavita could stop her, Reshma had bent and touched Kavita's bare feet.

"*Theek hai*, Reshma. It's nothing. *Kuch nahi.*"

There were tears in Reshma's eyes. "Memsahib, *yeh bahut hai.*" This is a lot.

Kavita was proud of understanding this. She quickly patted Reshma on the shoulder and walked away.

Why would Anand object to this tiny boy being in their house? All day the child sat quietly in a corner of the kitchen while Reshma cooked, and played with the bright plastic cars. Kavita resolved not to tell Anand about it.

From that day onward, Reshma's attitude toward Kavita changed. She behaved proprietarily, correcting Kavita's Hindi, and she insisted that Kavita come into the kitchen and learn to cook the dishes that Anand liked. Raju often spent the day with them. He never wore the purple T-shirt that Kavita had given him, but he became used to her and sat solemnly in her lap, looking up at her with his big eyes. He smelled of carbolic soap and something musky, not an unclean smell, just one that Kavita associated with poverty.

"Madam . . ." Reshma said one day, as they cooked together. "Why you don't have a child? You are married long time, no?"

"Oh, that." Kavita was quiet at first, but she felt safe with Reshma. "Well, actually, I did have a baby. A girl. I carried her for nine months. She was stillborn. You understand?"

Reshma covered her mouth with her hand, a gesture of sadness and sympathy. "Yes," she said, "I am understanding. Your daughter died. She is with god. It is a terrible thing. You miss her."

Kavita felt tears rush to her eyes. Nobody else had acknowledged the magnitude of her loss. They had all said, *It happens. You are young, you are healthy, you can try again.*

Reshma watched her, and then she spoke. "Madam, it takes time. You will be okay. I am sure of it."

"Thank you, Reshma." Kavita wiped her eyes with the back of her hand. "Really, thank you."

They cooked together in silence. After they finished, Kavita urged Reshma to take home some of the food, and she gave Raju a Cadbury chocolate bar. He never ate the treats, just handed them to his mother, and Kavita wondered if Reshma took them home for her older son, Ramesh. Maybe Ramesh was wearing the purple T-shirt too, the one that said JAKARTA FIELD DAY. Well, at least it hadn't gone to waste.

The monsoon continued in stops and starts. It rained for two days straight, and a torrent of water cascaded down the hill, pouring into the slum at its bottom. That morning, when Reshma appeared, she was alone, and Kavita heard her clattering around in the kitchen, furiously scrubbing the brass plates.

Kavita walked into the kitchen. "Where is Raju? *Raju kaha hai?*"

"Memsahib." Reshma looked out of the window at the pouring rain. "*Raju ka bukhar hai.*"

Kavita recognized that word from her Rosetta Stone. *Bukhar* was the word for fever. It could mean malaria, typhoid, dengue fever.

"Do you have medicine?"

Reshma looked blank. What was the Hindi word for medicine? Kavita went out to the living room and scanned her online dictionary.

"*Dawai.* Do you have *dawai?*"

Reshma shook her head. She started to say something and stopped.

"What is it, Reshma?"

The woman shrugged helplessly and went back to scrubbing the cooking pot.

"You can tell me." Kavita moved closer and touched Reshma for the first time, feeling how clammy her skin was.

"Memsahib, *paisa.* No *paisa.*"

Kavita went into their bedroom. All Indian houses had a metal security cupboard with a complicated lock—even though there were ATMs all over town, Indian families always kept cash in the house for emergencies. Anand had resorted to this practice and kept an envelope of five-hundred-rupee notes next to Kavita's gold jewelry. She counted out five notes—about fifty dollars—rolled them up and put them in Reshma's hand.

The woman recoiled, as though Kavita had put burning cinders into her palm, then she blushed deeply, nodded her head, and tied the money into a knot in her *sari*. Not wanting Reshma to touch her feet again, Kavita hurried back to the living room.

Reshma completed the cooking in record time that day, and soon the apartment was redolent with the smells of frying garlic and ginger. Before Reshma left, she stopped to say *namaste*, and then she pulled on her rubber slippers and was gone.

Kavita went out onto the wet, windy veranda and looked down. She watched Reshma's faded green *sari* as she walked down the hill, turned by the tea shop, crossed the open drain, and disappeared into the slum. Kavita wanted to stay out on the veranda, but it began pouring and soon the view was obscured by a thick curtain of water.

It finally stopped raining, and Kavita returned to school. The kids were noisy after being cooped up at home—Kavita had to scold them—but everybody felt a great sense of relief. The sun shone brightly, the lawns of the school were green and lush, and dark red flowers bloomed on the *gulmohar* trees. The Indian teachers shook their heads and said that this was just a respite: The winds had shifted, that's all, and the real monsoon was yet to come. A roil of gray clouds was sweeping across the ocean, gathering strength and moisture.

That evening Kavita returned home, and Reshma had not come. Kavita forced herself to go into the kitchen and wash the plates from last night's dinner. There was some leftover chicken curry for Anand, and she was happy enough eating an omelet. The idea of cooking again made her happy; it reminded her of their dinners in Boston, when they'd pile leftovers onto the table and fight over the last bits of greasy Chinese takeout.

But there was the usual evening call from Leela saying that Anand would be late, and she had eaten by the time Anand returned home, past eleven. He headed straight for the drinks cabinet and poured a stiff scotch.

"I ate something at the office." He sighed. "This damn client will be the death of me. He treats me like I'm his personal advisor, he wants things done at the last minute . . ."

"It's okay. I had an omelet."

"An omelet? Why? Wasn't there any dinner?" Anand was busy adding ice to his drink. His face was puffy, and his eyes were slightly unfocused.

She chose her words carefully. "Did you have drinks with the client?"

"No, just a bite at the office. Didn't Reshma make dinner?"

"She didn't come today. Her child is sick, I think."

Anand sat down with a sigh and kicked off his polished penny loafers. "Oldest one in the book. These people are always saying that. Don't believe it."

He pulled the cufflinks from his starched cuffs and rolled up his shirtsleeves; his arms were well muscled and thick with hair. When they first made love, she liked to stroke his strong, silky arms.

"No, her younger son—she has two—is really sick. She didn't have money for medicine. You should see this kid—he's tiny. I think there's something wrong with him—"

"Did you give her money?"

"Not much. About twenty-five hundred, she needed—"

Anand's face darkened with anger. "Kavi, that was stupid. You *never* give them money. That's a month's salary for her." He groaned. "Now she'll vanish, you'll see. She'll turn up after two or three weeks with some sob story . . ."

She felt her cheeks flush. "*Stupid* of me? *Stupid*?"

He leaned back in the chair, and it creaked under his weight. "Now, I didn't mean it like that . . . Come on, don't twist my words."

She turned on her heel and went into the guest bedroom and locked the door. In the old days, he would have come after her, and in the flush of reconciliation, they might even have had sex. Now she lay rigid under the musty sheets. A breeze blew through the room, bringing with it the scent of water. It was raining again.

⌐﹏

When she woke the next morning, later than usual, it was dark, though it was just eight o'clock. Anand had left already, though it was a Saturday; Kavita remembered something about a meeting at a resort outside Mumbai, in Pune.

The whole apartment was chilly. Feeling sick and hollow, she made some tea, warmed her hands around the hot cup, and watched it rain. The clouds were so low that they swallowed the tops of the apartment buildings. The streets were ominously empty, and the Indians in the apartment building, who normally braved all sorts of weather, were home—she could hear their murmured conversations.

She was stuck at home. She turned on her laptop and started to run through her language program. An hour later, as she was mouthing the phrase "*Mujhe bahut pyaas hai*"—I am very thirsty—she heard, distinctly, a hullabaloo from outside.

She went out onto the veranda and was almost blown over by the breeze, hurricane force by now. People on neighboring balconies were peering over the railings, and, following their gaze, she looked down into the slum at the base of the hill. An invisible hand was lifting up sheets of corrugated iron and flinging them about, as though they were paper. She saw tiny people pouring out into the narrow lanes, waving their arms, ducking as the sheets of iron whirled above them.

Reshma and Raju were somewhere down there. Kavita stood, clinging to the railings, watching the slum literally come undone; without roofs, the little shacks were like houses of cards, and their walls folded immediately.

She had to do something. She had to do something.

～

Kavita made it to the tea shop at the bottom of the hill. It was in ruins: The bench had been washed away, and one wall had fallen onto the charcoal stove. The proprietor stood glaring at the wreckage, water dripping off his thick mustache. She tugged at his arm, and he started. Her clothes were soaked, and her hair was plastered flat across her scalp.

"In there." She pointed at the slum. "Do you know Reshma and her little boy . . . Reshma, *aur bacha*? Where is she? *Kaha hai?*"

The old man stood helplessly, rain pouring down his face.

"Do you understand me? Reshma, Raju?"

He didn't reply. She took a deep breath, jumped over the open drain and walked into the wreckage of the slum. In the driving rain, men and women were moving silently, collecting a pot here, an umbrella there. One man carried a sodden chair on his head. Another tucked soggy photographs into his shirt.

Nobody seemed to notice her. She walked on. Her feet were covered in mud, and the hem of her jeans was stiff with muck.

She felt a hand tugging at her shoulder. It was the tea shop owner, his eyes bright with concern.

"No madam. Please come back. No good here."

She couldn't understand what he was talking about, was about to shake him off, when she noticed a group of people standing around a destroyed shack. Two men were slowly lifting up a large, rippling sheet of corrugated metal, and there was something huddled under it. A cluster of women in sodden *saris* began shrieking, and one of them fell senseless to the ground.

"Come, madam. No good, please."

The shrieking got louder. Kavita clasped her hands over her ears and allowed the old man to guide her through the alley, back over the drain, and out onto the road. He wouldn't let go of her arm and insisted on accompanying her. They walked arm-in-arm back up the hill, and rivulets of brown water flowed against them and tugged at their feet.

The old man left her under the portico of her building. She stumbled blindly into the elevator and rose up to their apartment, now empty and silent. Her hands were shaking as she found her cell phone and dialed Anand. She imagined his phone ringing in a conference room in Pune and was shocked to hear a loud ringtone here, inside the apartment. Following its melody, she found Anand's cellphone under a cushion on the couch.

She threw it down helplessly, then picked it up again, and her wet thumbs skidded across the screen as she pulled up his call history: There were many calls between him and

Leela, all after five or six in the evening. Pretty young Leela with her slim ankles and her young body undisturbed by childbirth.

Putting the phone gently back on the couch she walked into Anand's bathroom. From the laundry hamper, she lifted up one of his dirty shirts—strange how clean it was, still crackling with starch—and buried her nose in it, smelling his familiar scent, deep and masculine, and nothing else. No lipstick stains, no women's hair, no perfume. Leela was Anand's secretary. Of course, he would call her. She, Kavita, was being paranoid.

She leaned against the bathroom wall, feeling her clothes drying against her clammy skin. Pulling them off, she examined herself intently in the full-length mirror: She still had a swimmer's build, small breasts, long and lean, with muscle tone in her arms and legs. The only sign she had carried a child was a slight, soft paunch that wouldn't go away. Was she getting depressed again, losing her mind?

She turned on the shower and stepped into the hot spray. The stall filled with steam, and the scene in the slum came back to her: The sheet of corrugated iron rippling as the men lifted it up, the knot of women leaning forward, the sudden piercing shrieks that tore through the air. She closed her eyes and let the steaming water cascade over her head, erasing the image from her memory.

That evening, after Anand returned from Pune, Kavita spoke clearly and with great authority.

"I can't stay here," she said. "I don't like it. You said we'd try it out, and, well, I gave it a shot. Now I want to go home."

"But, Kavi, it's just been—"

"Either we go home, or else I'm leaving you."

Anand nodded. He walked over to the drinks counter and took a while fixing a scotch with ice. He came back, the ice rattling in his glass, and he nodded slowly.

"Okay, fine. I hear you. I'll see what I can do."

Kavita and Anand returned to Boston two months later. They stayed in a service apartment for a while and then bought a nineteenth-century brick townhouse in the Back Bay. Kavita threw herself into renovating it and insisted that they restore all the original moldings and buy period light fixtures. She spent hours choosing Carrara-marble countertops, custom cabinets for the new kitchen, and colors for the walls: should the bedrooms be teal or owl gray? She was even busier after she became miraculously pregnant and gave birth to a healthy baby boy.

She never thought about Mumbai. She acted like that time of her life didn't exist, but when her boy was three years old, the memory from the slum came back, and it wouldn't go away. The worst time was the early evening, when she had put the child to sleep and Anand had not yet returned, and she had a casserole bubbling in the stove.

She would be looking out of the kitchen window at their tiny back yard—she'd built a pergola at the rear and planted a Japanese maple tree beside it—when the memory, unbidden, would return to her, and there was no escaping it.

The rain fell. The silent men struggled with the huge, rippling sheet of corrugated metal. The pop and crackle of the metal as the men finally dragged the sheet away. A tiny body lay beneath it, lying curled up in the mud. Kavita couldn't be sure—no matter how many times she rewound the memory—but it seemed to be a child wearing a purple

T-shirt. She couldn't be sure, but maybe it had white lettering on it, and maybe it said JAKARTA FIELD DAY.

She couldn't be sure, because she never ventured into the slum again, and Reshma never came back to work. For the remaining two months of their stay, Kavita had done all the cooking and cleaning. She had refused to get a replacement for Reshma; till the day she left Mumbai, she'd hoped that Reshma would ring the doorbell and shuffle in and take off her rubber slippers. Till the very last day, Kavita had waited for Reshma to return and reassure her that Raju was fine and that she had not given the purple T-shirt to her elder boy, Rajesh. But Reshma never returned and didn't answer her phone, and that was that.

Standing in her shiny kitchen in Boston, amidst the deep silence of America, Kavita would hear Mumbai again: the roar of rain falling and wailing Hindi music and cars honking and people shouting. She would stare blindly out of the window, not sure where she was, but the moment would eventually pass. The boy would let out a whimper, or the timer on the stove would ding, or she would hear Anand's key in the door, hear him talking as he entered the house, saying, *Kavi, listen to this, you won't believe this fucking client*. Then Kavita would blink her eyes, wipe her face in her sleeve, and turn to the world again.

HOW TO BURY YOUR GRANDMOTHER

Your grandmother dies completely alone one muggy afternoon in Connecticut, eight thousand miles from her beloved apartment in Calcutta.

You can't even bear to picture it, can you? She is not wearing the crisp white *sari* that she has always worn, but a faded hospital gown. She has removed her ivory bangle, her small gold earrings, and the little stud that glinted in her nose. She has not applied her beloved Pond's cold cream or bathed with translucent Pears soap, and her very smell, the smell that signified Grandmother to you, has been replaced by a bitter, medicinal odor. The surgeons have removed the cancerous portion of her tongue and part of her jaw, and her pale, calm face has collapsed into itself.

No, don't turn away—I'm talking to you!

She dies completely alone in a sterile hospital room. Your grandmother, who cooked her legendary chicken *rizzala* in her soot-blackened kitchen, who knew everyone in the neighborhood, the beggars and the ragged slum dwellers and the grease-covered mechanics, who was always making *nimbu-pani* lemonade during the hot months, your grandmother, who took you with her in her rickshaw when she went to visit relatives in the dark, cramped rooms of Bowbazar, whose warm flank you curled up beside as she

listened to a mystery serial on her big, gleaming radio, who
told you stories about her childhood—about Chinese traders
in the Calcutta bazaars of the 1920s, their long plaited hair
touching the ground—this very same grandmother of yours,
she dies completely alone and in silence, in a hospital room
in Connecticut.

Where the hell were you?

You were supposed to visit a week ago, but it was the
end of architecture school, you were in the middle of your
final project, you were busy building a full-scale structure
out of plywood. It was a difficult project, because, unlike
the American students, you were not skilled at cutting wood,
and you had to spend extra hours at it, cursing as you picked
splinters from your palms. Besides, you had been to visit
your grandmother a month ago, and she was badly
deformed—the surgeons had removed part of her tongue
and her jaw—and she mumbled, but she was alive.

Every morning she rubbed coconut oil in her hair, then
bathed, and sat, like a cat, in a patch of sunlight on your
aunt's massive red couch. She peered out of the picture
window at the neatly trimmed suburban lawn, the glittering,
empty sidewalk, the blue mailbox on the corner. She turned
to you with her ruined face and mumbled, *Where are all the
people? What have they done with the people?*

You moved closer to her and pulled her to you, till her
mangled face rested on your shoulder. No, this is not true.
You did not move an inch. You were not your grandmother's
favorite; that honor went to your brother, who is fair-skinned,
like her. You could not find a simple way to answer your
grandmother's question about the missing people without
invoking concepts you had learned in architecture school,
urbanism and *density* and *demographic shift*. Your
grandmother's question hung in the air, till she said that

she was very tired. You helped her up, and she shuffled down the gloomy corridor to her room. She lay down, and you covered her with two comforters, because even in summer, America felt cold.

Your grandmother dies alone in the hospital because just that morning she asks your aunt to buy her a doll. Your grandmother mumbles that she has always wanted the kind of doll with hair you can brush, with eyes that open and close. Your aunt leaves her alone in the hospital and goes to Toys"R"Us and buys a huge doll with a pale, dimpled face and wavy blonde hair. The line is long, and it takes a while, and when your aunt gets back to the hospital your grandmother has already been declared dead.

Your aunt is inconsolable and cries steadily all day, even as she drives around Hartford with you sitting next to her. She sobs quietly on the road, and at traffic lights she lowers her forehead to the steering wheel and moans. You have to gently tell her that the light has changed. You direct her through the blighted, burnt-out streets, till you find the old-fashioned Italian funeral home that has started a sideline in Muslim burials. Your grandmother has already been taken there, and a group of squat, elderly orthodox Muslim women have arrived to wash the body and prepare it for burial. They have a lot of experience with this and take a brisk, practical approach. Interrupting your aunt's crying, they say that they need six yards of white muslin cloth. You and your aunt drive to a fabric store, and the people there understand immediately what the cloth is for and wrap it, with solemn ceremony, into a brown-paper package.

On the way back to the funeral home, your aunt says, *All she wanted to do was go back to Calcutta and die there. Why did I bring her here? Why? I should have let her be at 205 LC.* You understand what she means; your grandmother has a small, cramped ground-floor flat at 205 Lower Circular Road in Calcutta, and this is the heart of the family. This is where we gather for massive Eid lunches; the entire family overflows the divan and two battered leather armchairs and sits cross-legged on the beds. The door at 205 LC is always open, and there are always people arriving and your grandmother is always in the middle of cooking *biryani*, and the smell of roasting meat and potatoes and saffron fills the house. After lunch your grandmother falls asleep with grandchildren jumping up and down next to her and loud conversations being conducted over her sleeping bulk. 205 LC Road *is* your grandmother. Except that now your grandmother is dead.

Your aunt vanishes into the funeral home to help the women wash the body. You sit outside on a patch of crabgrass and look across the street at a gas station. Cars pull in and out, and you hear snatches of R&B on the radio and the *chunk-chunk* of gas nozzles cutting out. For long periods there is only the solitary swish of a car speeding down the block. Your grandmother found the silence of America unnerving. At 205 LC there was always the ticking of the pendulum clock, the cawing of the crows outside, the wail of Hindi film music from transistor radios, the shouting of women on rooftops as they dried clothes. Somewhere, there was always a man hammering. These sounds made up the basic warp and weft of her life, and to listen to nothingness upset her.

You are called back to the funeral home to see your grandmother. She is lying on a stainless-steel table, swathed in white muslin, her head covered, one long strip wrapped around her jaw. Your grandmother looks like a waxwork effigy of herself. You have the irrational thought that your *real* grandmother is back at 205 LC, squatting by her two-burner stove and wiping sweat off her face with the *pallu* of her white *sari*.

There is no question of burying your grandmother in America. No question of putting her into foreign soil, alone, exposed to snow and car exhaust. She will be packed into a pine coffin and then enclosed in a lead-lined box; this in turn will be encased in a sturdy plywood container. Then, covered in labels, with a customs clearance pasted on her, your grandmother will be air freighted—via London and Dubai—to Calcutta. Your aunt has a friend at Air India who is helping with this.

You do not stay to see your grandmother boxed up. When you return to your aunt's house, you stand at the doorway of your grandmother's bedroom. She must have left in a hurry, because her glasses are still on the dresser, as is a jar of her beloved Pond's Cold Cream, and three creased and much-read Agatha Christie novels. You get into your grandmother's bed. As you lie there, your body heats up the sheets, releasing your grandmother's distinctive smell, soft and clean. You try to cry, but you cannot.

Your grandmother dies in Hartford, Connecticut, and is buried, six days later, halfway across the world. You cannot travel to Calcutta for her burial. India is too far away and too expensive, and besides, you are starting a summer job in a few days.

You imagine the scene at the Muslim Cemetery: the beggars at the gates, reciting the Koran and asking for alms; the outdoor faucets where mourners wash their hands and feet; the tall, spindly palm trees rising above the rows of graves; the red, sticky soil; your Calcutta aunts gathered at the grave, heads covered, hands clasped in prayer. As is the custom, your grandmother will be buried, still wrapped in white muslin, on a plank, and her grave will bear no name, just a hump of earth.

No one has ever taught you to pray, but your grandmother made you memorize two lines in Arabic, and now you add them to the prayers being said, eight thousand miles away: *La illaha il Allah, Mohammad rasul Allah.* Lying in your grandmother's bed, you say them over and over, till you fall asleep.

She dies in Hartford, Connecticut, and a year later you travel to Calcutta to visit her grave. Your uncle picks you up at the airport and drives you to 205 LC, down the long, straight driveway, past the spindly mango tree that your grandmother used to nurture. Your grandmother does not come out to greet you, dressed in her white widow's *sari.* Her tiny apartment is exactly the same: once-yellow walls now gray; the pendulum clock ticking high on the wall; the clay figurines in their glass case furred with dust. On the dining table is the metal jug full of well water, and you pour yourself a glass, and it tastes the same, of earth and minerals.

That afternoon you visit your grandmother's grave. The *kabristan* was once far outside the city but now has been swallowed up by it. Inside the shady grounds you can hear the tinkle of bicycle bells and the *put-put-put* of motorcycles. Nearby slum dwellers use the graveyard as a shortcut and saunter through, freshly bathed, clutching plastic shopping bags. You try to feel something, but all you can think about is sitting outside the Italian funeral home, looking across the street at the gas station. You remember how the evening had darkened and the cars' red taillights looked like the eyes of wild animals.

In the evening your eldest aunt—the one who looks startlingly like your grandmother—invites you for dinner. She has made chicken *rizzala,* using your grandmother's recipe, and it tastes the same, rich and fragrant with onions and yogurt and scented with cardamom. You ask about your grandmother's funeral, and your eldest aunt says that it was raining that day. The mourners were gathered at the grave, but it was hard to cut open the lead-lined coffin. Lacking power tools, the gravediggers cracked it open with hammers and chisels, and it was dark by the time your grandmother was finally interred. You think of the wet, red earth, and the way it squelches between your toes and spatters your clothes. You imagine the scar of the freshly dug grave.

After dinner—you eat with your fingers, like everyone else—you wash your hands in your eldest aunt's bathroom, passing through her bedroom. She uses the same golden, translucent soap, Pears, that your grandmother adored. On the way out, you see that your eldest aunt has built a new cupboard by the door, a tall, handsome structure gleaming with coats of varnish.

Your eldest aunt sees you staring at the cupboard and says, *You know what that is?*

You must look confused, because she says, *This is the wood from your grandmother's coffin. It is solid American wood, a real shame to waste it. So I made a cupboard out of it.*

You walk over and touch the cupboard and feel, under the stickiness of the varnish, the soft grain of cheap American plywood. Your eyes fill with tears and your aunt notices and says, *There, there,* and, *It's okay, she's in heaven now,* but it is of no use. You are not crying for your grandmother; you are crying for yourself, because you have lost the center of your world.

It's easier to lie. You say, *I miss Dadi. I miss her so much.*

Your aunt says, *At least she had a good death. She didn't suffer.*

You know that she suffered. You know that she died alone, but you can never say this.

Yes, you say. *She went peacefully.*

You cannot bear to look at the cupboard as you leave the room: American plywood, covered with many coats of varnish, transformed from raw and white to a sickly yellow. Solid American three-ply plywood made up of subpar lumber, sliced into paper-thin veneers, then bound together with glue, American ingenuity creating something out of nothing, strong enough to fight off termites, strong enough to last another lifetime, at least.

CHINESE FOOD

B rando drove south every day, and when it grew dark, he pulled over and slept in the backseat of his Toyota, placing on the floor beside him a hunting knife he'd stolen from his father. It was slow going. One morning he woke and couldn't feel his feet: Winter was coming, and he needed a place to live.

On the outskirts of Richmond, he saw a sign in the window of a Chinese restaurant—*Delivery boy wanted, 18 plus only, good driving record*—and pulled into the parking lot. He was only seventeen, but tall, dark-skinned, wide shouldered; a pale scar across his cheek made him look much older.

Chen's Chinese was in a strip mall, wedged between a toxic-smelling nail salon and a check-cashing place. Brando opened the door and looked inside—the place was a total mess. The backlit display above the takeout counter had been removed, and an old, stocky Chinese guy covered in white dust was demolishing a wall with a sledgehammer. The old guy stopped and stared at Brando, who hooked a thumb at the front window.

"Yo, you need a delivery boy? I want to apply. I'm nineteen."

The old guy stepped forward. He had cropped gray hair and a creased, blunt face.

"You come back later. We busy now."

"I'm here. Can I fill out an application?"

The man ignored Brando and turned back to the wall; he hit it hard, and it crumbled away in big, jagged chunks.

Brando went back outside and stared at the sign. Too bad. It would have been a good job; he liked driving. Just then a white van parked next to him, and a middle-aged Chinese woman in an orange-fleece jacket struggled to unload some large cardboard boxes.

"Ma'am, here, let me help you with that."

The woman appraised Brando with frank, intelligent eyes. She had tightly permed hair, a round moon face, and eyebrows painted on in perfect arcs.

"Why do you help me?"

"I came here about the job, the delivery job. You work at Chen's?"

The woman laughed, a deep belly laugh, and her cheeks jiggled with mirth.

"I'm Mrs. Chen. I own Chen's. Okay, bring the boxes inside."

Brando loaded the boxes onto a hand truck and pushed it through an alley and around the back. He followed Mrs. Chen through a torn screen door into a small, filthy kitchen. The six-burner stove was coated with grease, and it smelled of stale cooking oil. He unloaded the boxes, stacking them neatly in the corner, and Mrs. Chen watched him with appraising eyes.

"Let's talk in the office, okay?"

The office was an alcove with a battered Formica table and two metal folding chairs. They sat across from each other, and Mrs. Chen folded her hands into her lap.

"You're Indian? Go to Virginia Commonwealth University? What do you study?"

Brando was surprised. Most people around here assumed he was Hispanic.

"My parents are from India. I mean, I was born there, but I've never been back. Actually, I'm adopted. My name is Neel, but I go by Brando. You know, like the movie? *The Godfather*? Like, *I'm going to make him an offer he can't refuse*?"

Mrs. Chen looked confused, and Brando hastened to explain. "I'm not at VCU. I mean, I want to go to college, eventually, but right now . . . I'm taking a break. You know, getting to know the real world."

He did not say: *I was kicked out of my prep school a week before graduation. I had a huge fight with my parents. I'm living out of my car.*

Mrs. Chen nodded slowly. "Yes. I thought you were Indian. I used to work with many Indian doctors at NIH in Maryland. You know, National Institutes of Health?"

"Are you a doctor?"

Mrs. Chen threw her head back and laughed uproariously.

"In China I was a doctor. Here, no, no, no. Here I am a lab tech. I take care of rats: I feed the rats, I kill the rats, I cut open the rats. Now my husband—he was a cardiologist in China—and I have bought this restaurant. Used to be called *Hunan Flower*, but terrible food, takeout only. Now we're going to make real Szechuan food, and Mr. Chen, he will construct a real dining room. Classy, you know?"

Mrs. Chen laughed again. She looked like a laughing Buddha. Brando had learned that the Buddha was from India, so then why did he always look Chinese? This was one of the many confusions that clouded his brain.

"So. You have a driver's license? You have experience?"

Brando did not bullshit her. He told her that he'd worked one summer back in New Haven, delivering pizza. He was so used to lying that it felt strange to be sticking to the facts, but he liked Mrs. Chen. She had a good laugh, and she was shrewd, but not judgmental.

Mrs. Chen said that the restaurant would be up and running in ten days, as soon as the construction was completed. They had to keep all their old customers—kids from the university who ordered orange chicken and moo shu pork—while attracting a more sophisticated clientele who wanted authentic Szechuan food. Delivery was their lifeblood; the food had to get to the right place and arrive piping hot. Mrs. Chen said that she had sunk their life savings into the restaurant. They could not afford to fail.

Brando's prep-school career counselor had said that body language and eye contact were important. He sat up straight, looked Mrs. Chen in the eye, and spoke slowly, with great intent.

"You can count on me. I can get around fast. I'm a good driver."

"Okay, you are hired. Five P.M. to three A.M. Thirteen dollars an hour. You supply car, gas. You keep the tips. This is a good deal, okay?"

They did not shake hands, but when he left, she bowed slightly, and he bowed back.

In the front room, Mr. Chen was breathing heavily, drops of sweat making trails through the white dust on his face. The wall was completely gone. He must have been sixty, but he was muscular, unlike Brando's father, who was flabby and always complained of back pain. Come to think of it, Mrs. Chen was probably his mom's age. He wondered if the Chens had kids.

As he drove way, he swore to himself that he would make Mrs. Chen proud. He'd be the best damn delivery guy ever.

~

Brando soon knew all the dorms and the frat houses on VCU's Monroe Park Campus. He left his car on the side streets and ran to the dorms, the brown paper bags boiling hot against his forearms. The kids at VCU tipped him well, which was great, because then he could move out of his car and into a small attic apartment.

The only problem were the Indian kids. They came to the door in their slippers, clutching a fistful of money, saw him, and stepped back in disbelief. Brando was their age, he was Indian, he was delivering Chinese food. He could hear their unspoken question: *What the fuck is wrong with you?*

So Brando grew his beard and shaved it into a long thin strip that ran along his jawline. He dressed in oversized, shiny football jerseys and baggy jeans. He slurred his words and said, *Chinese food delivery, You got a fryrice, two orders dumplin's, or-range chicken, si?* It seemed to work. The Indian kids assumed he was Puerto Rican, Dominican, Guyanese, something else.

One bone-chilling night in December, finals period, one-thirty A.M., Brando delivered beef with green peppers to a dorm on Franklin. The Indian boy who paid him barely glanced at him, eager to head back into the warmth of the dorm. The boy had thick eyebrows and spiky hair; he clearly hadn't showered for a while and smelled bad.

A name flashed through Brando's mind. *Aakash Patel.* They had been at Exeter together, before Brando was kicked out. Aakash was a dick, always talking about Harvard and Princeton. Brando wanted to lean in and say, *Hey Aakash, all that bullshit about the Ivy League, and you end up at fucking VCU? And by the way, do your tight-ass Hindu Brahmin parents know you're eating beef? Have a nice night, dickhead.*

Of course, he didn't. He pocketed the money and walked back out into the cold. He'd never wanted to go to college— fucking summer camp for rich kids—but something about Aakash Patel pissed him off, badly. He was one of those Indian kids who only hung out with the white, preppy kids. Brando's friends were black and Hispanic, on scholarships. They'd asked him, *What's the matter with the Indians, man? As black as us, but they think they white?* And he had answered, *They are whitewashed, man*, and that became their code for those type of Indian kids: *Whitewash.*

Walking back to his car, Brando's cheeks burned with anger. *Aakash Patel, whitewash motherfucker.* Brando's own people were the worst. His people? No, he had no people. His adoptive parents wanted him to be just like them: go to college, get a PhD in economics, teach at an Ivy League school. Sometimes he dreamed of his birth parents, but when he woke, he had no clear picture of them, just an overwhelming sense of loss.

Brando flipped up his hoodie, hunched his shoulders, and ran past a row of frats, old junky brick row houses. He passed an open front door where two figures were outlined against a bright rectangle of light. Talking—no, arguing—in low, angry tones.

He'd passed the doorway when he heard a male voice shout, *Cunt*, and he turned to see a girl in a black coat fall backwards down the stairs. She landed on her back, hard, and the door to the frat slammed shut.

Brando ran back to the girl. The padded coat had broken her fall, but she seemed winded, and her eyes were shut.

Her face was framed by her fur-lined hood: a long nose, thick black eyeliner, a smattering of freckles across her high cheekbones.

"Hey are you okay? What happened?"

The girl opened her eyes, tried to speak, but just gasped.

"It's okay, don't talk. You're winded. Just stay down for a second."

"*Ufff.* Help me sit up."

He grasped her under the armpits and hauled her to a sitting position on the sidewalk. She pulled off her hood and examined the back of her head. Her hair was as short as a boy's, and she had metal rivets in her ears, plus she wore jeans and boots. Was she queer? Sometimes alt girls dressed like this, too. It was hard to tell. Brando squatted down beside her.

"What happened? You slipped?"

She shook her head, *No.* She nodded in the direction of the frat house. "Fucker pushed me."

"Pushed you? Why?"

She stared at him with almond-shaped eyes. She was one of those white girls who somehow looked Chinese. Brando babbled on.

"I was just making a delivery, Chinese food, over at that dorm. Saw you talking to some guy. Next thing, you come flying down those stairs—"

She slowly got to her feet.

"Hey, delivery guy, want to make ten bucks?" She gestured at the closed door of the frat house. "Ring the doorbell. Say there is a delivery. Get him to open it."

The anger from seeing Aakash was still eating at Brando, and now some asshole had pushed this girl. Brando had delivered food to the frats during parties, seen the older boys getting freshman girls drunk, then taking them down to the basement. Scumbags.

He clomped up the stairs and leaned on the doorbell. A voice shouted from inside, *Get lost, you cunt.*

"Hello? Chinese food delivery. From Chen's. Fry rice, moo shu pork, two orders dumplings."

Brando heard footsteps inside. He looked back at the girl, and she gestured angrily to the buzzer. He pressed down hard on it.

"Hey, someone has got to pay for this. I'm not taking it back."

There was a *Fuck this* from behind the door, and it was wrenched open.

The girl was a blur. She ran up the stairs past Brando, through the open doorway, pushed a bearded white guy up against the wall, and jammed her forearm against his throat. With her free hand she rummaged in the pocket of his baggy jeans and pulled out a thick leather wallet. She flicked it open, yanked out some bills, and threw the wallet onto the floor.

"This is my money." Her voice was thick with anger. "You try to stiff me again, and I'll cut your balls off and make you eat them, understood?"

Her forearm pressed hard into the big guy's throat. He couldn't speak and his face turned bright red.

She let him go abruptly, stepped back through the door, and grabbed Brando by his sleeve. They ran down the street.

"Hey, delivery guy, you have a car?"

He nodded, and they ran down a side street to the Toyota. Its engine coughed into life, and they sped away, heading downtown.

He looked over at the girl. She was smiling, showing her pink gums, and counting the money she'd taken from the big guy. Hundred-dollar bills. He could smell her, a cheap floral scent.

"Yo, what were you going to do, if I didn't have a car? How would you have gotten away?"

She laughed. "I hadn't thought that far, yet."

He joined in her laughter. It felt good to have this strange girl in his car.

"You like Chinese food? Chen's has the best Chinese food in Richmond. I have a couple of more deliveries to make, but if you ride with me, we can eat in twenty minutes."

She brushed a strand of hair away from her angular face. "I think I'm free, Mr. Deliveryman."

Brando felt something shift inside him. He made his last two deliveries, and they talked as they drove to Chen's. Her name was Jocelyn. She worked as a butcher's assistant at the big grocery store, Kroger. She asked him his name, and he told her *Brando* and then his Indian name.

"Indian? Feather or dot?"

"Indian, from India. From Calcutta. It's in the east, I think."

"You think? You don't know?"

"I've never been to fucking India. I'm American, yo."

Jocelyn thought this was very funny and laughed till she gasped.

It was past two when he swung by Chen's again. Mrs. Chen made him some food to go: shrimp fried rice and black-bean chicken. She cooked with precision, deftly stirring the huge wok with chopsticks. She poured in a dash of vinegar, and it gleamed like lightning. He tried to pay her for the food, but she said, "No, no, no. It was a good night. On the house."

Mrs. Chen said that it was too hot inside the kitchen and followed him out for a breath of air. She saw Jocelyn sitting in his car and gave him a searching look.

"You have girlfriend?"

"Yes, she's a student at VCU. Economics major."

"Good, good. See you tomorrow."

This was the first time Brando had lied to Mrs. Chen. But what could he have said? That she was a girl who went around beating up guys for hundred-dollar bills? That he had no idea what had just happened?

They drove to Brando's attic apartment downtown. It was bare except for brightly colored cushions on the floor and a futon in the corner. Jocelyn said that she liked it. They ate the hot Chinese food while sitting cross-legged on the cushions. Then Jocelyn brushed her teeth, using his toothbrush, and they had quick, efficient sex on the futon.

Afterward, Jocelyn fell asleep, but he lay awake, looking at her. He tried to engrave her long, thin face into his mind: the freckles across the bridge of her strong nose, her nostrils still pink and flared with exertion. Under her pale skin he could count her ribs, and she reminded him of a carving he'd seen in an art-history class: A wooden Christ on the cross, with a long, mournful face and elongated body, both arms strained outwards in crucifixion. It was from the Middle Ages, which had been a dark time. But if everybody was ignorant then, how could they carve something so lifelike?

The next day Jocelyn woke early and left for her job at the Kroger grocery store.

Late that afternoon, before he began his shift at Chen's, Brando drove over to Kroger and waited for Jocelyn in the parking lot. She came out at three-thirty, squinting into the bright sunlight, a stained butcher's apron bunched up in one hand, a packet of menthol lights in the other.

"*Hola*, pretty lady. Need a ride?"

She put her face through the car window. Her hair brushed his cheek, and she smelled of cold, stale blood.

"Hey, hey, hey, it's Brando," she whispered.

The next day she moved into Brando's apartment, bringing a small gym bag stuffed with clothes. She said she had been staying with a distant cousin and had left the rest of her stuff there.

Because Jocelyn had no possessions, Brando's apartment stayed exactly the same. He never asked her what had happened at the frat house. She never questioned him about his parents or flunking out of prep school. He told her that he was adopted, and she said that she'd run away from Florida when she was fourteen to escape a crazy stepmother. She'd been on her own since then and done many different jobs to get by. This information was enough. They understood each other.

Brando continued working nights at Chen's. Jocelyn worked days at the grocery store and their lives intersected for a few hours. Sometimes when he returned home, late at night, she was gone, but she always came back before it was light and slipped under the covers and warmed her cold, bony hands in his armpits. They had a lot of sex, and her long, skinny body soon felt very familiar.

When Brando finished his shift at one or two or in the morning, it was comforting to know that Jocelyn was asleep in his bed. Sometimes, to prolong the pleasure of returning to her, he sat in the restaurant kitchen, chatting with Mrs. Chen. She was a night owl, like him. They ate thick, cold noodles, coated with delicious sesame paste or Szechuan beef with cumin and incredibly spicy red peppers. Brando thought that cumin was an Indian spice—his adoptive mother used to sauté it in hot oil—and was confused to find it in Chinese food. Had Indians traveled to China? He dimly remembered something about a Silk Route, or was it a Spice Route?

Mrs. Chen never asked him about his personal life or about Jocelyn. Instead, she talked about her own.

"The most important thing," she said, chopsticks paused near her mouth, "is who you marry. Take Mr. Chen and myself. We met in medical school, we were both young and idealistic. We realized that the Cultural Revolution was a disaster. We thought that we could change things, so we joined the opposition movement, and when that ended . . . we had to run away to America. But who am I to complain? At least we got out. A lot of our friends ended their lives in detention camps."

Brando's mouth was full of beef, and he just nodded. He must have looked confused, because Mrs. Chen went on.

"We were student activists. Then Tiananmen Square happened. You know the rest of the story, right?"

Brando nodded wisely. He had heard of Tiananmen Square in some history class. Some bad shit had gone down. It was in China. He saw the look of pain on Mrs. Chen's face and knew that she didn't want to go into detail about it, and he understood. The past was best left alone.

He quickly forgot all about it. Chen's was doing very well, and Brando had to hustle late into the night, making deliveries. Mrs. Chen talked about hiring another delivery guy, but Brando said that he could handle it.

The gray, cold winter ended. Spring drifted into summer and Jocelyn let her hair grow; it now fell down to her shoulders. She took to wearing big hoop earrings and long, flowered skirts. Sometimes Brando thought of how butch she'd looked when they first met. She seemed like a different person now.

One hot morning, he woke up to find Jocelyn painting her toenails. He lay on his side and watched her. There were puffs of cotton wool separating each toe, and she painted each nail with tiny, precise brushstrokes. He felt as though he was witnessing a secret ritual.

"Hey," he said, his voice still heavy with sleep. "What happened in Tiananmen Square? You know, in China?"

"What?" Jocelyn frowned down at her feet. "Why?"

"Mrs. Chen was talking about it again last night. She had to leave China."

"Hmmm." Jocelyn seemed preoccupied. "I don't really know. Hey, Brando, can I ask you a question? Where do they . . . The Chen's. People like them don't trust banks, right? The Koreans, the Chinese, people like that?"

"Mrs. Chen is pretty smart. She was a doctor back in China."

"Yes, sure, sure. But they don't go to the bank every night, right? So, where do they stash their cash?"

In the silence, Brando could hear the squeak of the nail polish bottle as Jocelyn replaced the top. Her ten toes shone, fresh and tipped with liquid pink.

"Are you awake? Are you listening to me?"

"Yeah. Well . . . I have no idea, really. No, wait. Mr. Chen does swing by the bank on his way home. Yeah, that's right, a drive-through bank. He leaves some money in the till, but it's not much, like, thirty, forty bucks. Why?"

"Uh." Jocelyn leaned over and blew on her toes. "I was just worried about you. All that cash."

Brando thought about the guy in the frat house. He knew Jocelyn was lying to him, but did she know that he was lying too? That first day he'd walked into Chen's, he'd noticed a section of the floor torn up behind the cash register, and over the last five months, he'd noticed how Mr. Chen would go over there with the day's take, and squat down. When he returned, his hands would be empty.

"So." Jocelyn squinted at her toes. "You really think he does a bank run every night? Doesn't keep it under his mattress?"

Brando shook his head, *no*, and headed for the bathroom to take a piss. He heard Jocelyn behind him, her voice sharp.

"You know your problem?"

He turned, and Jocelyn bared her teeth at him like an angry dog.

"You don't really know what Mr. Chen does with the cash, do you? You're just saying some shit to keep me happy." She drew a deep breath. "You act like you're all street, but basically, you're a rich kid, who doesn't know shit about the world and thinks that he doesn't have to. I dated this guy once—he was so fucking stupid. If you asked him about anything, he would say, *Naw, naw, I don't know that shit. I'm keeping it real.*"

Brando was amazed. "Where is all this coming from?"

"Tiananmen Square, you dummy. Everyone knows that the Chinese government sent in tanks and the student protesters were . . . Oh, fuck it. If you don't know something, why don't you google it?"

Brando closed the bathroom door and took a long, hot shower. His adoptive dad would say shit like: *Be curious, Neel. Look at the resources at your disposal. Other children would die to have them. Why aren't you curious?*

Brando stayed in the shower for a long time, and when he came out, Jocelyn had left for work. She came back that evening though, carrying a package of steaks, and she panfried them with onions, and he knew she was apologizing. The steaks were too rare for his taste—he didn't like blood oozing out onto his plate, and he didn't like the word *rare*. It just meant raw.

That night they had sex, and Jocelyn urged him on, and afterward, when they lay together, he could smell the meat on her breath. It was very hot, and he pulled away from her and slept alone on the far side of the futon.

Brando woke at noon to find two red-faced, sweating men banging on the door. They were cops. They were looking for Jacky Alvarado. Brando said that he did not know anyone called *Jacky*, and they showed him a creased color photograph: The girl in the picture was younger, had pink streaks in her hair, and wore a leather jacket with metal studs, but it was Jocelyn. She was smiling and looking directly at the camera. Who had given that photograph to the cops? Where was it taken?

Brando nodded, *yes*, this was the girl he lived with. Her name was Jocelyn, though.

The cops wanted to know where she was. Brando said that she worked as a butcher's assistant at Kroger. The cops stared at him. They said that Jocelyn had quit two weeks ago, after collecting her last paycheck.

The cops wouldn't tell Brando anything else. They took a look around the kitchen, the bathroom, even opened the closet door and then slammed it shut, as if that would startle Jocelyn into appearing. Then they clumped back down the stairs.

The apartment was so bare that it took Brando a while to realize that Jocelyn's clothes and her gym bag were gone. He rushed to the closet and checked inside his winter jacket, and the envelope he'd stashed there was gone: all his savings, six hundred and fifty-seven dollars in cash. He tried to be angry, but all he felt was sadness. He told himself that it was a mistake, that she would return later and explain it all.

Brando couldn't pay the next month's rent on his attic apartment. Mrs. Chen heard his story and shook her head sorrowfully, but she did not say anything negative about Jocelyn. She let him stay for free in a small room above the restaurant, with a bathroom down the hall.

That summer, Brando began saving his delivery money again. He worked like a demon and at the end of each night he fell asleep fully dressed, his clothes reeking of Chinese food. All he did was eat, sleep, work, seven days a week.

He started eating with Mrs. Chen every night and even learned to make a few Chinese dishes. He learned that Mrs. Chen always appeared cheerful, but sometimes she was faking it, especially after she talked on the phone with her old friends from Beijing; they were scattered all across the United States, and some were even in Australia.

Summer turned to fall and then deep winter. Chen's Chinese was written up by two foodie websites, and now on weekends they had a line out the door. A reporter from the *Washington Post* even showed to do a story about them. It would be in the national edition, and the reporter was accompanied by a photographer. Mrs. Chen insisted that Brando be included, and the photographer shot Brando behind the counter, cooking with Mrs. Chen, both of them wearing crisp white aprons.

To celebrate, they closed the restaurant early. Mrs. Chen made an entire sea bass for dinner, cooked in a broth laced with red Szechuan peppers. They ate as they always did, sharing the fish, each person with an individual bowl of rice. The Chens usually did not talk during meals, just ate intently, chopsticks clacking. Mr. Chen was a particularly fast eater and often would finish first and then go to his desk to sort through the day's bills. Today he did not leave.

When the fish had been stripped to a bony spine, Mr. Chen wiped his mouth and said that he had something to say.

"We have succeeded," he said, nodding his blunt head. "It is definitely time to expand. We will take over the check cashing space next door—I've talked to the landlord. We will close for two weeks this summer and redesign the restaurant." He paused, and his face reddened as he turned to Brando. "We are grateful to you, Brando. You have helped us so much."

"Yeah, yeah, no problem." Brando hated being praised. He changed the topic. "Mr. Chen, I don't think you should hide money under the floor anymore. It's not safe. Better to do a bank run every night."

"You know about that?" Mr. Chen's eyes widened. Then he guffawed, showing the metal filings in his teeth. "This boy. He sees everything. Okay. Okay." He reached out and touched Brando's shoulder. "I will go to the bank more often."

"There is something else." Mrs. Chen spoke quietly. "We have been thinking about your future."

"Me?" Brando looked at Mr. Chen, who just nodded. "I'm fine here. If you guys hire more delivery men, I can train them. Show them the fastest routes, where to park—"

Mrs. Chen reached out and touched his shoulder. She had never touched him before.

"Brando. You are a smart boy. We do this work, Mr. Chen and I, because we have to. But you can do anything you want." She squeezed his shoulder gently. "No, listen to me. One of our friends is a professor at Towson University, near Baltimore. He will help you, guide you. You need an education. Please consider this."

Mr. Chen stared down at the stained tablecloth. He raised his head and spoke in a gruff voice.

"You can always work with us during the summer and on vacations. You are always welcome here." He rose abruptly. "When Mrs. Chen and I chose our path, we decided not to have children. So we have savings. We will pay for your first year. After that, we'll see. No arguments."

He left to do the books. Mrs. Chen smiled faintly at Brando, and then her phone rang. She answered it in Mandarin and walked out into the parking lot and leaned against the van as she talked. She did this whenever her Chinese friends called; it was as though she was scared to talk inside, as if someone might overhear her.

Brando went upstairs to his room. He stood by the window, took out his smart phone, and typed into the search engine. There were many Jacky Alvarados. One was a retired nurse in Toledo, Ohio. One was a nail technician in New Jersey. There were five Jacky Alvarados in Texas. None of them were Jocelyn. He typed in *Jocelyn Alvarado*, but none of them were his Jocelyn, either.

Brando stared at the screen for a few minutes. He typed in *Washington Post* and *Chen's*, but the article hadn't been published yet. It would probably be online this weekend, and he wondered if Jocelyn would see the picture of him. He'd never seen her reading the *Post*, but she was smart and well-informed, and she had to get her news from somewhere.

Outside in the parking lot, Mrs. Chen leaned against the white van, still talking on the phone, and lit up a cigarette. It was a moonless night, and Mrs. Chen was reduced to a dark outline and the red tip of her cigarette.

Brando remembered what Jocelyn had said. He typed *Tiananmen Square* into the search engine. He misspelled it, but the search engine corrected it. There were many hits and many pictures. One image showed up a lot, and he clicked on it: A blurry black-and-white picture—maybe from television—of a row of huge military tanks, painted in battle camouflage, their long barrels raised. They had come to a halt, because a lone figure blocked their path, one hand stretched out in a gesture: *Stop.*

The figure's rigid, defiant pose made it clear that he—or she—would not move, no matter what. The figure's face was hidden, and when Brando zoomed in, the picture degenerated into a mess of pixels. He read some more. Tiananmen Square had been a bloodbath. The Chinese Army brought in troops and tanks to squash the student protest; at least ten thousand civilians were killed. Many dissidents fled to America, Canada, Australia. Brando searched for the name Chen, but there were so many names: Chai Lin and Wuer Kaixi and Zhou Fengsou.

Brando's head reeled with tiredness. It was late. Tomorrow was a Friday night at the restaurant, always busy, and he needed his rest. He took off his clothes and climbed into bed. Many thoughts crowded his mind, and it took him a long time to fall asleep.

Mrs. Chen remained outside, smoking and talking on the phone. When she finally came back inside an hour later, Brando, nearly asleep, heard the screen door screech. In his half-dreaming state, the sound was transformed into the clanking treads of tanks. He saw a young woman standing calmly in front of a massive metal tank, her palm stuck out. It was Mrs. Chen, many years younger, but definitely her.

Even in his dream, he was not surprised. When Mrs. Chen decided to do something—quietly, without a fuss—she was unstoppable. He had sensed it the first time he met her, and now he knew it. As Brando fell asleep, this knowledge filled him with a wild sense of power.

Acknowledgments:

"Barcelona" was published, in a slightly different form, in *The Missouri Review*.

"Mummy" was published, in a slightly different form, in *Slice Magazine*.

"How to Bury Your Grandmother" was published, in a slightly different form, in *The Asian American Literary Review*."

"The Architecture of Desire" was published in *The Columbia Review*.

This story collection was assembled across many years and cities. The Writer's Center in Bethesda, MD, and the late, great Writer's Workspace in Chicago provided me with shelter and community. Many thanks to those who read early drafts and sustained me: In Washington, DC, Angie Kim, Connie Sayers, Vicki Fang, and Amani Elkassabany. In Chicago, Lois Barr, Vimi Bajaj, Natalia Nebel, Rachel Gottlieb, Claudine Guertin and Anne Laughlin. Chaitali Sen in Austin, Maija Makinen in NYC, and Tom Miller in Boston. I couldn't have kept writing without you all.

I am grateful to BkMk Press for promoting emerging writers, and to Ben Furnish for his thoughtful edits.

Thanks to my son, Amar, for listening to endless story ideas, and for many illuminating conversations about storytelling. Thanks to my daughter, Naima, for showing me what it means to be fearless. Thanks to my in-laws, Doug and Carolyn Nash, for their endless faith in me.

This book would not have existed without Jennifer Nash, who said, "Send your stories out. What's the worst thing that can happen?" Jen is my lodestar, my own personal bodhisattva. It is her fierce love that allows me to explore the darkness of fiction, the knowledge that every evening I can return home to her calm presence. This one is for you, babes. Now let's go take a walk.

INTERVIEW WITH AMIN AHMAD

by Stella Bonifazi

BONIFAZI: Key characters in each story have some connection to India. Your characters comprise a wide variety of personalities. Do you pull inspiration from people or events in your personal life for the characters you choose to write about? How does your life in both India and America affect how you write about these characters?

AHMAD: As a writer, I'm always standing apart from real life and evaluating it for story potential. Whenever I'm talking to other people or listening to gossip, part of my brain is thinking: *Would this make a good story?* Of course, real life is the ground from which we all create, but it is always transformed by the imagination. I like taking real life situations and spinning them out, seeing where they could go, taking them in different directions. In the same way, I'm drawn to family secrets—the parts of stories that are skipped over or elided. When I feel that something is being covered up, I explore those blanks or erasures in my fiction and imagine what is being hidden.

I grew up in India and came to America when I was seventeen. So even though my entire adult life has been lived here, part of me is always an outsider. I'm an Indian, looking at America askance, observing American life. I am constantly evaluating what Americans take for real, as a given. For example, Americans waste a lot of food; growing up in India, surrounded by poverty, that was a sin. So in many ways, I am always chafing against American norms, always trying to find a way to live that will satisfy the Indian part of me. I'm most comfortable around people who come from two or more cultures, travelers like me, people who are a bit outside American reality. So it is probably natural that I write about people like that.

I'm also very interested in how immigrants here have to deal with whiteness. We are a minority in a white world, and we have to constantly code-switch, constantly reassure white America that we are respectable, normal people. As a minority, it is my job when I walk into a room of white Americans to find ways to connect. How does that dynamic seep into relationships across the color line?

BONIFAZI: All of your stories depict people confronting profound challenges: grief from losing a loved one, breakups, times of poor mental health. Is there a reason you are attracted to stories revolving around hardship rather than the happily ever after?

AHMAD: For me, the lure of fiction is that it takes life—which is often shapeless, senseless, random—and gives it some sort of shape. Stories do not have to end happily in order to create fictional satisfaction for the reader—but they do have to be shapely, they do have to create a pattern. Good stories often have a resolution at the end, a *click*, and it does not have to do with psychological insight (though it may), but more to do with a hidden pattern coming into view.

Once I realized this as a writer, then all kinds of material opened up to me. It could be shameful, messy, misogynistic, traumatic—and still, without providing a neat resolution, I could, hopefully, create a fictionally satisfying story.

So, for me, stories are a place where readers can experience darkness and loss and still have the pleasure of finding patterns that are often missing in the tumult of real life. In this way, stories become a safe way to experience all kinds of material that would otherwise be overwhelming and senseless. A good story will mesh with our own consciousness and perhaps later become a guide to navigating a particularly rough patch of our own lives. For example, when I was contemplating a hugely painful divorce, I imaginatively entered that reality by reading Hanif Kureishi's early novels.

BONIFAZI: Through your stories, you take the reader all over the world. From Chicago to Spain, India to Barbados, why is it important for you to include such a wide variety of locations?

AHMAD: I have lived in India, the UK, Dubai, Singapore, and up and down the East Coast of America. When people ask me where I'm from, they are often met with a confused silence, and then I inevitably say, "Cambridge, Massachusetts," because that is where I have spent the most time. In fact, when I return to Cambridge, I can recognize the cracks in the sidewalks, and I feel incredibly at ease. But I'm happiest in Cambridge during the summer, when the heat and the smells remind me of India. And then, when I'm in India, the heat there will remind me of a Cambridge summer. I'm simply incapable of being completely in one place at a time: there are always references to other places constantly being evoked. The locations in this book simply reflect my own peripatetic life.

BONIFAZI: Detailed descriptions of food are present throughout the entirety of this book. What does food in fiction offer your readers and how can it help to move a story forward?

AHMAD: Again, this is not a conscious choice. Indians, as a culture, are simply obsessed with food. It is a great source of happiness. Even now, after so many years in America, if I don't eat Indian food regularly, I feel dissatisfied. Particularly as an immigrant, food is not just nutrition but a way of recovering a part of my lost identity. For many years, I lived within traveling distance of New York City, and whenever I visited, I would go to an Indian restaurant called *Curry In a Hurry*, entering it and smelling the food was a great homecoming. It is still there, and even though there are many better options these days, I feel a great loyalty to it.

BONIFAZI: You write about people of all different social and economic classes. How does wealth play a part in how you write your characters and their stories?

AHMAD: Growing up in India, I was very conscious of the divide between the classes. I was part of the English-speaking elite, but the people who worked in our houses were often illiterate and had come to the city from their villages to seek employment. The irony is that while my own parents were socialites and were often out in the evenings, it was our cook and nanny who took care of me and told me stories and provided the emotional sustenance I needed. At an early age, I was admitted into their worlds, and I understood how powerless they were, how provisional their lives were. Secretly, my loyalty went to them. I try to honor them in my work and tell their stories.

BONIFAZI: How do family conflicts (e.g., with a clingy mother-in-law, a cheating father, an ailing sister) lead your work to confront larger topics like culture and class?

AHMAD: Even at age two, my daughter knew what a good story was. If I told her a story about a happy duck who had a good day, she would grimace and shake her head. I had to tell her a story about a duck who had lost its quack—then she would sit up and pay attention. I think we are all hard-wired for story, and without conflict, there is no story. Even the tiniest kids know that. When I'm writing, I don't parse out power and class and cultural conflicts. They're all mixed up in my life, and I draw from my lived experience when I'm writing.

I will say, though, that I was raised by women, and till I was eleven, I lived exclusively in a female world. My father was absent and had little to do with my upbringing: I think he thought it was women's work to raise children. So I spent many years around women—my mother, aunts, nannies—listening to them discuss men. And it was always a discussion about power: The men had all the control, and the women had to carve out lives for themselves, find some space for themselves in a man's world. As I grow older, I realize that this theme—a woman breaking free and creating her own identity—runs through my work. Fundamentally, I believe that women are more adaptable and stronger than men. Particularly in Indian immigrant groups in America, the power dynamics get disrupted, and I feel that the women adapt to life here faster—they improvise, they change, while the men remained wed to the old narratives of the homeland.

BONIFAZI: What is your next project? Are you currently working on it?

AHMAD: I'm working on final edits for a mainstream novel called *The Night Baby*. It's about a young surrogate mother in India who carries a baby for an American couple; she gets deeply attached to the child and travels to Washington, DC, to steal her baby back.

The novel features all my obsessions: outsiders, cultural displacement, a yearning to belong somewhere. It was a huge learning experience for me: I tried to create a complex, fast-moving plot but also delve deeply into character, which is not a luxury I had while writing my previous crime-fiction novels. I was also deeply influenced by movie/television storytelling and wanted the novel to be as cinematic as possible: I wanted to create a novel that could stand up to the most compelling Netflix show. Not a very literary goal, I know, but it helped me to create a very visual story.

Now that this novel is almost done, I'm interested in doing a first-person novel that is deeply imbued with the narrator's voice. That is the amazing thing about writing— one is always learning, moving on to the next challenge. It is truly a fulfilling way of living.

DISCUSSION QUESTIONS

Throughout all of these stories there are strong and detailed descriptions of food. What impact does food have on the stories, both formally and conceptually?

Beyond their ties to India, what other ties bind the principal characters in these stories to one another?

With one exception, all of these are written in the third person point of view. How does the story written in second person, "How to Bury Your Grandmother," differ from the others?

Many of these stories explore the tension between tradition, be it familial or cultural, and modernity. How do you feel about this tension? How does it shape these stories?

Which character do you most empathize with?

The locations of these stories span across the globe. How does this travel reflect the psychological journeys of the book's characters?

Which stories were your favorites? What made them enjoyable or memorable?

America has upended the lives of these Indian immigrants: a doctor addicted to the adrenalin rush of the ER, a genius computer programmer who always gets fired, a high-level bureaucrat outshone by his young wife, a teenage runaway, and a lonely livery driver who befriends a troupe of street acrobats. As they desperately seek solace in love, sex, and status, they discover that the journey to real belonging is much stranger than they had ever imagined.

Praise for *This Is Not Your Country*

Within the blur of the globalized world, Ahmad focuses on the "new immigrant"—familiar with many cities, but never at home. A beautiful, vivid collection.

—Chaitali Sen, *The Pathless Sky*

Ahmad is interested in dreamers, secret-harborers, country-leavers. They convince us that their world is not right, that much has happened before, that resolution and healing is close by. But Ahmad promises us nothing. Perhaps that is why we should read him, because he makes us want to believe.

—Deepak Unnikrishnan, *Temporary People*

The characters in this collection are at turns familiar and fascinating; their circumstances remind us that the human condition is simultaneously global and neighborly. In Ahmad's capable hands, the past and the future is perilous, prismatic, and joyous.

—Tarfia Faizullah, *Seam* and *Registers of Illuminated Villages*

Ahmad disrupts the standard narrative about India and Indian immigrants. His characters travel unknown territories, both geographically and personally. Urgent, original, and finely composed.

—Nina McConigley, *Cowboys and East Indians*

Amin Ahmad was raised in India, attended Vassar College and MIT, and has lived in Boston, New York, Washington DC, and Chicago. He worked as an architect before turning to fiction and now teaches creative writing at Duke University.

BkMk Press
University of Missouri-Kansas City